IN T
OF

★   ★   ★

HAYDEN STRAKER, *star captain.* He can win the respect of warriors, but can he survive deadly politics . . . or a forbidden passion?

YASUKO, *wife of Samurai Shingo.* In an empire of lethal whispers, her worst enemy is her own desire.

ELLIS STRAKER, *trader.* He'll deal with the devil and cheat the very saints—but can his schemes save Amerika's future?

ARKALI HAWKEN, *Hayden's fiancée.* She'll move worlds to find her lover—the wrong worlds.

BARB EASTMAN, *soldier.* Will his faith in destiny lead to glory and love—or madness and rage?

LADY ISAKO, *mother of Samurai Shingo.* At the Shogun's court, a mother's love can be a hate-filled sword.

★   ★   ★

Please turn the page for raves for
the saga of YAMATO.

YAMATO

THE WAY OF THE WARRIOR

PART 2

KEN KATO

WARNER BOOKS

A Time Warner Company

WARNER BOOKS EDITION

Copyright © 1992 by Ken Kato
All rights reserved.

Questar® is a registered trademark of Warner Books, Inc.

Book design by H. Roberts
Cover design by Don Puckey
Cover illustration by Royo

Warner Books, Inc.
1271 Avenue of the Americas
New York, NY 10020

 A Time Warner Company

Printed in the United States of America

First Printing: June, 1992

10 9 8 7 6 5 4 3 2 1

1

So there it was.

To Hayden Straker the omen of the yarrow stalks was that the Kan would now be made to leave, taking their ships out of the Osumi system if not entirely out of Kyushu. The Prefect's forces would blaze forth in victory, but one detail bothered him: no mention had yet been made of the amygdala.

A massive sense of guilt descended over him. The divines had asked the oracle and the oracle had spoken. There was to be a battle after all. A big one. Men would die. Many hundreds. In horrible ways. And was there not a tradition among the samurai of holding and then killing captives in the most barbarous fashion?

Wasn't the real truth of it that the situation was all his doing? All his fault?

No argument.

There were shouts of banzai, then Hideki Ryuji summoned

Hayden Straker forward and bade him sit in the middle of the dais before him.

"Tell me your opinion."

He looked at the Daimyo, his mind simmering with sick disappointment as everyone strained to hear him. At last he cleared his throat. "It would not be appropriate for me to comment, my Lord. I am not experienced in your ways of war."

"Nevertheless I want your opinion."

"I don't believe I know enough to—"

Hideki Ryuji cut in on him peremptorily. "Do not argue with me, insolent man. You are commanded to give me your opinion."

The excited gathering listened intently until the silence deafened them. His face burned under the Daimyo's stare. How could he say that now he only wanted to avoid bloodshed? That he desired Sadamasa-san should meet with the Kan functionaries and arrange a demonstration of force that would send them scudding all the way back to the Three Thirty Degree Boundary? That there was no need to wipe out a thousand or more human lives.

"My Lord," he said slowly, realizing now that Hideki Ryuji was not asking for honesty at all but merely demanding his obedience before the assembly. "I think it is likely that your army will destroy the Kan reinforcements." He paused. "However, their garrison in Kanoya City have excellent beam weapons—"

"We also have excellent beam weapons!"

It was said with such unexpected volume that he winced. He was aware that the generals and nobles who flanked him, and the sons of Hideki Ryuji who stared at him from his left and right, were watching him closely even as they showed their enthusiasm to their master. It was as if his words could seal their confidence, or somehow break it. As the hubbub fell away, he knew he would have to say what he believed, whether it upset them or not.

"Yes, my Lord, I know that, but the weapons the Kan have are better than yours."

There was silence, then Hideki Noboru jumped up indignantly. "That is an insult! Kan weapons cannot be better!"

The Daimyo flashed his younger son a warning glance, saw the young man subside into eye-popping silence, then the Prefect leaned forward on his knee, his eyes steely. "I apologise for my son. He is young and hot-headed. And because I have been remiss in my duty as a father he has grown up with manners that affront the senses like dog dirt."

Amazingly the youngster spoke again. "Father, I request permission to commit—"

Instantly. "Denied."

"Father, I claim—"

"You will compose yourself!"

The youth was stricken. He stared at a point on the tatami two feet ahead of him. No muscle moved.

Hideki Ryuji detected the ripple of approval among the *fudai* for the way he had corrected the waywardness of his youngest son. I had hoped that one day Noboru might become a satisfactory person, he thought with regret. I now doubt he will live that long. He has learned that the Way of the samurai is death, but he has yet to learn that a retainer is worthy only insofar as he shows devotion to his master. Noboru is shallowly self-interested. Because of this he is also sordid, weak, narrow, and inefficient. His teenage mouth constantly plunges me into questions of face.

He considered for a moment, smoothing the material of his *jinbaori*, then he turned pointedly to the Amerikan. "Answer me this: What is the most powerful beam the Kan are able to deploy from orbit?"

"I do not know about the Kan, my Lord, but as you must

already know, the biggest weapon in Kanoya City has a ninety-five GeV injector.'' He made an ''O'' with his thumbs and index fingers to show the diameter of the argentium tube. ''That is, its beam has only to dwell on full-phased reflective plex for three to five milliseconds before the motes will fail to black or clear, my Lord. Think of the death and destruction that is bound to follow on both sides if you—''

Hideki Ryuji nodded once, cutting him off. ''On Edo there is a beam weapon, the 'Summer Lightning of Tohoku.' I have seen it fired with my own eyes. Its mount alone weighs five hundred eighty of your tons; it has a power cell twenty-two of your inches in diameter, and it releases a beam that can overcome the intramolecular bonding energy of pure supraform plex at a range of—more than two hundred thousand of your miles.''

Hayden Straker shook his head amid the proud silence, almost unable to believe there could be such an immense beam weapon, but knowing that even if it was true, and even if it could be brought here, it could not prevent the slaughter that must take place tomorrow. The way the Prefect had crushed the spirit from his son had shocked and disgusted him. *I didn't think it was possible,* he thought, *but this man makes my own father seem like an angel. I wonder if I can soothe the damage to Noboru's self-esteem?*

The Prefect leaned back. ''Now you understand why I think you should never boast about foreign weapons in Yamato.''

A stir of amusement surrounded him.

''Yes, **my** Lord, but—'' he began, his words petering out.

Hideki Ryuji glanced around his kneeling nobles, his face impassive. ''So? You have more to say?''

''My Lord, you commanded me to tell you my true opinion.''

''Then say.''

He turned to look at Noboru. ''Sir, forgive me, but it is

true to say that the Kan weapons are better. Though they are smaller, they're very well designed, and ideal for their purpose here.''

He wanted to say that because of their size they tracked more accurately and fired faster. He wanted to shout out the immense rumor—only a rumor, but what a rumor!—that the Kan had finally developed the singularity gun. The horrifying weapon had been used by both Amerika and Yamato ten years before, but had been totally banned by interSectoral treaty in 2442. No one could have any knowledge of secret technical advances made in Xanadu since that time, and since Ganesh Ramakrishnan had left Amerika for psi-knew-where, it was possible that singularity gun technology was what had given the Kan the confidence to declare war on Amerika so easily. What if that rumor was true?

He looked at the impenetrable faces around him, the magnificence of the war gear they carried, and wanted to make them understand that there was no need for any of this. That it was insane to send these squadrons of terrifying glory seekers down on the city. That the aim was only to oust the Kan from Kanoya City so honest trade could start up again. That calm negotiation was the proper way! Men of goodwill settling their differences across a table! That's sense and true dignity! But his words died in his throat when the Daimyo pulled a familiar-looking blaster out from inside his *hakama* and pointed it at him.

"Do you recognise this?" Hideki Ryuji demanded. Again there was instant tension in the air.

"Yes, Lord," he admitted, sudden terror seizing him. It was one of his own blasters.

"And this?" Another appeared.

"Yes."

"And this?"

An impossible third.

The Prefect chuckled deeply. Those who could see him began whooping and laughing. Then Hayden Straker made the whole place erupt as he looked down involuntarily at his own belt and saw that his blasters were there, intact.

They shrieked and howled as Hideki Ryuji tossed the new side arms down before him.

"Please. Pick them up!"

He did so, turning them over one at a time in damp hands, inspecting their plexwork and their engraved tube plates and the special Aquila eagle pattern on their grips. They were identical in every way to his own.

"My armorer made them for me in two days," Hideki Ryuji said. He inclined his head indulgently, extracting another morsel from the humiliation. "Do they not appear to be selfsame and one with your own? Consider then: Perhaps everything you hold in esteem is illusory. In fact, these copies will outperform the originals in terms of range, accuracy, and burning power by ten to twenty percent. Therefore, please do not tell me of the ability of foreigners to manufacture superior weapons." He stood up then, and began to address his Council of War as Hayden Straker listened with a sinking heart.

"I have listened to the oracle," the Prefect told them ringingly. "And it has spoken to my heart. I have meditated upon the matter and it is my judgment that we must now seize the initiative! We have *sente*, we need only to play one more white go stone to kill the enemy. Tomorrow we will move and gain a great victory . . ."

As the Prefect made his formal address, Hayden Straker found himself shaking. He could feel the sweat running down his back, and his face felt as red as the M1 red disc of Antares that decorated the Sectoral symbol of Yamato. He felt like a man who had unleashed a tiger. All control of the situation had slipped from his grasp and there was nothing he could do.

Suddenly he stood up. "Please, I beg you! Reconsider. You will only reopen a wound that will bring disaster to everyone!" Hayden Straker heard his own voice as if it were that of a stranger. It was a reed compared to the Prefect's stentorian harangue. "Please. You must resort to negotiation. As the supplicant in this matter, I demand that you—"

The adherents of the Hideki clan were mortified. Not only had he, a *gaijin*, interrupted the Prefect of Kyushu when he was speaking, he had actually called into question the lord's authority.

While everyone was frozen in shock at the astonishing outburst, Noboru seemed to awake from his hypnosis a terrible and haunted figure. He leapt up, slicing the longer of his two swords out of its scabbard and over his head in a rigid two-handed grip. Then he bellowed fearsomely and sprang forward at a crouching run.

Hayden Straker watched him rush across the tatami towards him, unable to react to the threat. There was not time for horror to grip him. There was not even time for him to avoid the strike. He had hardly locked onto the truth that Noboru's attack was aimed at him when the sword began to scythe down at him.

Hideki Ryuji had been watching the pressure building in his son. The shame of public censure had pushed him towards the Void and for the last few seconds he had stood on the brink, wearing the look of a young man who was facing the ultimate conflict. With a massive effort the Prefect had blotted out the parts of his mind that viewed Noboru as his son and his analysis came into atom-fine focus. For any samurai that look could only mean the Void: the choice between life and death. All Noboru's instincts had been shaped by the Manual of the Hidden Leaves, and its central koan that "In the moment of living or dying, a samurai must choose death."

The secret hand signals of *ninjutsu* were the subtle code by which Hideki Ryuji had communicated with Goro and his pages, and they had relayed instructions via outer-ear implants to the blind guards who stood ready, concealed behind paper screens at his back.

"Cover Noboru-san and await my command!" he had signaled, so that from the moment the youth's *katana* came soughing from its scabbard he was marked.

Hideki Ryuji's bark was instant. The blind Zen archers released the tension in their strings.

From three different directions yard-long arrows punched through the opaque screens and sped into Noboru's flesh, burying themselves in his neck and skewering his forehead and right eye. He crashed down, his shout still echoing like Rinzai's *katsu!* The point of his sword dug freakishly into the matting and his whole weight bore down on the hilt, so that the ancient blade snapped as he fell.

It was clear to everyone in that instant that Noboru's peculiar destiny had completed its circle. It remained only to meditate upon what his existence had meant in the greater context, and how that destiny fitted with the much more intricate destiny of the *gaijin*.

"Look, Mister Straker!" Yasuko said, pointing over the starboard skirts of the *sora-sensha*. "Amerikan buildings."

He looked in the distance at the white columns of Jos

Hawken's mansion as they banked and overflew the outskirts of the Lease. Nausea rose in him again, displacing the discomfort he felt from being confined inside a borrowed suit of body armor and the hefty webbings that kept him jammed into the weird little seats. Last night he had stared, terrified, as Hideki Ryuji stood over the lifeless body of his son and roused his generals into a martial fury once more. The Prefect had finished by sending them back to their troop encampments sure in the victory, but some remembered the yarrow stalks and quietly speculated about how what had passed with Noboru had surely altered the judgment. The oracle had told that the eldest son would command and the youngest would carry away the corpses. Now that Noboru-san was dead, it was Shingo-san who had become the youngest son.

And what of me? he thought. When the battle is done am I just to go back to the ruins of Kanoya City as if nothing has happened? When the Kan are punished, am I going to go back and submit to my father's domination once more?

He watched all the familiar landmarks slide by, the tension in him screwed tighter by the taut warrior anticipation of those inside the sky tank's gondola. Before them the dusty strip of the Nakasendo, the Kanoya City land road, ran away toward the Takigawa River and the lagoon beyond as they passed into the Lease. Like most of the surface routes on Osumi, it was a poorly repaired track, a factor that would limit the mobility of peasants and other potential rebels. To their right the hill where the Hideki clan ancestors were interred in their jars stood above a sleepy town of mean wooden shacks and bamboo fences. Beyond it the sea stretched, green as jade, to the horizon.

There were maybe fifty warriors in full battle gear inside the gondola. Though the vehicle itself was technically smart, there seemed to be a pilot and also another crewman whose job was to take orders and coordinate with other units. The reason for the rest of the personnel had mystified him until Yasuko explained.

"These seats are dispersion pods. They can be jettisoned from the vehicle. That way our soldiers are able to come into fighting range, to pick their moment and go."

"You mean these boys want to get to hand-to-hand fighting?"

"Of course. There is much less honor in killing anonymously, at a distance. The samurai ideal is two closely matched opponents standing two sword-lengths apart, armed only with edged steel."

Lightning flickered briefly on the southern horizon.

It's another omen of doom, he thought. Hard starlight, attenuated by rolling masses of cloud, strange shadows flitting across the waving green rice fields, the breeze restless in the treetops. Every time I experience it, I never fail to wonder at the change brought over land, sea, and air by something so simple as a critical nexus configuration! Physical effects on the weather; psi effects on the mind. Aurorae and Saint Elmo's fire. Hurricanes and madness. The roots of proto-historic Old Earth astrology and the psi anomaly that was found on the Moon. Surely they know the nexi are approaching quadrature. Sweet psi, why did it have to come to this? A bloody battle and another thousand humans sent to their graves. And it's all at my request.

The white-iced cake of Hawken's mansion became their pivot point again and it circled up there in the tilted panorama as they banked round, dizzying him. In back of the mansion had once been tall stands of blue bamboo. They had been sickled down by some stray beam, and lay scattered like yarrow stalks. The mansion itself loomed up close, deserted and ransacked by God-knew-who, its contents pulled out and strewn across the lawns, its shutters and ornamentation ripped down. A fire burned at the foot of the steps where an encampment had been improvised. I should have been married in that house, he realized with astonishment. Married to a woman— no, a girl—an Amerikan girl called Arkali Hawken whose face and voice I can barely remember now. Did I really sit with her here and walk with her in the groves of longan and persimmon trees and tamarinds and throw a gold *koban* into the lake with my promise and hers on it? How long ago was that? It seems part of another age, a lifetime ago. He shivered. It was another lifetime. It's as if time itself doesn't flow straight in Osumi.

"Our advance parties found these merchant palaces abandoned," Shingo said gleefully, following his gaze towards the other big estate houses. "See how the Kan troops have run away."

"They've gone for the safety of the Kanoya shield," he said, sickened by the destruction. But he was thinking, no Kan force has ever tried to stand against a samurai army on one of its home planets before. Once it's brought into action can it be stopped? Or will these war-loving lunatics pursue the Kan to Satsuma and destroy that entry port and spill over the Boundary like so often in past disputes between Yamato and Xanadu? What have I begun?

He tore his eyes off the Hawken ruin. "We're getting close."

"We shall join battle very soon," Shingo said.

"Perhaps it's a pity Haigo Gozaemon-san is dead," he said, his nerves showing. "If it's true you intend to fight one on one, he would have been invaluable." He swallowed hard as they powered out of the turn. "Still, if Gozaemon-san was alive now, then none of us would be here."

"If! Then!" Shingo grunted irritably. "What you say is meaningless. There are no ifs or thens. You *gaijin* live inside your own crazy, arrogant minds. That is why you have no understanding of the real world around you. Only Zen teaches the true reality—that in this universe there are no 'would have been's or 'could have done's, there is only what is and that too is an illusion. You should learn to accept that.''

What if he's right? he thought, seized by the bleakness of the idea. What if everything is an illusion and one where our choices don't matter a damn? What if we don't have free will? What'd be the point of trying to do anything? Surely it's a madman's doctrine to think no consequences flow from your own actions? Totally irresponsible. But maybe comforting too, because if I believed the samurai creed, then the guilt of Danny Quinn's death wouldn't weigh so heavy on my soul, nor would the notion of causing an army to come here be eating me away like it is.

A stream of gibberish came over the talkback.

"Excellent news! The way is open for our attack."

"You're going to make a frontal assault on Kanoya?" he asked, aghast.

"The Kan have no dome, and no shields."

"No shields?"

"Perhaps the generators were sabotaged." Shingo laughed abruptly. "Good psi, as you say. The pure stream of it!"

"Jeezus!"

He licked his lips, his mouth crab-apple dry. I guess that's another difference. An Amerikan psi-astrogator thinks in terms of bending all psi—of whatever kind—to his will, while the Tao mathenaut tries to discover a pure stream of good psi to drift in. Shee-it, talent or no talent, can't say I like the feeling of today one little bit!

He sat stiffly in the webbing as the sky tank carried him and Yasuko and Shingo unstoppably towards battle. Behind them, other units had already begun to form up into battle order. On the near side of the apron, more ground units had concealed themselves in the maze of buildings. Beam weapons were covering the terminal. Their own vehicles ranged along a long figure of eight, zigzagging back and forth along the apron in close cover, a deadly display of maneuverable force waiting to fall on the enemy.

There they strutted and roared, while the main ground force sneaked in out of sight, suited up under radio black, and frogging quietly down the lagoon, hiding out deep in the sucking mud of the paddies just a quarter mile from the ramparts.

The paddies lying between the city, the apron, and the place the native town had once sprawled were now sparse on cover. Beyond that a maze of stinking fish pools, just mud now and a mesh of tangled eel skeletons, the beds harder baked and more cracked the closer you got to the city and the black ashes of the old wooden township. The steady play of beam weapons had boiled out the pools, turned the fruit trees to charcoal stumps, raised a million tons of brackish water into steam. The land was like a preview of hell. Even with radio black the Kan might just see the mining teams approaching across that wasteland, then it would be hell for real.

Hayden Straker sweated inside his helmet, anxiety rising in him as Hideki Shingo issued commands to his squadrons over the talkback. Then the main Kan emplacements began to open up and angry red swords slashed the sky. The sky tanks threaded the beams skillfully. Still Hideki Ryuji's ground army moved forward in concealment, the whole force hidden ready to attack the ramparts with meson cutters and mines and beam rifles, silent as death. Kan beams coming from the city weaved in and out of the circling horde, dispensing certain death to the machines that got too near. The pilots had eaten snap-drugged tofu for courage and ferocity, insane saucers buzzing the gap in the dome and stabbing a beam inside. Then they roared eerily into the distance, swaggering with bursts of colored trail decorating the sky.

The Kan fire halted, then two squat vehicles issued from the main portal, the leader moving out ahead a few feet above the ground, the turret fixed on a sky tank wheeling overhead, and the shield glowing like a red soap bubble. The pilot of the sky tank gained height, as if sensing something was amiss. The Kan machine scanned the sky for a long moment and turned to rendezvous with the second. Then both machines moved off again.

In Shingo's squadron, the pilots were handpicked men, fanatical worshippers of Hachiman, the God of War, who lusted for blood or death, blasting forward to throw themselves on the Kan. They wore headbands proclaiming that they were resigned to dying, were dead already, and therefore beyond death and beyond fear. Then the engines on their own vehicle rose to a roar and began to beat out the rhythm of war, and as they banked left, Hayden Straker saw Hideki Ryuji's elite squadron of sky tanks move into a chevron formation along the apron, laying down what looked like a trail of bombs, but bombs that briefly flowered in retro-fire and soft-landed. A hard-to-see infantryman hatched from each pod and melted into the crete. The last craft began to trail turmeric-colored clouds. The yellow smoke blotted out the view as they briefly flew through it. The sight of the pods going down had raised the hairs on Hayden Straker's spine. He knew that his turn would come soon and the fear of battle dried his mouth.

More and more Kan ground vehicles came out from the city and began to move forward, and Hayden Straker saw the astonished delight on the face of Shingo.

"They've decided to engage!" he exulted.

A message came in over the talkback. Code for Shingo.

"My father's scouts report that a second Kan force has

come out from Kanoya City," he said. "Good. They will pay dearly for this decision."

"An airborne force?" Hayden Straker asked, white-faced.

"No, armed troops. On foot."

"How many?"

"Hundreds! I hope there are thousands! The more the better! For they will all die!"

"That's crazy! They wouldn't do anything as suicidal as that! Unless—" He stared to the back corner of the gondola where Yasuko sat silent and immobile, two grave-faced *ashigaru* webbed in beside her. Suddenly all their suits began to scintillate like untuned screens. Her strength helped him overcome the claustrophobic terror whipped up by the tight confinement and the deafening roar and vibration of the motors and the knowledge of what he was waiting for. An order was barked and Yasuko took two assault snubs off the gondola's central hub. She selected one and passed it to him, put the heavy triangular butt of the other to her own shoulder, sighting it and checking the action as did the other troopers.

"We'll be going down very soon! When the pod hits, try to get clear immediately!"

He gawped.

"You will draw their fire otherwise!" she shouted. "In the smoke it is often hard to see what a target you are making of yourself!"

"Why is Shingo-san's suit lit up like that?"

"His men must have a clear view of him!" she shouted back. "Or their morale will fail!"

Suddenly his confidence snapped as he got his first clear view of the Kan weaponry and he realised what must be the truth.

"Jeezus, Lady! We've got to get out of here! Tell him, because he won't listen to me! If the Kan are bringing guns out they're not beam weapons!"

"Don't concern your—"

"He must break off the attack!"

"We are taught that attack is more honorable than defense!"

"That's singularity technology down there! I'm sure of it! My father told me about what they do! Those crews can annihilate you! They'll cut your samurai army to butcher's offal if they've got singularity guns!"

"No one can stop the attack on Kanoya City!" She stabbed her finger furiously at the scanner, at the Kan infantry massing on the other side of the apron. "These are our enemy. They have no singularity guns!"

Down below the Kan infantry were spreading across the apron now, their assault weapons quartered across their chests, silver suits glowing inside protective fields seven or eight feet across. Their helmets turned this way and that like praying mantis heads, sensor clusters trying to penetrate the radio black of their enemies. Samurai troopers' fields lit up visibly as they closed, beams splintered off their bubbles, fast-moving high inertia projectiles pancaked or exploded on them, but something with the momentum of a man running at a sprint could struggle through a shield and when the bubbles of friend and foe merged they became locked into their own private war.

Hayden Straker steeled himself as the vehicle under him blasted into a multiple-gee swerve. In front of him Shingo was shouting like a madman at his commanders, one hand on the com selector, the other on his sword hilt, urging them forward. The gondola bounced wildly, almost shaking them out of their webbing as the vehicle braked into a ground run. Its gray and pink mottled undersurfaces shed vortices of vapor in the humid air, the straps and loose metalwork inside clattered.

This is it, he thought, his guts locked tight. But it wasn't.

Half the seats in the gondola suddenly vanished into the floor with a rush of stinking air, then the base iris sealed and the pods were gone. The saucer banked again and reared up at a ninety-degree angle so that suddenly the ground was a vertical wall just outside the dome of the gondola, flashing past his right ear. All around them a sea of troopers broke out of radio black and streamed past, screaming, carrying their shining protective auras with them.

The wave descended like surf onto the two ranks of Kan soldiers whose emplacements fringed the apron. The oncoming flood was a fearsome sight, yet still the Kan held their ground, as if unaware of the shock that must come. They closed in that last terrifying moment, a hundred yards, seventy-five, fifty, until the charge had coalesced into one surging mob. Then the Kan officer raised his arm, bringing a hundred or more men out of the perimeter ditch with long, tight-beam rifles such as snipers used. They climbed up onto the crete and the ranks of silver suits began to pour raw beam energy into the attackers, but without effect. The officer stepped back between the two battalions, fighting for control, and leveled his aiming laser. The first rank knelt all together, leaning into their stock plates. The second stood and leaned in also, harrowed into the gaps so that their personal shields were merged like a chain of bubbles.

Hayden Straker watched with horror from the bucking gondola as the entire line of silver troops disappeared, engulfed in violet light and then yellow smoke. The additive firing that zapped from the beam weapons penetrated the personal shields and burned down dozens of the leading *ashigaru*, thinning them and obstructing others so dozens more were cracked to the ground, the force of their charge completely shattered. But even so, more samurai came doggedly on, eventually reaching the first Kan emplacements and getting to grips. Terrified Kan troopers threw themselves back, pirou-

etting in panic, some dropping their cumbersome weapons to
the ground as the samurai shock wave smashed into them.
Then the Kan line opened up again briefly until they were
engulfed and the bloodbath began with the burning down of
dozens of hapless Kan soldiers.

Those that resisted the unflinching attack fell to the swords-
manship of the samurai, others made off. Some fled for the
cover of the charcoal town, where narrow service portals
might be opened to provide sanctuary from the lethal on-
slaught. Others retreated after their broken battalions. On the
right, the other Kan units had met the same fate, leaving the
gunners on the squat weapons platform to withdraw. The twin
barrels of the vehicle tracked aimlessly from side to side now,
surrounded by a mass of men hoping to take cover on the
strange weapon.

To the south the samurai infantry were jogging on in their
indestructible formation, their discipline taming the Kan and
dominating them. But now the sky tank in which Hayden
Straker rode accelerated with gut-wrenching power, scudding
north. Shingo was marshaling his men, directing the saucer to
a more vulnerable front. There the Kan troops were reloading
power tubes and leveling them once more at an unseen enemy.
They had finally realised that a substantial force was coming
up out of the lagoon under radio black.

Hayden Straker recalled they were Sadamasa's division.
He began to regret his useless appeals to Shingo to withdraw,
knowing it had only been seen as cowardice. Maybe the Kan
don't have singularity guns after all, he thought. If they did
have, surely they'd have used them by now.

The samurai were winning. Everything was going pretty
much according to the Hideki plan. But something terrible
still gnawed at him. Then he saw the squat weapons platform
move forward.

As the tide line of samurai started to fire, the squat Kan machine zeroed in on the ground behind them. There were a couple of thousand men out there hidden in the landscape. The strange double-barreled cannon blasted out raggedly, ten unworldly reports in half as many seconds, filling the air with a humming shriek and great violet streamers that soared out in an arc above the mud beds. The Kan and their officers hit the deck, their gun bus pushing out in front, keeping the flux of quasi-singularities directed at the enemy. The effect was that of a scatter gun. Thousands of little discs of nothing, sizes ranging from grape to grape pip propagating in a cone of maybe thirty degrees. Each firing spattered the mud beds with thousands of perfect black circles, the tops of perfect slender cones that would penetrate hundreds, maybe thousands of feet slanting shallowly into the ground. One wet paddy was drained instantly in this way, revealing tracking footprints sloshing behind radio-blacked troopers, who once revealed were easy prey for the big beam weapons on Kanoya's ramparts.

Each vital hit that a singularity made blipped the falling victim into view, some with their guts punctured or their spines severed or a neat hole in the heart with a patch of tissue a foot across all the way around drained white of blood.

The Kan had taken few casualties from the samurai beam weapons, guns that were too light to punch through a personal shield with any speed. The second wave of Sadamasa's men went in in assault formation, ground vehicles in their midst, and as they reached the scattered corpses and kicking, wounded men, they too were shattered and repulsed. Hayden Straker saw the samurai charge break below him as another volley blasted into the troops. Twenty men went down. Shingo was screaming at his men to drive on when the vehicle was hit by something that had no right to hit. Its nose went up and it slewed to a halt, screaming as air blasted in through twenty small holes. A bright blossom of fire enveloped the skirt. The pilot stared suddenly at the clean hole that had appeared in his own knee. Yasuko's eyes were shut, her face slack.

"Yasuko-san!"

But then the vehicle slumped, and the holed canopy flipped its latches and flew off, blinding them.

"Jeezus, she's rolling! Eject!" Straker shouted. The stink of lube was in his mouth, ruptured gas lines spurted all around. The assault gun went off in his hand moments after the shattered canopy flew off. He felt himself knocked backwards as the gondola lurched aside, but he fought for balance and recovered himself just long enough to throw his gun at Yasuko's release handle and shoot her clear of the crashing saucer.

When his own pod blew, the jar almost blacked him out, then his head hit the ground with a stunning impact, and the wind was knocked right out of him. He scrambled clear of the busted webbing on pure adrenaline. Yasuko's suit sprawled beside him, hard to see on account of the autochrome, then it started to move. Thank psi she's alive, he thought, grabbing her and whirling as he heard another machine bearing down on them.

Then the next attack wave engulfed them, soldiers hurling themselves onto the Kan in one final show of insane bravery as he heard the moaning of that damned evil weapon again, and he hit the dirt.

He checked himself for damage, then stared out of stinging eyes, all sense smashed from him. He saw the victory they had engineered dissolving into ruin. What if a pinhead-sized disc of nothing cut through your head? he thought suddenly. Would you notice it? Depend how much blood and tissue it sucked in as it went through. Maybe hit you like a stroke. Maybe just a sudden loss of sanity. Where's Shingo-san? he thought, his head ringing. Then he saw Yasuko's suit fail in flash mode, a spectacular crash, beautiful even in normal circumstances, but tremendously dangerous here. She was trying to drag her husband's suited body from the overturned gondola. His helmet was gone and his face was streaming blood, and he lay with his arm trapped at the shoulder by the gondola's rim.

Shingo's dead, he thought. And Yasuko will die too unless I can reach her. We've got to get out of here. The felled vehicle writhed, two blunt control surfaces beating the air in spasm as the organix began to die. Yasuko tried again to pull Shingo's trapped arm free. Then samurai troops began to stream back past them, some staggering in balls of dense smoke that had become trapped inside their fields. Someone had finally ordered them into withdrawal.

As he ran in towards the twitching heap of junk, another singularity volley blew some more holes in the vehicle wreck, but the direction of fire saved them. Yasuko heaved at her husband with every last ounce of her strength. Then Hayden Straker saw that she had unsheathed her sword and severed his arm to get him out. He pulled his side arms and waved them at the billows of smoke and crete dust beyond to cover her, and then watched horrified as the regular shapes of the Kan line appeared out of the thinning murk now no more than fifty paces away. At any moment they might break, and charge for the crashed command saucer, scenting the honor to be had from presenting a General's or even a Daimyo's head to Hu Tsung.

"Yasuko!" he shouted. "Leave him! Get back!"

But she continued to pull single-mindedly at the inert form of her husband. She had moved only a few yards when he

turned and stuffed the side arms into his belt, and as he came
up beside her he also began to heave at Shingo's jazzing
body.

The Prefect's son was a dead weight, and all effort to move
him faster was futile. He pulled the body back ten yards,
twenty, twenty-five, then ran forward again, sweat sliming
his whole body under his suit. He was determined to protect
her as long as he could. Maybe I can draw their fire. Maybe
I can—

He fired a snaking purple bolt once into the shapes, and
then again, seeing both splinter and burst on the merged
shield, and filled with impotent fury he cursed Osumi for a
stinking ball of shit on which to have to die, and threw his
useless blasters into the swirling dust.

As if in response the murk began to clear. He saw the
sinister mantis-headed infantry and the silver of their suits.
He saw their long sniper weapons and the smoke swirling,
captured inside their fields, and the light striking dimly off
their gear. Astonishingly, they had halted. They were reloading.

Then another *sora-sensha* was wheeling down out of the
sky and they were suddenly pressured by the shock wave of
its shield field. Then they were surrounded by samurai who
jumped down out of the machine on lines and lifted Hideki
Shingo up into its belly and yanked Yasuko off the ground
and dragged him away too.

Then motors were thundering around him and he found
himself hugging the plex-armored legs of one of the bodyguards. Suddenly the death resignation in him had turned to
a vast and euphoric relief, but with it had come the fear again.
Laugh if I got hit now, he thought wildly. Just like fickle psi,
that. To get hit in the gut after a peak of hope. He heard the
singularity gun fire once more, and cringed down inside
himself. Couldn't do otherwise.

And as they accelerated into clear air he saw that thousands of samurai were switching to radio black again, fleeing back across the paddy fields to their transports, pulled out by the Daimyo's order.

Hayden Straker knew that the battle for Kanoya City had been lost and won, and that the army of the Prefect of Kyushu had been utterly devastated.

BOOK 1

[Ref. Module MCDLXII-012.111931 /Engl.]

[Cross-reference to other SEC modules in CAPS.]

AMYGDALA

*** REQUEST CLEARANCE CODE ***

*** THANK YOU USER PLEASE PROCEED ***

First, see [Ref. Module MMMDCCI-011.846107]
CHRYSOID.
  Begins: #ough most requirements could be satisfied
by organix technology, or bioprocessors, or the brains
of synthetic quasi-human life-forms, or often a mixture
of these techniques. Nevertheless, many important
high-level operations had still not been achieved by the
turn of the century, and some eminent authorities,
among them R. L. KISCH, took the view that artificial
psi-activity was simply not accessible. Implementation

had been tried by workers at both of Kisch's laboratories at RISC, though these remained secret. Experiments were run on chrysoid arrays summing to greater than ten mensa, over a five-year period. The stated goal was to record modifications in the local psi-index, but no statistically significant results were published. Beneficial applications that could be developed from a cheap, industrially available psi-active chrysoid were clearly manifold. Psi-astrogation was thought to be the majo#

. . . HACK INTERRUPTED . . .

#sulted in Kisch's death. Ramakrishnan, on the other hand, introduced psi-active meta-crystals (which came to be known as amygdala) that were not based on the chrysoid array principle. The technology originated, in part, on Varanasi in the Hindostan Sector, but little is known about their origin prior to development work carried out at RISC by the Europan brothers HANS and PATRICK VAN HOORBECKE. Since only a very few specimens (or, as some authorities maintain, fragments) of the original Hindostan meta-crystal were obtained, efforts were made to disassemble them, but the failu#

. . . HACK INTERRUPTED . . .

#coming originally from the Latin word "*amygdala*," meaning an almond, possibly via the late English word "amygdule," a geological term used to describe almond-shaped agate pebbles. Named for their shape#

. . . HACK INTERRUPTED . . .

#A psi-active specimen was reported to be contained in the Yamato royal jewels, implying an origin considerably older than the usually assumed date of circa A.D. 2350, though no firm evidence for this claim has been confi#

. . . HACK INTERRUPTED . . .

#plications are that a device rated at several hundred mensa could be extremely dangerous, and should therefore be suppressed, or at least restricted. Opponents argue that as with all technological developments, the scientific principles on which they are based are morally neutral, but that the applications themselves are rarely so. Supporters of the post-apocalyptic irredemptionist school point out that there are ways to use Tri-Vee or gravometrics in both constructive or destructive ways, but that this applies equally to hypodermic syringes, phosphorus matches, or even large rocks.

Whatever the result of the moral debate, it cannot be denied that the widespread introduction of psi-active devices would alter our present social structures out of all recognition. Since early man abandoned the practice of sacrificial rites in which local psi was artificially manipulated by selective murder, human attempts to use psi influence has#

. . . LINE ABORTED

3

Arkali met Barb Eastman in the ghostly glow of the dome two hours after sunset and one hour after the sounding of the curfew siren had ceased.

The place of their meeting was secluded and high up, the deserted roof of Hawken Inc., right under the gap in the dome. Huge clouds rolled outside the gap, blotting out the stars. The wind sang against the cut edge of the dome, filling the air with a ghostly aeolian whistle and fine crete dust that settled on the lips and eyelashes. The air was humid, but the warm wind was gusting from the south, fluttering their clothes and carrying away the shouts of the sentries squadding the skids below. Apart from those sounds, a dreadful hush had fallen over Kanoya City since the battle; a morbid expectation, but of what Arkali couldn't say.

It had seemed impossible that so few Kan resources could have broken so impressive an attack, but they had. And in so doing, not only had they defied the Lord of Kyushu, but they had broken his power, leaving themselves in complete control of Kanoya City and the whole planet, without any fear of being forced out of the system.

"And that's why we have to get offplanet," she whispered, her eyes full of pleading. She knew that her suggestion to escape to Fort Baker had staggered him. "See, Lieutenant, we can't do anything here ourselves. That much is obvious. And now the Kan have blown out the samurai army, they think they're invincible. They'll grant us no concessions now."

"Is that what your father thinks?" Eastman's face was a conspirator's, his cap pulled down, the collar of his uniform jacket pulled up around his ears. His white leggings and black boots were hidden under an ankle-length cloak, giving him the look of an Adventer preacherman.

"I don't know what my father thinks. It's not important!"

Eastman studied her suspiciously, and his gaze was so coldly penetrating that she pulled the edges of her own dark coat tighter around her, hiding the white flashes on her garb.

"Where's your father now? Can't think I've seen him in two days."

"He's at his mansion."

"Outside the city?"

"Yes. You know the Kan Admiral's staff left it when the Daimyo's army appeared. It's now so smashed up that the Admiral doesn't want to stay there anymore. He's given in to Ellis Straker: we're going to be allowed to live in it again. That's only right."

Eastman's suspicion deepened. "C'mon, why would Hu Tsung do that?"

She twitched her shoulders. "It's their crazy sense of honor. Face, or whatever you want to call it. He made a promise."

"Yeah?"

"Oh, who knows what they think and believe? Perhaps he agrees it's not decent that women should be here inside the city after . . . what happened. We can't escape to anywhere. Or so they think."

"Eh?"

"Don't you see? This is our chance!"

"Sure it is."

She sighed, knowing that she needed his help, exasperated at his stubborn refusal to see things her way. "Listen, Lieutenant Eastman, how can I convince you? There were some . . . some dealings between my father and the Chinese Admiral. That's how they bargained the mansion back from him. It's real obvious that since the attack the Kan have got careless. Their grip on us isn't exactly tight. We can escape to Fort Baker. Don't you see—"

"Miz Hawken, I'm going to ask you one more time: Will you go and talk to your father about this?"

"Listen! We don't have that much time! Will you forget my father?"

He put out a hand to her, anxious about revealing his feelings, but she moved away from him anyway. "Listen to me," he said again. "I know that your father and Mister Straker have been talking to the Admiral. I believe there's a plan to take us all to Seoul in a Kan ship. I heard that—"

"No!" She shook her head. Her dark green garb and coat shimmered in the security light. "It's only what the Kan want. They'd like nothing better than to see the entire MeTraCor establishment and all the other troublesome Amerikan traders shipped off wholesale to Seoul, I'm quite sure about that."

"Yes, but—"

"Will you hear me out?" She grasped the edge of his cloak urgently. "Ellis Straker and my father talked with Hu Tsung all right. And that's what was offered—safe passage. That's what the Admiral calls it, but it's no more than an attempt to free himself of his biggest problem: what to do with us. We can't go along with that. Don't you see that?''

''Why not? If it gets us away to Seoul, what's wrong with that?''

She stared at him, her exasperation turning to bitterness. The lights of Kan requisitioned vehicles glittered down the skids below. ''Don't you believe it's your duty to cause the Kan maximum pain? They've taken Kanoya City from us!''

Eastman chewed on his lip. ''Sure, but I don't see how doing what you say is going to help matters. Fort Baker is an orbiting station. It's in plain sight of the Kan battle fleet—by all that's real, Miz, how d'you plan on getting there?''

''You're just afraid!''

''No!'' He checked the parapet below quickly, and then spoke softly. ''We ought to keep our voices down, or the Kan squaddies'll hear us. But, c'mon, what's the point? Why go up to Fort Baker?''

''Because we can fight on there, Lieutenant. Show the Kan what we're made of.''

He sighed. ''We can fight on better at Seoul.''

She twisted her hands together, maddened by his pudding face, his particular obtuseness. ''And to think I had you down as a man of of decisiveness and courage,'' she said, a hard and sour twist in her voice suddenly. ''You're not. You're like the rest. Now you think the battle's over you're all standing like sheep. Mister Eastman, this is Yamato. Seoul's in the Zone! Don't you see the distinction in that?''

''Seoul's an interSector trade depot. Huge. And there's a big Amerikan presence there. Not like Baker, which is tough as a walnut, but that's about it. With a garrison of a few dozen—fifty at most—what do you expect to achieve? We've got to carry the news of what's happening here out of the system.''

''We've got to stay here. A toehold in Yamato. It's a treaty system Yamato never wanted. The idea was thrust on the Emperor's government by defeat. Lose it now and they'll find some excuse never to let Amerikans back here. Fort Baker's our last hope.''

He rubbed his face tiredly, like he wasn't quite grasping her psychology, and backtracking to make her understand. ''I can see Yu Hsien wanting to smash Baker as soon as he can . . .''

''Yeah, and he'll do just that if he has an aluminum won's worth of strategic sense. That way he'll have erased the last Amerikan presence in Osumi, and the whole of Yamato. We've got to go up to Fort Baker to reinforce their garrison!''

The hopelessness of her plan was reflected in his eyes. ''Just the two of us? Jos Hawken's daughter and a MeTraCor factotum who'll eat more than he's worth on an orbiter?''

She turned away, thinking about what she had been told by Ellis Straker, that the Kan Governor of the Satsuma Lease, Yu Hsien, had departed the Satsuma system and was now here, or on his way here. If pleading wouldn't sway Eastman, perhaps there was another way. ''Did you know that Yu Hsien intends to destroy Kanoya City completely?''

Eastman digested her words thoughtfully, as if comparing it with what he himself had heard, or perhaps gauging what he could tell her. ''By all that's real, I heard from Mister Straker that Hu Tsung wants to ransom Kanoya City.''

''Neither Mister Ellis Straker nor anyone else here has got the resources to pay a ransom,'' she said too quickly.

''That's not what he says.''

She stared at him accusingly. ''And what does he say, Mister Eastman?''

''That he's prepared to turn over a stock of aurium for Hu Tsung's private purse, if only he'll take his ships and troops out of the system.''

''That's not going to happen,'' she said, thinking about the fifteen tranches of aurium. The way her father had been furious with her and had railed at her madly when he had come back from his meeting with Hu Tsung still shocked her. Perhaps his feelings had exploded because of the incitement he'd endured watching a Kan Admiral eating off his best Cantonware, and sitting on his furniture, and making the lovely white mansion his own, but there had been no need to shout at her the way he had. Now the mansion was a ruined husk. All he had worked for over the years. Gone.

"Whatever possessed you to tell Straker about the aurium?" her father had snarled.

"I thought he ought to know," she had said, then stripping the flesh deftly from his argument. "You told me that aurium was your own. But it was really his. It was, wasn't it?"

"You stupid girl!" he had raved. "Do you know what you've done? Do you know? A lifetime's credit. Destroyed! Straker was ruined anyway. But now you've broken both our chances!"

The beast inside Jos Hawken had come out, fierce and uncontrolled. He had brought her to tears before he had finished, shaking her and making to hit her, but then just as quickly he had squeezed her tight and begged her forgiveness. It had been eerie, a demonstration of the unreasoning power one human being could wield over another so long as there was a love bond.

She stared at Eastman, her hand straying to the pocket of his cloaklike coat. "Won't you help me, Lieutenant? Won't you?"

He looked down at her in an agony of indecision, then slowly he said, "Soon a Kan ship will take you to Seoul. Then it'll all be okeh. You'll see."

"But it could be weeks before the Kan allow a ship to leave the system with us on board!" She turned, her mouth set. How could she tell him the real reason she wanted to get to Fort Baker? How could she say it was to find Hayden, and that the finding of Hayden was the most important thing in the universe? There was no reasoning to explain. No logic to lay out for him. It just was. If Barb Eastman could not be won by sound arguments of strategy, how could a declaration of her intuition make any difference? She longed to tell him that she knew beyond any question that it was the right thing to do, but she could not find the words to tell him.

"Fact is, I've been told I show a little talent," she said, trying on a thin lie.

"They say it's not something found in the genes."

"I don't feel safe in Kanoya. We must get out. Soon. Tomorrow night."

"I've given my parole as a MeTraCor—officer—not to attempt to leave the Kanoya City bounds."

The excuse was lame and she saw he knew it. A MeTraCor officer! she thought. He told me his father was an impoverished Arizona lawyer, and he himself is nothing but a clerk, for all that he struts about in a lieutenant's jerkin. By his own admission he scores absolute zero on the talent scale. How can he say he's an officer? You only have to look at him, the slob.

She lifted one eybrow, seeing what her reply must be. "You gave your word as an officer to observe the curfew. So you're not supposed to be here. But still you came."

"I couldn't turn you down, Miz Hawken. I thought—"

"You thought what?"

"I don't know what I thought," he said, embarrassed. "That perhaps you had something to tell me. Y'know—about us."

It was as if he had slapped her face. "You came because you thought I was suggesting taking you up? That it, Mister

Eastman? You sure don't have the least speck of talent, do you?"

He pressed his lips together, deflated by her remark, and looked at her as if trying and failing to comprehend what that night of terror must have meant to her. "Miz Hawken, I told you about my talent scores in confidence. I'm no Ellis Straker, but then he ain't perfect. One thing I can assure you is that the Kan are not planning to murder us in our beds." He smiled his crooked, patient smile, an unbeautiful smile. "And I'm here to protect you. I swear I'll stand guard on your strap post until we light out if it'll ease your mind."

"I don't want you anywhere near my strap hammock." She shivered. "Get me to Fort Baker. That's all I want."

"You know that's impossible."

"You're a coward, Lieutenant Eastman. Just a snap-hearted coward. What's wrong with you?"

He looked at her a long moment, stocky and lumpish, a look of appraisal in his eyes. "You know, Miz Hawken— Arkali, if I may. I think you've changed quite a lot inside in the time you've been here."

She looked away, fraught now with emotion. "I'd say that quite a lot has happened to me in that time, Lieutenant."

"Please, why don't you call me Barb?"

"I must get to Fort Baker—Barb. For reasons you can't understand. If I strike you as a little wound up . . . can't you just trust that I'm telling you the truth? I have to go there."

"What reasons? Can't you spell it out?"

"I can't expect a man like you to understand." She hunted about for a way to put it, sighing with frustration. "It's no use telling you about feelings or instincts, I suppose. Oh, I'm a daughter of Jos Hawken all right. I've got his talent. Since I first stepped aboard a nexus ship, I've known that. I've realized that talent's not something to be taken lightly. Things don't just happen. And because I was born the way I was I know there's something going to happen. Always. Don't you see? I just know we ought to make for Fort Baker. Please help me, I'm begging you.''

Crete dust made the air piquant. The wind ruffled her hair, hair frosted by the blue city light. She wiped at her eyes. Her face was oval and upturned and very white. He regarded her physical fragility, knowing what it cost her to abandon her dignity this way. But now she was beginning to shuffle her pack of lies.

Why do the children of ex-Navy people believe they have a monopoly on psi-feelings and presentiments and emotions? he wondered. How can I tell her of my talent when I can't even tell her about the feelings I have for her? If she ever finds out what I am—what I really am—that'll be an end to it all. Men like me are despised here. Banned from Yamato by a special clause in the Treaty, like the very thought of us is a repugnant idea. And it's not just the locals. Who out of those who know-me-yet-don't-know-me would save my squatting ass from the lard-maker if once they found me out?

He knew he should have left her, then. He knew he should have gone straight down through the Hawken building, and taken himself stealthily away, but he could not bring himself to part from her until she forced it.

"Can it be," he began slowly, "that you think, just because a man rarely shows his emotions outwardly that he must be as tough and as cold as a stone through and through? By all that's real, it's easy to think that pretty, flighty, nervy people are sensitive. But it'd be plainly ridiculous to expect a goy like me to quiver like a butterfly in sympathy with every squatting psi ripple in the emotions of those around me! But that doesn't mean I don't feel things inside."

There was a chip of regret in her voice. "Lieutenant Eastman, I'm sorry if I have offended you, but—"

"I didn't tell you this," he said. "But earlier this year I tried to end my own life."

She stared back at him silently, and he looked down, shadowing his face with his cap-peak.

"Yes, I know it's maybe hard to believe. But I had no use for this world or any other. I wanted to transit out of it with all speed. And so I tried to shoot myself in the head."

"Lieutenant Eastman!"

"It's quite true. Arkali, I put a Wesson 220i to my temple and pulled the trigger."

"And what happened?"

"Nothing. Just that. The trigger operated perfectly. The actuator made contact. A couple of sparks flew out the spout. But there was no discharge."

"What did you do?" Her voice was morbidly curious.

"I opened it up, examined the mechanism, and reseated the clip in case it was a problem—which it wasn't. Then I tried again."

"And it failed to discharge again?"

He laughed shortly. "As you see."

"That's terrible." She turned so that her face was also hidden in shadow. "I'm very sorry I called you a coward, Lieutenant. I didn't mean to say—"

"But that's not the best of it," he went on, not listening to her. "After that second try I remember I experienced more than a little irritation that the damned fool mechanism wouldn't do its duty. I was about to examine it again when a fellow MeTraCor employee—Bosco Shadbolt, perhaps you've met him?—he came into my room and asked me quite innocently what I was doing."

"What did you tell him?"

"Only this: I told him to point the blaster out the window and fire it. Which he did. Without any difficulty."

"No!"

"Oh, yes." He shook himself from his reverie, coming back to the present like a sleepwalker. He felt eager to open himself to her now, feeling she would understand. "So you see, I may not have any psi rating, nothing written down, yeah? But I do have a notion about something peculiar taking a hand in my fate. The peasant people of this world call it karma, and understand it implicitly. No one would believe there was anything to a tale like that if you told it in Amerika, but here it makes perfect sense! According to Zen everything has a meaning—everything and nothing. I'm sure you understand what my escape from death really meant?"

She shivered and drew her garb close, despite it being warm enough on the roof. Something in his deep intensity troubled her. "What did it mean?"

"Isn't it obvious? I was being saved up for something special. If I would have died, then you would've died too. Because I wouldn't have lived to rescue you. You see that, don't you? It was meant to be. By all that's real, our destinies are inextricably twined together."

She gazed at him, fragile and dew-eyed in the blue security light. Suddenly her relief was tangible. "Then you will help me get to Fort Baker?"

He pursed his lips suddenly. "Arkali, how can you ask that?" He asked it with impatience, adding, "After what I've told you, doesn't it all fit with Hayden Straker's inexplicable madness? With the fall of every last barrier that's stood between us? Every turn of events since then has brought us closer and closer together. Isn't it clear that we'll light out for Seoul soon, that here's the opportunity for us to start a new life, you and I, together?"

"Lieutenant Eastman . . ." She was shaking her head. "Lieutenant Eastman, no. You don't understand."

"I understand everything. There's a flow in psi and you must feel it and go along with it."

"Lieutenant Eastman, I—"

"Hush!"

He seized her and turned her away from the light that flooded suddenly from a sensor post.

The steps were unmistakable in their approach. Boots on the crete stair flagging, coming up from below, a hand skimming on the plex railing.

Eastman put a finger to his mouth. Suddenly sobered, he tried to enfold her in his big cloak, but she pulled away from him. The boots had almost reached the top when they stopped warily. Automatically, he felt for his blaster, then realised that he had not carried any weapon for days as a condition of his parole. He felt Arkali's warmth, heard the rustle of her garb, and smelled the clean sweetness only a desired woman gives to the air as they waited in the silent shadows. By all that's real, how tremendous she looks, he thought. I want her. I'd do anything to help her, anything to make her want me like I want her, but what she's suggesting is squatting crazy! Against the flow of everything. There were more steps.

A sudden fear froze him. Jeezus, perhaps she's going to be proved right! If that's a squaddie I'll have no choice but to choke the devil, then we'll have to go to squatting Fort Baker, and tonight! That's a thought!

The stairwell echoed.

"Bosco?" She had hissed it into the darkness before he could quiet her.

A shape resolved itself in the blackness.

"It's me."

"Shadbolt?" Eastman hissed, his relief that it was not a Kan soldier second only to his annoyance at the intrusion.

"Yes. By Jeez, Eastman, that you?"

"It's all right," she said. "I asked him to come here."

Eastman tried to shake the killing tension out of his muscles. He had been prepared to launch himself bare-handed onto an enemy and his heart was beating like a war drum. He watched her explain to Shadbolt, saw her move closer to him, and felt the jealousy begin to burn in him.

Part of him was amazed at his own foolishness. This was Bosco Shadbolt, a good man, his closest friend, a moral soul. But Shadbolt, with his black hair and boyish face, was also very attractive to women. He normally affected an unlit snappipe in the evenings, and would suck it with a judicial air, as if considering a friend's problems with a depth of understanding that outstripped his twenty-five years. Yeah, Eastman thought venomously, and all that squatting stuff serves to cover a streak of indecision in you as wide as the Mystik River.

She had taken his hand in hers. "Will you help me, Bosco?"

"I'd like to help," Shadbolt said uncertainly. "I suppose Barb's already told you what MeTraCor will have waiting for us on Seoul?"

"What?"

"A brig, most likely. You see, we were both a little too eager to offer our views to JJ. Foster during the siege." He smiled, abashed. "When Ellis Straker was in command things seemed kind of different. I guess we were both a measure too liberal with our opinions. If we're shipped off to Seoul, we'll be reprimanded and probably get sent back to Amerika at the first opportunity MeTraCor can open up. They don't tolerate troublemakers." He looked to Eastman. "What do you think?"

Eastman shrugged. He had totally forgotten about Foster and his own defiance on the night of the mutiny. Then he heard himself say stiffly, "I've already told Miz Hawken that I'll give her all the assistance she needs. We've agreed that an attempt to get to Fort Baker has got to be made."

"Oh, Barb."

She moved to him and touched him and the touch gave him the kind of shock that could only come from the voltage of love. What he had promised was madness. Total madness. But he knew at once exactly why he had agreed, and the gratitude she showed delighted him, and the warmth was already beginning to blot out the belief that what he had agreed to was entirely insane.

The air was heavy and electric and full of the influences of quadrature. The wind had stopped and everything was still; distant blue flashes lit the south and east silently, and the stillness was the stillness that foreruns a storm. Inside the MeTraCor building the atmosphere was equally tense. Red Bowen, standing like Ellis Straker's chief retainer, waited just inside the iris with a pair of blasters stuffed into his belt, his hands resting on his hips close by the weapons.

"Well then? Which of you sonsofbitches is gonna come along with me and get a taste of glory?"

There was no movement in the assembled group. No assent from them. The ranks of MeTraCor junior staff reluctantly made space in their assembly and Ellis found himself staring round thirty faces, the whole scene banded by blue security light and the slash of louver blinds. He hadn't told them the half of it and none of them knew what he was being asked to volunteer for.

Some of them looked at Bowen and back at him suspiciously.

"C'mon, c'mon. A half dozen out of the lot of you, that's all I'm asking."

Again there was silence.

"Where's Eastman?"

"He ain't here," one of the younger MeTraCor teks said.

"Yep, breaking the curfew again, eh. Now there's a man worth it. He ain't afraid of no Kan squad. And I'm certain he'd tell me yes to my question."

"What exactly is it you want?" The questioner was a tall, blond-haired man of six years seniority, Prawley by name, one of the go-playing crew who wore his gaiters tight and thought himself close enough by blood to the Frastleys and the Markovish families to have adopted senior MeTraCor affectations. The rest were disposed to listen to him. Their mistrust was strong, but Ellis knew he needed them. Half a dozen. Better a dozen. Willing to tote-gun for him and to fight. If the plan was to succeed, he would need to talk them round for sure.

"Just a bit of fun. I want you to come with me through the ramparts and get away from here tomorrow night."

"Break our parole? Our word of honor to our captors?"

Ellis hated MeTraCor for the way it trod the enterprise out of youngsters. He hated its hell-damned monopoly and the heavy hand of the state that lay across it like a dead weight.

"By God," he hissed, his voice curdling with disgust. "Hell's fire burn MeTraCor and all its ruling maggots! What kind of deaf, dumb, and blind titan takes raw, spirited men like yourselves and deliberately crushes the life out of them?"

Those nearest him recoiled in the darkness, but they couldn't tear their eyes away from him as he cursed their reluctance.

"MeTraCor's in the wrong business, eh! Should be like

Halide. Should be in synth genetix. Should be making fucking servants, yeah, if it wants to manufacture complacent, self-satisfied lick-asses that can't stand up so's never to rock the ship! Your chiefs never want to give young men their run, nor let them say their say, when once in a while that's a necessary thing for young men. No, they want to make their people subordinate and dependent and cowardly and out of synch with psi, like some kind of synth servant. They want to bore them out and stuff their skins with gloop and thin piss and stuff its own hierarchy chock-full of eunuchs and yes-maggots so that it don't ever do nothing but creep forward at an inch a year, never risking, never venturing, which is what they call 'good business' and 'sure and steady progress.' Eh? Eh? Am I right?''

He stared around at them again, raising his voice now as if he was careless of the curfew.

''Well, let me tell you where you're at! MeTraCor burns out young men's souls when there ain't no Earthly need. And their yellow gutlessness seeps out like a blinding fever to cloud their vision. The Kan've been gaining on us for years, and MeTraCor's blind to that. Then a war comes and they're unprepared and they lose all they've built up and again they're blind to that. And when war passes into peace as it surely will, all trade'll be knocked back a decade and they're blind to that too. I ask myself why must it be, when there's an obvious and a better way.''

An obvious and a better way.

He could almost hear the phrase echoing in their heads.

''Yes, a nexus ship to Seoul,'' Prawley said.

''You're not going to sit here and wait on no ship to take you to Seoul,'' Ellis said, grinning ghastly in the half-light. ''There ain't going to be no ship, by psi. And that's a fact!''

''Hu Tsung's promised us a merchantman,'' one of Prawley's friends said definitely. ''The Council told us so.''

"I said there ain't going to be no ship! And Jos Hawken, he says so too. Governor Yu Hsien has left Satsuma two days ago real time to come here." He stared at the staffers and ops and teks evilly, thinking of the aurium he and Cornelius Morgan and the McBrides had just finished unearthing at the Hawken mansion. The only problem was how to get so great a weight of superheavy credit away from Kanoya City and Hu Tsung. "Make no mistake, when Yu Hsien gets here he'll have every last one of you strung up with a meat hook through your jaws for your disobedience."

"We've heard your scare stories before, Straker! We know about you!"

"You don't know nothing," he told Prawley. "You don't know that the Prefect's army only came here because of my son. It was brought here by a bribe delivered to Miyakonojo by him. It wouldn't have come without him. All that was his doing, yep, and mine."

"What does it matter? Look at the result! A whole system's army utterly defeated at the hands of a force less than one tenth their size! They're whupped. And with them our last hope is gone!"

Ellis stared back, angered by their defeatism and apathy. The stinking singularity gun's melted their wills, boiled the virtue right out of their bones, he thought. He knew he had to whip them out of their listlessness. "That the Yamato army failed to relieve us was because Hideki Ryuji and his sons've got the same chance as cockroaches when it comes to facing an enemy with the singularity gun. I agree with you there, Frastley. But they came to help us, and you're all witnesses to that fact. I don't owe MeTraCor an aluminum won. I promised them an army and an army they got!"

One of the staffers spat, muttering, "That rabble of sword-swingers can hardly be called an army."

Ellis cuffed him smartly. "Zip it, boy. I won't have one of you lickspittles calling coward on anyone else when you don't have the balls to do anything yourself."

"What do you want us to think?" the youngster blurted. "Coming here with your man with illegal side arms in his belt and all. You'll get us killed."

Ellis shook his head as if astounded, as if holding in a great urge to violence. "I'm telling you, Yu Hsien is going to flatten Kanoya City and you listen and want to do nothing about it. All you do is complain about events that're dead and gone! What kind of Amerikans are you? Not like the boys of my day when we'd crack the whole of Known Space open like an egg soon as spit to get at the guts inside." Ellis smacked his hand on the arm of a chair. "Listen! I'm warning you: Yu Hsien has told Hu Tsung what he intends, and now Hu Tsung has told me. The Governor don't want Amerikans on this world, and he means to get rid of you as cheaply as he can."

"Sure, but we're all accountable to MeTraCor here." Another of the staffers had spoken up, his voice drawling and unperturbed, his accent that of the minor plutocracy. "We answer to Miz Foster and to no one else."

"That's not the opinion I heard from you a week back, Lennards!"

"As you yourself pointed out, Mister Straker, we have to look to our futures now," Lennards said, sighing heavily. His face was wet with sweat in the still, close air. "MeTraCor brought us here. And it's MeTraCor that keeps us. We came across the Boundary to this damned Sector where they don't allow freezees and they don't allow synths, whore or not, and a million other essentials of modern life. And we come here for no other reason than to build us a credit rating, and I got to tell you that those of us five-sevenths through our tour of duty are looking to our futures more than you're prepared to admit. We been climbing the ladder long enough. We're owed a lot, and due to realise it soon—if we can reach Seoul.''

"Yes," another behind Lennards said. "You might be able to whip up the Independents with your gobshit, Straker. And guys who don't fit in like Barb Eastman might follow you, but we have to consider MeTraCor's rules. Miz Foster has said we should have no more contact with you."

Ellis's lip curled. "Ah, Foster's gasping on her deathbed even as we talk! Strung out on her strap, with her ass hanging out and her liver black as tar from something she picked up on Cagayan years ago. She'll never see Seoul, ship or no ship, and like you say, the Treaty don't let freezees in here."

They began to look from one to another.

"When you think of your futures consider this: There was never a man who fought his way to the top of life's ladder with his soul intact. I'll tell you now, you'll go nowhere but to blazing mediocrity by standing in line to kiss fatsos' backsides!"

They lounged in the sweaty heat, enervated and wilting, their real-silk shirts open to the waist and sodden at the armpits. Their faces displayed dull-eyed ennui. The eldest staffer stood up languidly. "Why should we trust what you tell us, Straker? You hoodwinked the Council into making a defense against the Kan and look what it's gotten us. A smashed-in dome. And it could've been a whole lot worse."

Ellis's contempt was livid. "Ah, but you're a real MeTra-Cor man, ain't you, Prawley?"

"I don't mind admitting that, Mister Straker."

"Well, listen tight, and you may learn something. I've put up a ransom of ten tranches on Kanoya City and Hu Tsung has accepted it!"

There was disbelief.

"C'mon!" Prawley said. "Are you saying he's just going to light his squadron out? Just like that?"

"For ten tranches of aurium, you bet your ass."

"I don't believe it!"

"Okeh, ex-tek. Check, check, check."

They looked at the macro he pulled out and propped on the table. It looked out through the ceiling, through the twenty floors above their heads, through the layers of supraform plex that made up the injured dome and two hundred miles of clouds and progressively thinning atmosphere. They watched as they began putting their faces to the glass-less space between the ranging bars, none of them with the least idea of what they were meant to be looking for. The blackness of space swelled vast and starless, lit only by a constellation of stationary ship's lights.

"The Kan ships are there just like they always have been! What's different?"

Ellis's laugh was derisory. He flung open the drapes and walked out onto the big balcony, waving a charismatic hand so that they followed him out. Overhead, between the gap in the dome and the gaps in the cloud they could just make out occasional starpricks of light that were the Kan. "Yep, they're there, all right. But what else is out there? D'you see it?" He laughed again, damned near a cackle. "No? Course you don't! Well, I'll tell you: The Index is as high as you like! Not a peep out of the nexus! And because you got no talent you don't know what's going to happen at quadrature. But, see, Prawley, Hu Tsung ain't like you. He can feel it in his pores how the Index's peaked. He's been here well long enough to know the signs of the local atmospherics. He knows there's fast brewing a state of affairs between Two-Eight and Two-Nine that can squeeze his robbing squadron like Scylla and Charybdis. And he knows what this calm signifies. He's got no choice but to leave. He'll take himself away if he has to astrogate every vessel out of the system himself.''

They thought about that, imagining Kan crews throwing their ships out across the stillness, astrogators sinking into agony in their cockpits. Suddenly they felt the humid mugginess close in around them. It was heavy and dead. Sweat drenched their bodies; it could not evaporate into the moisture-laden air. Breath came shallowly. Everything was sticky, there was no respite from it when the breeze died, as it had. The clouds had closed suffocatingly over the city like a hot, damp blanket, containing them. The calm before a storm. They hung at the balcony rails, wretched as scarecrows, prisoners of MeTraCor, of the Kan, and of Osumi.

Then they felt it.

They began to feel movement on their damp faces. Like the lightest caress of a mother's hand, on their brows and on their cheeks. A stirring in the air.

"It's a breeze!"

"By God, he's right!"

"I can feel it."

"Jeezus, I can feel it too!"

Lennards turned back from the rail. "Mister Straker, if the Kan Admiral has got to leave, why did you promise him a ransom?"

"You got to offer a man something if you want him to tell you his secrets. See, it takes half a week to ready a fleet properly. He has to hand over to Yu Hsien. I had to know the time UT he planned to light out, so that everything could be made ready.''

"Made ready for what?"

Ellis made a gesture of frustration. "I see I'm slinging jewels off my front porch, trying to talk to the likes of you. Perhaps you've more respect for hard metal than for words.''

He patiently tried again, as if laying it out for three dozen obtuse children. "Take it from me, Hu Tsung'll light out the day after tomorrow. There won't be any ship for you. So you've got two choices: You can stay here with this yes-maggot, Prawley, and be treated to some more Kan hospitality when Mister Grand Functionary Yu arrives. Or you can come with me tonight and get the pay you all so richly deserve." He dug a handful of heavy aurium-plated medallions from his pouch and scattered them so that they rang and shimmered on the polished table. Some of the staffers scrambled for the coins and began to scrape at them with their fingernails.

"Red!"

The astrogator came up. "Yeh?"

"Tell them how much more of this you've seen."

"Plenty more, fifteen tranche."

They gasped. A staffer's official salary was less than ten thousand spending units of Amerikan credit per real-time year—a barely livable slice of the cake after tax and inflation and hypo. The credit Straker's astrogator had quoted was as much as each of them would earn in ten thousand years!

"Because I need you to come along, I'll give you a hundred thou in hard cred apiece. And the promise that anybody who lights out with me'll be heroes at Seoul when we carry back the news of what's happened here."

"You're going to go to Seoul?" one of them asked.

"Yep. Just said so, didden I?"

"But how?"

"'Board the *Chance*, Prawley. How d'yuh think?"

5

The two groups met on the apron the following night an hour after curfew. The breeze was getting up, and the cloud was moving and parting in huge canyons in which the stars hid like diamonds. Bowen with his lads for one lander, Ellis with his for the other. It had taken them two hours to retrieve the last of the aurium from Hawken's mansion and get it to the rendezvous. Now they had met up on the dark north side of Kanoya City. The two guards who had stood point on the landers were now lying trussed in the storm drains that fringed the apron.

It was smooth as tearing silk. They loaded the two forty-two-foot landers, faked Kan ID with a pirated datachord, and lifted off. The routine interrogations were diverted without difficulty. Ellis took the patch stick in his hands and passed an eye over the flashing and blipping chaos that was in front of him. Kanji 'graved on everything, but he knew enough about piloting to get by.

A dozen staffers and ten others were crammed into a hull that felt like a sumo wrestlers' den. The aurium was in ingot flasks in the aisle, all webbed down against shifting and upsetting the gyro fields. Sitting astride it there were Cornelius Morgan and the McBrides, and, in the other lander, two or three other independents who knew what they were doing. Jos Hawken was not present. He knew nothing about the undertaking, nor about his daughter's intention to go with Barb Eastman and Bosco Shadbolt and steal a lander of their own.

Ellis grinned in the darkness, his mind relishing the coming confrontation. Earlier, during the hours of daylight, he had listened to Eastman's regretful excuses. They had been sharing a mess of curried gloop cooked up in Ellis's antique Dovermat. A last supper before parting.

"I'm proud of this old black box, Lieutenant Eastman."

"Sure you should be eating what it synthesises, sir?"

That had wounded. "S'matter? It tastes, doesn't it?"

"Yeah, but . . ."

"But what, feller? Eat up. I'll tell you, John Oujuku gave me that. Birthday gift. You heard tell of Admiral Lord John? It was stolen off a Korean who stole it off an Estates liner. Real high-class kit, is what I'm telling you."

Eastman had shrugged, looked hang-faced a moment, and then got to saying what he wanted to say.

"You know Miz Hawken won't be talked out of it, sir. She keeps repeating that she must get to Fort Baker, whatever the risk. I believe she'll get herself burned down unless she's tied hand and foot."

"What's the problem, Eastman? Can't you find anything to bind her with?"

"That's not what I mean, sir."

"And I ain't talking about webbing." He had looked up from shoveling at his plate, his expression dispassionate. "Promises, lad. Women're best brought round by promises."

"She won't listen to any alternative. It's an obsession to get to Fort Baker. I can't say what could have fixed such a squatting silly notion in her head so strongly, but there it is."

Ellis's eyebrows had lifted innocently. "Ah, the gel's just as mad as a MeTraCor astrogator on a ten-year contract. Now, I can't stand to see calf love making a fool of a feller like yourself. Why don't you forget Arkali Hawken and come along with me and we'll war on the Kan in tandem, as the lawyers say. Now there's an offer. What do you say?''

"I'm sorry, Mister Straker, but I have to go with Miz Hawken.''

"She's real pretty, ain't she?'' he had said slyly, an encouraging leer larding his mouth, and Eastman had gone suddenly prim on him.

"Sir, I feel it's my duty.''

"Sure, sure.''

Ah, he's well and truly lost, Ellis thought now, remembering that comical glazed look he had seen in Barb Eastman's eye. Lovestruck! Just spoiled rotten! Daft as a bog brush now, all the sense driven right out of his head, and him once with so much promise as a fighting brain too.

Ahead on the forward scanners the familiar stars of the Scorpion's tail distorted out of any shape resembling a stinger: Wei and Lesauth, Shaula, Sargas and Girtab. The only visual star in field with an inhabited system was Admiralty 155203, Eta Scorpii, an okeh F3, primary to Satsuma, a world terraformed over a quarter millennium ago, the world where the Kan concession was now to be found.

He felt a pleasurable little mental frisson as he figured the physics of it. The light photons from Eta Sco had labored "overland" the fifty-plus parsecs to his eyes. Strange thing the physical cosmos. Unbelievably slow. Incomprehensibly far. So this antique light was older than his prize Dovermat. He was looking back one hundred sixty something years into history, before Yu Hsien had set up shop there, and well before the good people of Yamato had set up on Osumi. And even so, by the magic of the nexus, Celestial Meatball Yu had left there in real-time a few days ago and apart from a few days dilation would arrive here in all his pomp and glory in a few days time. Just before quadrature. Amazing when you thought about it.

A faint phosphorescence shimmered in the lateral scanners where the lobes of the lander's magnetic sweeps stirred synchotron radiation up out of Osumi's belts. The sight of those aurora swirls vortexing repeatedly in the star-silvered screens lulled him. But there was a warning in them. Spiraling particles meant a flare on Zeta CrA. The star had put out its magnetic tongue at them some time ago, which could only serve to remind Admiral Hu how fine he was cutting things. It was a light-hours pathway from Teth-Two-Eight to Teth-Two-Nine, to the primary and back to Osumi. And quadrature was creeping up slow and sure.

Symptomatically, he thought of his Reba: the look on her face when she had presented him with a son half a lifetime ago. He felt a twinge of guilt over Hayden before his heart scarred over once more.

See what a wound I've taken there? he thought bitterly. Ah, why did you have to die, Ree? Why does my heart open and bleed at intervals for the love of you still? Don't you see how the thought of you impedes me when I need to be ruthless?

His grip hardened on the stick. Emotional tide's coming in, he thought. Fragile as eggshells. Quadrature approaching is all. Phew! Hot in here.

A hard thought bubbled up out of the black sludge at the bottom of his mind. It's plain to any fool that romantic love's the game of imbeciles and fools. Ain't that so? There's no winners all round and no lasting advantage to it. Ain't that just so? What a force of effort spent on dandying and prettification! Yeah, and in the end it's a game where young men and young women're the only prize—youngsters who don't know nothing and can't defend themselves against the advances of a decent talent. That's the problem with human kind. Always worrying about reproduction.

And what for? So your offspring can bite your ass, and

quit on you. Not like trade, where a man gains wealth, and you get to see something for your trouble at the end of it all. The samurai are in accord with our own aristocrats on that: marriages should be arranged for mutual profit. Yep.

He pulled out a wad and blew his nose to clear his head and to check for signs of bleeding in the mucous membranes. That had always been his problem. Lost half a pint of blood on one transit once. Came out of the cockpit looking like a syko victim.

Ah, Barb Eastman should know better. He's too anxious to get himself killed on Arkali's behalf. He might come to some sensible conclusions one day—if he lives that long. I hope he does live, because there's got to be some convenient way to disengage Hayden from his promise to marry Arkali.

He watched the distorted Scorpion's tail pick up an extra star, moving slow, and looked over the rear scans to check that Bowen was following the right distance back. Ah, yes, Hayden. My disowned son. You completed your task after all. I wonder where you are and if you went along with old Ryuji's army. What do you hope to accomplish now? Now that the Kan have the singularity gun beyond any shadow of doubt. Oh, Duval Straker, you loosed a Pandora's box on mankind when you conjured that piece of kit from your equations. That's the trouble with weapons. It's real hard to treaty them out of existence again once they've been invented.

He saw his half brother's disapproving face rebuke him silently.

Hell, it ain't my task to explain to Eastman the reason Arkali wants to go to Fort Baker so bad, he told Duval's illusion as it transmuted slowly into the face of his son. Neither is it my duty to go calling on Jos to put him right, by God! His credit's gone for good, and when I come back to Osumi and the Kan vacate Kanoya City, I don't see what purpose can be served in merging with Hawken Inc. now.

Maybe we could've rolled his daughter up in a bunch of webbing and brought her away with us, but I want Arkali Hawken and Barb Eastman hidden away together aboard Fort Baker for preference, not least because you'll never find them there, Hayden. It's a small place—intimate like—and Eastman'll be able to impress himself on her as much as he pleases, and she'll have nowhere to hide from him. Ha! And as for me, after tonight's work I'll be free to go where I like while Jos Hawken'll be stuck fast to the planet Osumi. Without his daughter he'll have nothing to dote on, and if he's hurt, well that's justice for his deceit over my fifteen tranches of hard-earned aurium . . .

"You all right, sir?"

"Hmm?"

"You feeling okeh?"

He shook the question off gruffly. "Keep your eyes on the forward scanner, Ripley."

"Sir."

The regular humming of the engines fell away and the forward attitude fields turned their angle of attack. They looked to him as the deceleration squeezed them. The interrogators began to chatter and squawk on hailing.

"Why are we stopping, Mister Straker?" Lennards asked.

"You want to get suited up now?"

Suddenly everything went deadly.

"I said, why're we stopping?"

He tossed a helmet at Lennards. "I've got something to say to you all. Some of you think we're rendezvousing with the Kan flagship, but if you think that, you're wrong. We're heading straight for the *Chance*."

"What about the Admiral's ransom?" one of the staffers asked.

Ellis took out a cheroot stub and clamped it in his teeth. "What about it?"

"Do you mean we're going to hand the Kanoya City ransom over to Admiral Hu aboard the *Chance*?"

"Nope."

A pause. Then a panicky kind of anguish from one of them.

"But I thought that was the plan. To buy our freedom with that aurium."

"A waste of good superheavy, don't you think?"

"But surely his men won't let us get aboard the *Chance* unless the ransom's been paid!"

"Then we'll have to persuade him another way, won't we?"

"Now just a minute! That wasn't what we agreed," Prawley said.

"There's a price to everything, mister. You should know that."

"You want us to storm your ship? From these landers?"

"What if they see us coming?" another of the staffers asked, plainly terrified. "What if they've called up already?"

Ellis stared at them. "They won't fire on us. It's like this: Hu Tsung's ships have been readying for the last twenty-four hours. They'll light out at 14:00 UT. *Chance*'s been hooked up to a maintenance station for the last two days, taking on fluids. No point getting aboard her until she's fully made ready. Then it's a quick disengaging of her umbilicus and the retractors fore and aft, out with my *suifu* from confinement and away before Hu's people have time to lock on with their armaments, or haul ass to pursue us."

"But how do we get aboard?"

"Never hear of egress hatches? Never hear of a cargo hold?"

"Cargo hold? But they're sealed by law offplanet! What about the antipersonnel measures?"

He dangled an ion key and smiled. "Switch them off. We'll coast up quiet and surprise the watch. Swarm on her hull and get into her through all the egress ports. Then open the day doors and do the business.''

"But what if they see us coming?"

"Don't you worry. There's boys here has done what we're about to try dozens of times. No power shooting. Just scorchers and pig-sticking. I like the way *Chance* is decorated. She's my property, remember. That's why I brought nothing but side arms.''

He pulled out two sacks and upended them on the deck. Inside the bigger bundle was a half-dozen 100 series Wessons; the smaller contained a couple of dozen dinner knives that had been ground to sharp points.

Prawley groaned. "Straker, you're insane."

"Ah, we'll be all right. Even a yeller-gutted bastard like yourself'll be all right.''

"I won't do it!"

"What'll you do instead? Fly home?"

Prawley tensed, but then looked down and saw the blaster in Ellis's lap and thought again.

"Now, suit up, boys. And do 'zacly what you're told, or we'll all find ourselves swimming in the same shit.''

6

Admiral Hu Tsung lay awake in the Controller's big bed, his skin gleaming with sweat, his queue hair recently disheveled by acts of abandoned indulgence with the golden-skinned

Osumi girl who lay beside him. She sighed as she resettled her slim and naked length against his arm and leg. On the table close by her head was the half-empty bottle of perfumed oil and the cataplasm she had used on him so skillfully. It had been delightful! Her name, he felt sure, meant Peach Blossom. He would call her Mistress of the Sea Slug, or perhaps Princess Orgasm.

How strange the mysteries of fashion, he thought, toying with the excellent notion of the cataplasm. Most ingenious clever, these people. How quickly a man's taste begins to deviate from the norm when separated from the center of culture by so great a distance! But soon I'll have sufficient credit to return to Gu Gong and pass through the Gate of Supreme Harmony. Then I shall make my possession of the Fortunate Weapon known, and after that it is possible that I will be accorded the status to compete with the functionaries of the highest rank for office in the Dowager's government.

He looked at the girl as she lay on her belly, her eyes closed, her entire form relaxed after her primitive exertions. To take back a genuine Yamato geisha mistress! Or is the idea too outré? This one's too tall and thin and feline for Gu Gong. She's a blank-eyed devil-ess! One cannot see her wicked nature—there is no truth in her eyes at all.

Naturally, it is her inferior genes that are to blame. In the Central Realm only the poor are as blank in the eyes as she, and there is a matter of ignorance of form! A courtesan such as she would never pass in Gu Gong. She's far too—exotic.

He resettled himself, careful to avoid catching his finger cones in the courtesan's luxuriant hair. What awesome auspiciousness! To have what must be the very last Fortunate Weapon to survive the Amerikan war fall into my hands. And at a time when we are in dispute with Amerika. Perhaps they will be enraged enough to tear up the Limitation Treaty and to make more Fortunate Weapons—which they surely could—only in that case they will surely be Unfortunate Weapons. But then the result would be a capitulation of current ruling elements in the Dowager's government, and their replacement by others who would show me greater favor. So possession of this weapon is very fortunate indeed for me.

Yet I do really want to make my bid for political power now? Do I really want to abdicate this life of war to make a new one in the Dowager's palace? Am I not extraordinarily fortunate? To fly through the Dragon's Eye is not given to one man in a thousand million. I shall miss the exhilaration and the peculiarities a happy voyager encounters. As a ship commander I may go where I please, and do as I please, with whomsoever I please, and no one cares if my consorts are not appropriate—or if they do care, they dare not communicate that thought to me. I am the ultimate authority in all our possessions beyond the Zero Degree Boundary, in what the Amerikans call the Neutral Zone, and I answer to no one but the Dowager herself!

Beside the bed, the cataplasm slithered, black and garish purple inside a porcelain bowl, rippling and hunting about like a leech. A relief molding of an eagle head stood out imperiously from the ex-controller's "plaque of mandate" on the wall beyond the cascades of silk drapery surrounding the bed. The Admiral regarded the pale hook-beaked features and blank eye of the officialistic MeTraCor trademark with disapproval.

In the subtle lighting of this room that profile bears more than a passing resemblance to Yu Hsien, he thought, except that behind the black contact lenses of the real Yu Hsien's eyes there is a mind as adept at political intrigue as any Yamato Daimyo. But in this matter he has met his match. He is forgetting that I have the ships, and that I have the power, and that I have the Fortunate Weapon. He does not yet realise that I do not care about his lofty aspirations to build a personal empire in Yamato.

He reached out through the drapery to the panel, and phased the lighting, refiguring the cast of light and shadow on the eagle's head. With the illumination coming from the right, the effect was grotesque. How much grimmer the real Yu Hsien will look when he hears that a deal on the future of Kanoya City has already been sealed, he thought. How much paler than pale will he turn when he arrives to find that my fleet has departed and that his unfortunate troops will have to find their own way back to Satsuma!

What will happen to the Amerikans when Yu Hsien arrives? he wondered fleetingly. Doubtless they will have to take the brunt of his considerable disappointment. Too bad. Yes, just too bad!

Hu Tsung closed the drapery and lay back, resting his hand on the girl's bare bottom thoughtfully. It's quite simple: Yu Hsien, Celestial Functionary, Executive of China Products, and Governor of the Lease of Satsuma—though he calls himself Governor-General if you please!—remains firm in the deluded belief that he outranks me and may call me to heel like a running dog. Furthermore, he thinks he can prevail by using his lackeys to paralyse the situation here until he himself can arrive to take charge of everything, but I will not allow that. I am like the wind. I go where I please and I do as I please . . . whenever I please! That has always been my ideal. I believe in making war—and I also believe in making war pay!

"Yen you yi si!"

He slapped the girl's bare bottom sharply, pleased with himself. She let out a delightful squeak and slyly met his eye, then she began to stroke him. He listened, his senses heightened: a rumble of thunder told him the weather was still deteriorating. There was a commotion in the main square below. From the sound of it security troops were arriving in their commandeered vehicles, officers were shouting indistinct orders, and there were other urgent sounds. How the military made such a great fuss about psi-storms and every fluctuation of the Heavenly Balance! Ignorant men! Primitive minds! Slaves of superstition! Anyone would think troops who had been brought out of suspension for a battle and then gone on to win it gloriously would find more cause to delight in their brief freedom.

He examined the back of his hand. But I have to admit there is no getting used to major psi phenomena. Quadratures in two-nexi systems are always spectacularly impressive—and strategically important—especially to the timing of this particular withdrawal. The ransom discussions with the Amerikans of MeTraCor were a waste of time. Those weak and ineffectual men of the Council were unable to offer terms, and I was on the point of beginning Yu Hsien's labor of destruction, starting with the dome of Kanoya City, when the Amerikan trader, Ellis Straker, announced his ten-tranche offer. It seems that irritating bargainings have filled all my days since the moment I first agreed to meet with him!

What a scorpion dance it has been! Our claws locked, circling and sidestepping, both stings arching and striking! Ten tranches of aurium had suddenly become a regrettable five! But, after rage, five had grown to six; then threats and blank refusals, so seven; then a space of silence, so eight; then, after delays and maneuvers, with great difficulty, nine. Finally he had held up his hand in front of Straker's face and rubbed his fingers against his thumb, giving the angry ultimatum: Ten tranches, despicable snake! Or else I shall lose patience! And no more to be said about it!

He had shown the trader what bargaining was!

The next day Hu Tsung had sent his most trusted servant,

Ah Quei, into the lime caves of Shinju Horaana to meet with Straker's servant in order to verify the existence of the superheavy metal. The passages of the Pearl Cavern ran for miles under the Lease. Ah Quei had been blindfolded and taken to a secret location where sensors could not follow, but he had returned with bulging eyes. There had been ten tranches stacked up on display on the melted stones of a twenty-year-old ancient shrine. They had showed Ah Quei all of the ingots, and he had estimated it accurately, despite his loathing for enclosed places.

Hu Tsung shifted his weight comfortably in the bed and laced his hands behind his head. What was that excessive noise? Why, in the name of the August Personage of Jade, were the troops getting so excited? The storm was troubling them. They had some vague idea about the connection between atmospheric disturbances and the state of angriness of the Dragon's Eye.

"Oh, oh, oh . . ."

She moved her mouth across his body. His eyes traveled up and down the folds of the drapery as the girl's hair spilled across his belly. Mosquitoes from the lagoon had come in through the shattered dome. They patrolled the silky seams overhead. He looked down at the purple bruise the girl had enthusiastically raised below his navel.

She met his eye, and then, very deliberately, she bit him.

"Aieee! Zhuyi!"

He tensed but relaxed again as she coyly began to kiss the place she had bitten.

"I am surrounded by people who want to suck my blood," he said. "And now you too?"

He sighed. All day Lao, the garrison commander, and Wu Shen, the officer who had purchased the Slumbering Soldiers in Guang Dong, had been busy tightening a tourniquet around his neck.

By eight o'clock tomorrow morning there will be nothing left of their plans, he thought, relishing the meeting with Straker planned for seven. Kanoya City will have been sold for ten tranches of the finest Sado aurium—and I will be leaving the Sector of Yamato, richer by two hundred billion in yuan . . .

He heard a discharge and something beyond the semi-phased panes lit up violet in the night.

A hammering on the door made the girl look up.

"Hao," Hu Tsung said without hesitation, despite the fact that he had left definite instructions not to be disturbed.

Ah Quei came in, knelt daintily, and bowed so that his shaved front pate almost touched the bed. He was perturbed neither by the girl nor by the news he had brought. He offered a tray on which the note lay folded like a mantrap.

Hu Tsung opened it and read his garrison commander's message. Then he exploded from the bed and began to throw his robe over his shoulders with great haste.

"Tell Lao to call the flagship! And tell Wu Shen I'm coming!" He tugged violently at a long silk belt. Ah Quei disappeared instantly. The girl stared at him as if he had suddenly gone mad.

The firing he had heard had been his troops summarily executing the apron guards. The *Chance* had disengaged from the provisioning station and lit out for the Dragon's Eye the Amerikans called Teth-Two-Eight.

"I can't believe it!" he shouted as he dragged on his slippers. "Burn Ellis Straker! Burn him! Burn him! Burn him!"

7

Dream terror beat through Hayden Straker as he sprang awake. Everything around him was blindingly bright, and for a moment he wondered where he was, and whether he could now muster the strength to look at the perfect hole cut through the center of his chest. He knew that if he did look he would see that his own heart was missing, and that must mean he was dead.

Momentarily the horror of the paradox froze him. Then he searched his chest, unable to breathe, and at last he realised that another vile dream had visited him and he collapsed back into the futons, thankful beyond reason that this was Edo, a world many light-years from Osumi.

The battle of Kanoya City was now many months in the past, but still it haunted him. It had been his battle, the battle he had bought and paid for, the one that had ended in total rout. So many men killed, an unknown number—hundreds, perhaps thousands bleeding and dying on the ground, and many more wounded crawling back in screaming pain, limbless or seared open by a monstrous weapon. For them there had been no waking from dream, no return to wholeness. And no glory.

He breathed rapidly, gasping like a man drowning in his own blood. As he closed his eyes the terrible memory of the attack lived in his mind again: the magnificent panoply of war shattered, so many men blasted into carrion by the singularity gun, agony upon agony, and the insane, panic-stricken retreat raked by snaking beam fire from the city ramparts. It had been his fault. He had wanted it. Had demanded it. Vehemently. All of it. And it had been given. Against Hideki Ryuji's better judgment. God forgive them both.

"What is it, Mister Straker?"

He opened his eyes into the glare of afternoon, and a pain seared his head. A huge bronze dragon cut across the sky. A figure stood over him, her voice concerned for him. He remembered now. It was a festival day. He had been the honored guest of Honda Yukio, sitting with him and two of the Shogun's generals atop a classical white castle, a ziggurat tower of many steps and steel-gray pagoda roofs, except for the top tier that was unroofed. It was remote from the main palace, in the midst of the terraces of the Daiten astronomical gardens. Below were armillary spheres of Known Space, twin skeleton globes, hooped bracelets of phosphor bronze defining the galactic equator, the twelve boundaries, the ecliptic of Edo, and the local celestial meridians. Elsewhere, there were geometrical granite blocks engraved with graduated lines, many kinds of sun dials and moon dials for Edo's satellites and gnomons to fix and set the direction of the primary and the system nexus. Above was a great star-sighting quadrant standing in the center of the tower platform, its crescent free-swinging on a balanced axis like an enormous weather vane, or a gigantic version of one of his father's jealously owned astrogation instruments. At night, when the multicolored lasers shone from it, the observatory dominated the sky.

This was the place the court astrologers came at night to take their readings from polished scales of deeply incised Chinese numerals, to plot the progress of the system planets across the zodiac and read what was written for the future.

But the walled platform of the tower had been laid with rich silk carpets and scattered with cushions and hung with delicate curtains; it had been transformed into a pleasure pavilion.

There had been displays and sake and expensive delicacies and white-faced geisha and maids waving paper fans over them for cool. And there had been the sensuous courtesans of Edo with their eyebrows painted high over their eyes, lips painted with brilliant crimson, extravagant gowns of the most gorgeous color and pattern, loose to their waists so that their small but perfect breasts were frequently glimpsed. They all possessed tresses of the most astonishingly long black hair, talking as they played and sang and danced and joked and plied the male guests with sake. It had been a gentle noonday relaxation without politics but with snacks and an endless supply of aromatic rice wine instead, and they had come out here where the hot, humid breeze of Edo's north temperate summer blew from the east and the Blue Ocean.

He had endured the entertainment patiently, hoping that Honda Yukio might be able to put a stop to this endless waiting and arrange for him at last to present his petition to the Shogun. He had come armed with a letter.

"Drink, Mister Straker. Drink and enjoy. Drink and enjoy and relax. Here we have everything for you. So drink and be content."

"I thank you, Yukio-sama."

"And please enjoy my doves too. Here we say that no man can be expected to function in a proper manner unless he unburdens himself regularly. Is that not so?"

The favorite grandson of the great Sakuma Hidenaga had been a forty-year-old, overweight boor, his smile insincere, his eyes hooded and impenetrable as he spoke, and he sweated perfume. Nevertheless, his luxuriousness had been skin-deep. He had asked some penetrating questions about Osumi, about the battle and exactly what had happened in it before he had allowed his giggling girls to feed him melon slivers and consume him with their laughter.

"May I at least ask you to pass on this letter to the Shogun at your first convenience?" he had asked finally, smothering his frustration with Yamato indirectness as best he could. "Surely he cannot be so taken up with affairs that he has not the time to read what is a very short letter."

Honda Yukio's eyes had slid behind their lids as his toad-like grin had spread. He had waved a careless gesture at the universe. "What is time, but the revolving of the heavenly bodies in their courses? We shall have to see how the first moon sets, Mister Straker. And see also how it rises. For sometimes today's moon is grown more plentiful by degrees than yesterday's, and sometimes it is grown slimmer."

"I hope that tomorrow's moon is full, Lord. I have been expecting that phase for too long."

The grin broadened and the words came again, caressingly, from his throat. "You may hope. But please do not be surprised if tomorrow's full moon is darkened again by eclipse."

"That will not surprise me, Lord. Indeed, I have schooled my mind to expect delays to the end of time."

"That is strange, for is not time endless?"

He had sighed. "Lord, in the Amerikan world we have another view of time. It has been brought down from the heavens in the observatories of Liberty. Our time has been captured and contained. Thus tamed and regulated, time is our servant and not the other way round. My Lord, that is what makes us what we are."

Honda Yukio had swallowed the criticism whole. "And in the Central Realm of Xanadu too, we have heard, there is also an observatory where time is unnaturally regimented. How fortunate for you that you do not live there." He had rolled his eyes up, then he had snapped his fingers and a woman—the most wanton of the courtesans—had instantly produced an expensive gold and steel wristwatch. Yukio took it and twisted the winder out with his thumb and forefinger, to spin the hands against a classically worked oyster perpetual datejust dial.

"You see! In the days of our supremacy we collected such a wealth of things! There is something about very ancient machines that appeals to us. That is why ninety percent of artifacts manufactured before the twenty-first century are now to be found in Yamato. Toku-toku, toku-toku . . . Do you hear it? It is a useless thing, of course, of no purpose or consequence to me, but it is pretty, is it not? Such a thoughtful gift."

Hayden Straker had taken the watch and examined it, and slowly a brooding sense of unease had crept over him: the crown embossed on the backplate was absent. In its place were the words "Flying Horse Brand" and "People's Republic of China."

Honda Yukio had made his point as he had intended, but Hayden Straker chose to risk a disaster of face.

"My Lord, it's not bad at all—for a fake."

"So sorry, but these Flying Horse fakes are more valuable than real Rolex antiques. So many were thrown away when the batteries failed, you see." He grinned, then, soothingly, he said, "Perhaps we will soon be able to do something to advance your interests. We have some small influence with our exalted grandfather at whose name all except fools bow low. Now please allow this beautiful creature, whose name is Myobu, to wait on you. Drink and talk as you please. Tomorrow, if the merciful gods will it, you may be gone from this timeless place, perhaps to return to your own world."

He had obeyed. Self-consciously at first, but as the extraordinarily fine sake thinned his blood he had allowed the women to take off his jacket and cap and then his socks and gorget. He had propped himself on his elbow with the fragile *choko* of wine between his thumb and first finger, and sucked in the warm pungent drink appreciatively. It was instantly refilled.

"Tell me about yourself, Mister Straker. Tell me. Tell me all."

He had seen the toad grin broaden. Things had begun to swim in the heat. The emerald folds of the robe of the most beautiful courtesan glinted, green as a serpent's eye. "Lord, there is little to tell . . . about a humble man . . . but I will tell you . . . whatever you wish."

"Come, Myobu. Put your hands on the Amerikan's brow. I want to know how he came here. Before that, how he came to Osumi. And why does he accompany this extraordinary embassy now?" Among the caresses a jowl-heavy face loomed. "I have heard about some gem that you brought to Hideki Ryuji. It is said to be very special. Yes, perhaps you would like to tell me about that."

The pleasure pavilion atop the ziggurat was deserted now. The shadow of its cusped pagoda roofs had moved with the sun-star of Edo. The samurai had gone from the astronomical garden to some other part of this huge and fantastically impressive palace complex. They had gone—whether by design or not he could not tell—leaving him alone, asleep and exposed. He had lain directly in the F2 sun-star's powerful noonday rays for more than an hour.

"Yasuko-san? Can it be you?"

His mouth was dry as dust. He tried to get to his feet, ashamed at his sore, sweat-dampened face and disheveled hair, but succeeded only in falling back. His heart still thumped. "Excuse me. I fell asleep. I had a dream."

She was a black shape eclipsing the light. She wore a formal kimono of many layers that fell from her obi to her ankles. Her midriff was bound by the close-fitting sash, and the lapels of the robe crossed over just below her neck, obliterating the shape of her breasts. Her hair was pinned up with delicate wisps escaping at each side, carefully combed out to suggest exertion.

She said, "I was walking among the sculptures below and I heard your cry. I thought you had found a scorpion, or perhaps one had found you." She paused, then asked, "What was your dream? If you tell it to me I shall tell you its meaning."

"I . . . it was nothing. I'm all right, thank you."

"Do you not realise that it is dangerous to go to sleep in the open on Edo? That it brings problems for those of very white skin?"

"I did not mean to do so."

Around him was a wreck of pummeled cushions, spilled *tokkuri*, a tray of half-eaten sweetmeats; grains of white rice sullied the tatami. He looked away, feeling ashamed.

The paper screens hanging around them were a painful white. They obscured the view over the mountainous valley, but also protected the pleasure pavilion from vulgar gaze. From this vantage point they could see anyone coming up the steps, but no one could see them.

She approached him. "Your face is very red. Let me see it." She knelt and took a bottle of lotion from between the cushions, then she poured some into her palm and delicately applied it to his cheeks and forehead. "This is a special oil the courtesans use. It will kiss your skin and prevent it from peeling away."

Instantly, the burn left his face and the touch of her fingers lingered as he looked at her.

"That's very kind of you, Lady," he sighed, surrendering to the delight. "Very kind."

"You did not go with the others," she said matter-of-factly.

It was not a question, but still he felt he had to reply. "Go with them? No. I fell asleep and . . . I think it must have been the sake."

"Yukio-san's—hospitality—is not what it seems."

"That's very true, Lady." He smiled, calmed by her. "I underestimated how much alcohol was in it. I assumed it was quite weak and I was very thirsty, and because of the warmth I suppose that I . . ." He moistened his lips and looked up. "I drank too much."

"Perhaps."

"I thought the Shogun forbade strong drink here," he said sheepishly. "And the way his grandson's ladies were dressed . . ."

She adjusted her kimono, which was chaste and confining. "The Shogun gives guidance on many matters, but on his own capital world each person is under oath to take only what his or her strength or vanity allows." She ran more oil into her fingers and rippled them against her thumb. "I think that the courts of the Shogun are intended as a paradise. It is as if we were already dead, no? In such a place mundane or homely thoughts have little meaning."

He looked at her for a long moment, and when he spoke his voice was stronger. "However, we are not dead. And it has surprised me, Lady, in our time here, that there is no prohibition on the taking of snap at the Shogun's court. Nor on the smoking of tobako—which appears to be enjoyed by the nobility without restriction. There is also the open practice of prostitution."

"It is true that the Shogun is samurai, and an upholder of the traditional Way, therefore his Court observes the principal laws of Yamato." She gestured with her hands, like the seesawing pans of a weighing scale. "But he is also a mindful ruler, who enjoys the festivals and the observance of religious ritual as well as the practices you say."

"He sees no inconsistency in that and the asceticism of the Way?"

"On Edo, or Osumi, you will find many different interpretations of the Way that arise from the personal idiosyncrasies of individual Daimyo. In Yamato all people have a place, and unlike Amerika, in our system all people know what that place is. I think that after hundreds of years the Amerikans still have not grown up. They make a virtue of altering status. In the Kanoya City Lease they make a big mistake trying to teach this way to Yamato people."

"You think so?"

"Do not forget that the samurai Way has been ruling for fifteen hundred years without interruption. The Way has been in us for a long time."

"Without interruption? What about the late nineteenth and twentieth centuries?"

"It is true that the wearing of swords and other outward signs of samurai status were temporarily banned under the rule of the Emperor Meiji, but this was to concentrate the energies of the people on modernization. You would not deny that during the first half of the twentieth century the Way was strong in Old Japan."

"But Japan lost the World War."

"Do you know that within a few hours of the exploding of the first *genshi* bomb, a meeting was held in which it was agreed among men of impeccable samurai lineage that the World War would be switched from a military to an economic front. In the decades that followed, Japanese rulers adopted what seemed to Amerikans to be democracy. But that was done deliberately to make Old Japan appear more acceptable to her commercial customers. What happened when Old Japan became the dominant world power is history that we both know, Mister Straker. Democracy has always been an obsession confined largely to the Freemason caste of Old

Europe and Old America. It is true to say that neither Yamato, nor Old Japan, ever gave any thought to democracy."

Yes, he thought. She's right about that. And history is always written by victors. That's why it's so hard to make sense of these people. Their history's made them unique. They're not remotely like the Chinese, nor do they think like us. Our religions and our laws, our governments and our gods, our traditions and ideals, they're all completely different.

"But all people are the same, underneath," she said, sensing his thoughts. "Is that not your belief?"

"I don't know." He regarded her thoughtfully. "If you mean that we all suffer pain, I'd agree. If you mean that we all experience joy, or grief, or ecstasy, or sadness, or delight, or torment, or inner peace, again I'd agree. If you mean that we all pursue those things or hide from them, I'd agree once more. But if you mean that we think the same, your people and mine, then I'd say that we almost certainly do not."

"So! You are a reader of minds?"

"I simply observe it as a fact of behavior."

"Do not forget that you too have behavior." She inclined her head. "By the gestures of your hands I see you are a man who finds it hard to reconcile what he has been taught he should believe and what he knows he believes in his heart. Am I correct? Do all Amerikans have this problem?"

He smiled shallowly. "I'll say only this: That is a question you would not ask if you were Amerikan."

There's more to it than that, he thought, prickled by her criticism. We're from a culture that's like an oak—strong and upthrusting in the trunk, yet diverse also, branching in a thousand different directions, each end a leaf, individual and unique. Whereas this civilization's bamboo, the strength of its single stem is immense, yet it grows in one direction only; its character comes from the way every strand and fiber is closely bound in tiers. I've only understood that since I've been here in Edo. I've begun to see also that its heart is hollow, only the outward show continues. They're at the end of their glory, a hollow stem fated to fall—or to be cut down. My father always believed that, but I could never before understand what he meant. I could not see how a stem so manifestly strong and powerful and so deeply rooted in the soil as Yamato could be so fragile. He said it was, and he was right. Now, I see that.

Ellis Straker had warned MeTraCor many times that Yamato was sinking into decadence. He had called it a natural process that afflicts all empires. "You should learn that in any living creature the vigor always fails eventually, no matter what or who it is. It will in me one day! Yep, and in yourself! Which is why you have to grasp today! Strive while yet you can!"

And empires?

"Ah, empires are like the men who build them. They grow old and decayed and too weak to defend themselves. So you must expect the Kan to find this Sector of Yamato an increasing attraction."

As Hayden Straker remembered his father's words, great articulated wasps banded in black and lime-green visited the browning cores of apples in the bowl beside him. Their comma abdomens breathed fast on needle-slender waists— golden eyes jeweled as they ate. They buzzed away in relays to their brood hive built in a ruined Shinto shrine.

According to Ellis the fissures had begun to yawn open forty years ago, when Mutsuhito's father had handed on the Imperial throne, but long before that the samurais' Empire had been dying—from the inside out.

Anyone can see it now, he thought, looking out over the basking glory of the Shogun's palace. Despite all this, their industrial power is shrunken and enfeebled, the four Quadrants of Yamato have split away, and Kyushu, Shikoku, Honshu, and Hokkaido are all but independent fiefs. Their colonial possessions in the Neutral Zone have been freed by Amerikan power, and the Boundary States along the Three Thirty Degree Plane are running out of Edo's control. What else? If the rumors are to be believed, new incursions from Xanadu and Hainan are set to sweep away Yamato's sham administrations. It's only a matter of time before the whole of the Sector falls into chaos. I'm learning so much here, so much that I'm beginning to make sense of my father's ideas, and of Hideki Ryuji's policies too.

After the debacle at Kanoya City, it had been strangely clear to him how to carry events forward on his own initiative. For the first time he had felt able to grasp events, and edge them a little towards his design. First thing's to have a goal, he thought. Sounds so obvious, but unless you've got a goal you'll never find psi. I never knew what was wrong with me before.

After the battle he had known that he must enlist the help of a higher authority than the Daimyo of Osumi for help in making Yu Hsien relinquish Kanoya City. In Miyakonojo, he had asked the Prefect for permission to take his request for assistance to the Shogun on Edo, the bearer of the Sword of State himself.

At first, Hideki Ryuji had refused, not wanting to give Sakuma Hidenaga any reason to send a fleet into the Osumi system. But then he had chosen to send an ambassador to Edo, knowing it was imperative that the Kan be disciplined as soon as possible. And now, that could only be done by Sakuma Hidenaga's forces.

As soon as an official pretext could be found, Hideki Ryuji had sent Shingo and the Lady Isako and Yasuko and their full establishment of women, servants, and guards on an official embassy to Edo. The official reason had been the failing health of Mutsuhito, the Emperor on Kyoto: Shingo was to consult with the Shogun's Court on what arrangements should be made in anticipation of the Emperor's death. Of course, the real reason was something else entirely. Only on the eve of departure, after very careful thought, and for reasons he could not yet discern, had Hideki Ryuji decided to allow him to pass along the Chain of Hidden Leaves also.

They had been on Edo for many months now. The elaborate negotiations had dragged on and on, and two days ago Honda Yukio had told him casually that the forty-year rule of the Sun God, His Imperial Majesty Mutsuhito, was ended, and had been for some time.

His son and successor, the new Emperor, had so far been unwilling to move in the matter of confirming Sakuma Hidenaga as Shogun. The reasons were political: Sakuma Hidenaga was old and in ill health. Two potential heirs were waiting in his shadow, already vying for the shogunate. Favor shown now, however slight, could backfire later, and to delay the reconfirmation of Sakuma as Shogun was a definite signal that the new Emperor wanted a new generalissimo. It seemed that he was prepared to accept either candidate, so long as he could prove himself the stronger.

Honda Yukio was one of those contesting lords. He was much sharper in the mind than he wanted people to believe, and perhaps he too was signaling that the time had come for events to move forward, that the diplomatic paralysis was, at last, coming to an end. Perhaps.

He thought of the Chinese-made electromechanical watch again and queasy misgivings bubbled in him. *The antique is significant. Honda Yukio is taking presents from the Kan. And there is still the amygdala—what has happened to that? But isn't its usefulness spent? Since the rout at Kanoya City there had been no point in thinking about it . . .*

He put his hand to his temple. The brightness and his overindulgence completely robbed him of strength and his head raged. "Oooohhh."

"The Shogun says that in strong drink and gambling there is both usefulness and sin," Yasuko told him pitilessly. "But that the sin of them is greater than their use."

"Your leader's thoughts are very wise, Lady."

"Perhaps you should take heed then. Especially concerning gambling." Her eyes flicked carefully right and left, then she continued, an edge of warning in her voice. "The Shogun's Court is a caldron of intrigue that makes Miyakonojo seem as pure as the waters of a crystal stream. Honda Yukio-sama and Sakuma Kiyohide-sama are the two main players maneuvering for position here. The stakes are very high and growing higher every day, so be careful, Mister Straker, and for your own safety, do not be seen to back the wrong side." She urged him to lie back more comfortably and produced a second oil to put on his face. "You said you were dreaming. The dream made you shout. What was its substance?"

The dream . . .

After the battle the ragged remnants of Hideki Ryuji's army had gathered, then dragged their battered vehicles back to Miyakonojo. Hideki Ryuji himself had been pale-faced and silent in his war-tattered *sora-sensha*, shocked and humbled by the unexpectedness of the defeat. He understood only partially the immense implications of the outcome. It had been a total humiliation for a Prefect. His authority had been defied and his army smashed into retreat, and by a force perhaps one fifth, perhaps even one tenth, the size of his own.

But it was much more than a humiliation. It was a precedent. For the first time, a few Kan officers and their low-grade suspended troopers had withstood the massed assault of a much bigger samurai force. The charge had broken and fled under the fire from the despicable weapon, and with that army had fled also the ultimate sanction of overwhelming force that lay with the samurai overlord of Kyushu.

"It was a war dream that made you shout."

Again the question that was not a question. Again it laid his guard low.

"I was dreaming about the battle," he said distantly. "In the fight. It was a terrible dream."

"You have very little taste for war, Mister Straker."

He looked at her hollowly. "The truth is, I don't have the stomach for it."

She took his admission without comment. Another long moment passed, then she said slowly, as if reciting a verse stored for years in her mind, "Warfare is ordained for you, though it be hateful unto you; but it may happen that you hate a thing which is good for you . . ."

He gazed at her, mystified by the paradox.

". . . and it may also happen that you love a thing that is bad for you."

She looked back now, into the depths of his eyes, and he saw her compassion, and he could not stop himself from reaching up to her to touch her cheek, then she looked away again and his hand fell away also. "The gods know your destiny, but you do not," she said.

She did not rise as he expected, but stayed and worked more oil into the skin of his face, and he closed his eyes and considered her words. The danger of his situation fogged his mind: it's beyond the strict laws of the Court to be alone with a lady of the First Rank, or even to be in her presence without the express permission of her husband. Even on a festival day such as today, and with the dispensations granted to me by Hideki Ryuji, even in a place such as this astronomical garden where both men and women may walk freely—if Shingo-san were to come here and discover us, he would be within his rights to have us both punished.

It's true that their punishments are incredibly severe. I wonder what the punishment for adultery is? Has she thought about that? My God, we've been here months, and each time we meet she talks to me using less and less formality, we converse with greater and greater enthusiasm, covering all kinds of subjects, where else can it be leading?

Why did she happen to come by this particular place when I was alone here? Perhaps she's right that in this world we choose to obey whichever laws we please. And perhaps I am beginning to love a thing that is bad for me. She's so beautiful that I could . . .

He reined in his thoughts sharply, but he could feel her supple fingers on his cheeks and neck, he could feel her eyes on him, smell the sweetness of her breath, and the longing in her. No! No! That way lies only destruction! Think about why you're here. Think about the battle. Think about hell-damned samurai politics. Think about anything except Yasuko-san.

He sat up suddenly, the excitement of his body an ache pulsing in him. He began to gather up his clothes and cap and don them hastily. "Thank you, Lady. I should like to go down now. Alone, if you don't mind. Thank you again for your attention. Thank you."

He got to his feet and descended the steps as fast as the dizziness in his head would allow him, and she looked after him as he staggered, wondering if he could really be so susceptible to the rice wine he had drunk. If he had slept so heavily and awakened so unhappily and so confused after just a little sake. Perhaps the legendary capacity of *gaijin* for handling strong drink was greatly exaggerated.

She smiled at the embarrassment he had shown at her

touch, and the astonishing way the shape of his penis had begun to show inside his tight white trousers. She had seen that. It had betrayed him, showed what his thoughts really were. For a moment his eyes had glazed under her tender ministrations, and he had seemed about to make a grab for her. But he had not.

What would I have done if he had? she wondered. But she already knew the answer to that.

It was strange how men behaved when the moons of Edo were in a certain aspect, especially since he had been enjoying the company of Honda Yukio's courtesans before he fell asleep. Doubtless the rest of the men in the drinking party had retired with the choicest women to private apartments to slake other thirsts, why then had he not followed?

A sudden suspicion overcame her. Which courtesans? I wonder. Oh, you'll have to be more careful than I thought, Hayden-san, she told him mentally as he staggered down to the garden and began to cross it. If you can be drugged for your secrets—and perhaps you were—you can just as easily be poisoned.

She capped the lotion bottles, and wiped her hands, and started to descend the steps also. She saw carrion birds wheeling and winging on the hot airs above the landscaped valley.

So, she thought, hurrying from the star garden, the Era of Kanei is over. Shock was still reverberating in her. The Tenno Mutsuhito, the Emperor. Dead. That's what Yukio-sama's women are saying, but Yukio-sama is a grasping, ambitious, treacherous schemer even by the standards of Edo and everything he originates has to be examined and compared with other reports. The reports of what that gross and filthy-minded Daimyo did with the courtesans who consented to go with him had been the staple gossip of Edo for almost a year. They were always paid huge sums, and always obeyed the courtesans' code of elaborating and half divulging so that even one such as Goro-san could not begin to unravel fact from fantasy.

The calling of birds had ceased in the noonday blaze.

Yasuko approached the guards who stood at the door of the residency and waited for them to bow and allow her entry. It was a guard's duty to protect the privacy of the incumbents and to prevent the hostaged families of certain lords from leaving. Some women were kept prisoners because their husbands could not be trusted by the Shogun. She remembered her own confinement in an Edo residency, and the first homesick months she had spent under guard at Miyakonojo in case she should rebel against the marriage into which she had been ordered.

It was horrible, especially those first nights, she thought. But then the other women gradually won my trust, and I have accepted my sequestered life patiently. It might have been worse. On the world of Sendai, the perimeter of the residency is patrolled by samurai carrying beam weapons. At least here, as at Miyakonojo, the guard consists of expert swordsmen, but since I am not of the Shogun's establishment but rather a member of the embassy of the Kyushu Prefect, I may come and go past them as I please.

She made her way through the corridor of the residency to the spacious quarters where the rest of the Osumi women were lodged. Besides herself, there were twenty ladies accommodated in the quarters, the Lady Isako and the courtesan Myobu among them. As she came to her landing she met her older maid, Niso.

"Is Myobu-san within?"

"No, Yasuko-san." Niso grimaced. "The tigress hasn't been here for hours. She's out sharpening her claws somewhere, but I don't think she went at Shingo-san's pleasure."

"Oh?"

"She and the Lady Isako spent some time talking this

morning. They're planning something together. I can sense it.''

Yasuko considered the conclusions she and Niso had already reached concerning the courtesan. Myobu-san was Isako-san's purchase, but it was doubtful that she had been perfectly frank with her contract-holder. Of course, before settling the figure, Isako-san would have demanded to be kept fully and exclusively informed in all matters relating to Shingo-san, and naturally Myobu-san would have agreed to her conditions, but the courtesan was not the type to divulge everything.

"She's devious," Yasuko said. "She's spent too long on Edo for her own good. My guess is that she came to Osumi because of some embarrassment, the rumor is that one of her maids is a poisoner."

"That witch, Tamae-san, her so-called masseuse!" Niso's eyes flashed. "Some say they have seen Tamae-san practice the skills of *ninjutsu*. Those whom Myobu-san protects say Tamae-san was employed because she is expert in the skills of the *kunoichi*."

"Indeed?"

Niso shrugged. It was a delicate matter; *kunoichi* were women, brought up in the ninja tradition, schooled in the erotic arts as well as the secret fighting techniques of their male counterparts. "Of course, she may be here to assist her mistress in the matter of Shingo-sama's personal difficulty. She has certain methods, so I was told. But I don't believe that's the real reason."

"No. Shingo-san has no problem with size or stiffness, and he never wanted for vigor with me. I wonder if he . . ." She shook her head. "But that's not what I wanted to know. Tell me, does Myobu-san ever wear a poison ring?"

Niso pursed her lips. "It is quite possible, but so difficult to tell. Tamae-san could obtain one easily. And it wouldn't surprise me if the tigress goes habitually about the palace with deadly powders hidden in every fold of her clothing. She is a walking arsenal of deceits!''

"Do you have any idea where she went this afternoon?"

"No, Lady. But I know that she went out by the Gate of the Star Garden before local noon. Do you know if there were any pleasure picnics planned by the men there at that hour?"

Yasuko bit her lip. "Tell me, have you heard any more about the Tenno?"

Niso's face became instantly grave. "The Emperor? Only the horrible story that he has become a spirit at last."

"Do you believe that?"

Niso nodded and stared tearfully at the tatami out of duty to the late Emperor's name. If it were true, there would be a month of wailing all over Yamato as soon as an official announcement was made. Astonishing to think that Yamato was now so big that the mourning would be over on Kyoto and Edo long before the announcement had been shipped down the chains to the newest frontier worlds.

"And what of the Shogun?"

Niso swallowed and their eyes met. "The *tayori* is variously that he spends his waning days in prayer, or that he is insane and maintained in a drug trance in a secret chamber under the palace, or that his son, Sakuma Kiyohide, has put out his eyes and has him tortured daily to try to make him confer the *katana* Shori on him, or again that it was Honda Yukio who did the blinding." She sighed with dissatisfaction.

"Yes, I agree. The rumors are without focus. Stay vigilant, Niso-san. I want to know what Myobu-san is up to. But also be careful!"

She kissed her cheek and left.

So, she thought as she made her way towards the door to Shingo's quarters, Myobu-san was not with my husband as I thought. She could have been with Mister Straker, after all—

could have. And she could have drugged him—again, only could have.

I must talk urgently with Shingo-san. He must surely now believe the Lady Isako when she tells him that I am spying on him on his father's orders, but perhaps even she underestimates the degree of confidence that exists between the Prefect and myself. Does she realise, for example, that I know Shingo-san is really here to dispose of the new amygdala? Does she know that truth herself? She must do. I know that Ryuji-sama has charged my husband with the task of choosing who shall receive the jewel of power. There are only two possibilities, but Shingo-san must now be guided to the correct choice.

As she threaded her way through the crowded residency she was bathed in comforting domestic noises and smells and sights. She smiled at those she saw, and they smiled back at her. During her stay on Edo, she had talked with the Shogun's women, and had learned many invaluable facts. For one, it seemed that Sakuma Hidenaga had not appeared in public for almost ten months, creating all kinds of scares and rumors. For another, the Shogun's eldest son was Sakuma Terutoshi, but he was not the heir. According to the most reliable sources, he had abandoned himself to a life of decadence and voluptuous living at the Kyoto Court. He had no desire, it seemed, to take up the heavy responsibilities of the shogunate, nor any wish to bring the curse of the evil-eyed jewel that was fixed in the Shogun's sword down upon his own head.

He had prevailed on the Emperor to issue a decree appointing Sakuma Kiyohide, his own much younger brother, as heir, but that information was disputed by the women who had allied themselves with the noxious Honda Yukio. They thought Sakuma Kiyohide was trying to usurp the shogunate in a well-timed fait accompli.

It is a fascinating power struggle, she thought, and we are

now at the fulcrum of it, able to affect it to our advantage—
if we are clever. That is why Hideki Ryuji-sama sent us here,
and why he sent Hayden-san too.

She considered. Honda Yukio himself was already Daimyo
of Shinano and Mino, two territories in Honshu Quadrant; he
was also the favorite grandson of the Shogun and the main
contender in the battle for ultimate power on Edo. His campaign had been gathering pace. Already he had worked himself into a most advantageous position militarily. Now he had
begun to claim that Sakuma Hidenaga had promised him
prefectship of Kyushu.

That changes everything, she thought. The critical move
has been made and I must inform Shingo-san and then cause
him to move in the correct way. He is such a changed man
that he can no longer be relied upon to do what he must, and
that worries me.

She turned into a long, narrow corridor that was cool and
paper-walled. The wear-polished planks underfoot were wax
slippery under the soft cotton of her socks so she did not
hurry, but she did not linger either: the opalescent panels on
both sides concealed watching guards. One last piece of *tayori*
occupied her mind as she walked. She had discovered that
Myobu's contract had once been owned by Honda Yukio. I
wonder if he's using her to get at Hayden-san, she thought.
And if so, why? What exactly does Yukio-sama want from
him?

In sight now was the door from the Osumi residency. At
the portal she bowed and spoke to one of the guards, and he
sent a goofy-toothed ten-year-old boy with her message to
Shingo. Moments later the boy reappeared and whispered to
the guard. Of course they would not admit her to the sacro-
sanct inner quarters of the lord, but one of them showed her
to a waiting chamber, where Shingo appeared within the hour.

Since the defeat at Kanoya City a great change had come

over him. He was quiet, and he had seldom emerged from his quarters. She had not seen him for weeks.

He was stiff in his bearing, his new arm still held strapped-up across his chest, and he was grim-faced as he approached the window. She felt a pang of guilt at the thought of his decline. To have been defeated by a small force of Kan using cheap, resuscitated troops was dishonorable enough; but to have been dragged from the field of battle by a woman, leaving his sword arm behind, had been ignominious. She should have left him to die a warrior's death, but she had been unable to do that, and in rescuing him she had robbed him of his whole destiny.

That had been a terrible crime. One for which Shingo would never forgive her. More terrible because of Hideki Ryuji's horrifying commands when they had returned to Miyakonojo after the battle. On the night of preparations, when the capital had been ringing with the shock of the defeat, surgeons had grafted a new arm onto Shingo under strict orders from his father.

Illicit Amerikan technology had been used. But the surgeons had been far from competent with the medical cabinets and the cabinets themselves had been stocked with *gaijin* tissue. Mistakes had been made. First, they had claimed the device was only equipped to deliver the limbs of women. Then, when the Prefect had offered one of his bodyguards', mistakes had been made again.

The man's arm had been severed cleanly by one of his colleagues. The guard had then received the woman's arm, and Shingo had been prepared to receive the guard's. Only then had it been noticed that the freshly severed arm was a left arm. A second guard had been summoned, and this time a right arm procured. The operation had been successful, but the surgeons had said that it would take a long time to heal properly. They had implied that he might never relearn his sword skills.

With his samurai dignity in shreds Shingo had been unable to hold his head up. Without full health, and his daily meditations on the Book of Hidden Leaves, he had become lethargic and morose, and the heavy rice wine and rich foods of the Edo Court had burdened him with extra flesh. He stopped six paces from her and she smelled the acid tang of his breath. He had been drinking.

"Well?"

"Thank you for coming at my asking, Lord," she said formally.

"You must kneel when you speak to your husband!"

She sank to her knees obediently.

He looked at her with hate in his eyes. "What is it you want of me?"

"Ask rather what I have to give you."

"I know you have nothing to give me." His voice was icily vacant of emotion, but his words were still cutting. "You never give me anything."

She lowered her eyes. "I have brought you an important piece of information."

He went to stand unsteadily by the opening that overlooked the garden, his back to her as if he could not bear to face her. "As I said: nothing for me."

"It is important. Very important, my Lord."

Suddenly he turned, his voice was filled with a grinding rage. "My name is Shingo! Shingo-sama! Or have you forgotten?"

She waited as she always waited, silent, head erect, maddeningly superior, secretly laughing at him. He had been told by one who had seen her go to the Star Garden and mount the steps of the tower, and that some minutes later Hayden

Straker had come down from there, dressing himself as he descended.

"Well? Speak!"

"It has come to me today that Honda Yukio-san has laid formal claim to the Prefecture of Kyushu. If the Shogun can be persuaded to sanction it, it is possible he will attempt to oust our lord from Miyakonojo."

He stared at her, his eyes traveling her face. "Anything else?"

"Is that not enough, my Lor—Shingo-sama? I think it is significant enough to warrant immediate communication to your father. If you sent a messenger ship today—"

"I asked if there was anything else. Confine yourself to passing on what you have heard! Your opinions are of no interest to me! Now, do you have anything more to tell?"

"No, Lord."

"Then get out of my sight."

She got to her feet and backed away elegantly with bowed head, not even trying to show humility, and then she looked up. "Perhaps . . . perhaps there is something else."

"Well?"

"Some of the women believe that Yukio-san has a secret plan to help him gain Kyushu. It is a complex game and you and Mister Straker are both bound to be key stones in it. If I am to make sense of what I hear, I must know about the new amygdala."

"I have it safe," he murmured, torn inside by her mention of the *gaijin*'s name.

"But I must ask: What do you intend to do with it?"

Hideki Shingo looked accusingly at her. "Why? I hate the filthy jewel! It is a foreign thing. A dirty thing. It is truly cursed and truly it has brought disaster down upon our house! I shall shatter it into fragments and grind the fragments to powder and scatter the powder into the nexus!"

"With respect, was not the amygdala entrusted to you by your father? I wonder, what did he want you to do with it?"

He studied her in silence, enraged by the knowledge that she knew Ryuji-sama's intentions as well as he did, but that still she continued her conniving game. You owe your loyalty to my father, not to me, he thought. You never treated me as a wife should treat a husband. Never. He said carefully, "You may also wonder about this: My father has now given up his ambitions to gain the shogunate."

"Was that ever his intention?" she asked softly.

"It was." There was triumph in his voice now. "But after the defeat, the reputation of Hideki Ryuji is as dirt. He and my brother are marshaling the pathetic remnants of the army of Osumi, using them to assist the Amerikans at their last stronghold. They are groveling at the feet of foreigners! And yet I am sent here to dispose of the filthy jewel in a way that might save my father's dishonored neck from the *katana*'s cut?" He raised his head dangerously, and his gaze had the amber fire of a tiger's. "But of course you know this already. For you are my father's eyes and ears, and you boast that you know his mind better than I do myself."

The bitterness in his voice was intense. She looked away and kept her eyes averted. "Both Sakuma Kiyohide-san and Honda Yukio-san want the Amerikan amygdala for its power to oppose the Shogun's own jewel. Which of them shall have it? And what shall be the price?"

"I have yet to decide the answer to either question."

"Give it to Honda Yukio," she said levelly, "and you arm him with the advantage he needs to take the shogunate. If he can be Shogun he will no longer want to be Prefect of Kyushu."

"Enough! How dare you attempt to counsel me!"

She stared at her feet again. "I apologise."

"You cannot apologise!" he said, thrusting his face into

hers. "You have no sincerity! You have played with me all these years! You have betrayed me! Your heart is black! Why do you deliberately torment me?"

The strike was as fast as a cobra's. He grabbed her jaw and forced his mouth on hers. She staggered under the sudden passion of the movement, but tried not to turn her head aside in disgust. But her standing still, unresponsive as a wooden Daruma doll, only enraged him. Her teeth gritted as he grabbed at her throat with his left hand.

"If you will not love me, then you must fear me!"

His fingers dug into her neck, his thumb pressing hard on the vein. She pulled away, gasping. Without the use of his right hand he was powerless to drive home his attack, unless he could throw her down and pin her, or pull out his sword with his left hand. With an agile movement she put six paces between them.

"Why? Yasuko-san? Why do you hate me?"

"I do not hate you! But I can never love you. And I refuse to fear you."

"You prefer the company of that filthy *gaijin* to mine! You are my wife!"

"Shingo-sama, I am myself!"

He sprang at her like a tiger, and his left hand slammed into the side of her face, the power of it throwing her bodily through the door and to the ground.

"Then go to him! Go to him! And take him!"

Her *tabi* socks slid on the waxen timbers of the floor as she got up. The back of her hand was red with her own blood, but her dignity was whole. "Remember you are our lord's ambassador here!" she gasped back at him. "Please try to conduct yourself accordingly."

She turned and fled, and all the way along the translucent corridor that led back to her quarters the terrible broken crying of Hideki Shingo followed her.

8

It was night, and the lights that lit the rampart walkways of Edo's vast palace complex were naked flames, torches made from the skulls of famous enemies with whom the Sakuma clan had had disagreements.

Tomoki the falconer was a small man, gaunt, in his forties, very dark-skinned, and with glaucous gray eyes. He was a *sangokujin* by blood, from a strange little world in the Zone, in the Coma Cusp. He had adopted a Yamato-style name after being accorded chonin status because of his extraordinary skills. He had kept Sakuma Hidenaga's birds for twenty years.

Hayden Straker took the hawk from him and held it firmly on the rough leather of the glove, gripping the varvel jesses attached to its legs. He was impressed by the powerful grip that the bird's claws exerted, and the weight that his hand was obliged to support. Tomoki grinned at him proudly, a man totally absorbed in his profession and anxious to explain its secrets.

"You like, Ren-san?" he asked.

"He's superb. And quite heavy."

"Oh, no! He is a she, Honored Guest!"

Hayden Straker raised his eyebrows, taken by the majesty of the bird and the perfection of her plumage. He looked to Yasuko; after more than a week the swelling on her face had gone, but there was still faint bruising on her neck and cheek.

He turned back to Tomoki. "How old is she?"

"Two years and three months, Honored Guest. There are many kinds of hunting birds on Edo. All are either long-winged birds that kill in the air, which are falcons, or short-winged birds that kill on the ground, which are hawks. My beautiful Ren-san is a falcon—she kills in the air."

Hayden Straker's eyes strayed to Yasuko's, and back to the falconer. He asked, "Can you tell by looking at her which way she kills?"

"Yes, Honored Guest. You can tell because a falcon has a dark eye, whereas a hawk's eye is always yellow." Tomoki spread the wing expertly and the bird screeched at him. "See also the second wing feather is the longest. So this bird is most certainly a falcon."

"The training of a hunting bird demands infinite patience," Yasuko told him, adoring the bird. "A falconer must choose the exact moment at which to take the young eyas from the nest, just as the brown feathers have replaced the down. Earlier, and the eyas will never learn to hunt properly; later, and she will revert too easily to wild ways."

He turned and looked into her eyes, seeing once more the burnished darkness and recognising that in one of her previous lives Yasuko-san must surely have been a falcon.

Yasuko said, "The young bird must be taken straight to the loft, and bells put on her jesses, but then she must be given her freedom. Do you see, Mister Straker? She must fly at hack with liberty, so she gains strength of wing and confidence in herself. Only then can she be happy and ful-filled, and do her duty by her master."

He nodded, but it was more than understanding. He felt he had taken more from Yasuko's words than she had intended him to take. He had learned to read the parables of her thoughts, and the knowledge warmed him.

Tomoki showed them the hawks' feeding platform, still

intense, zealous to convert him to the joys of hawk rearing. "The Lady is very correct. If the falcon is given this vital freedom and is relied upon to return at sundown to her food, she will not fail."

The hack board had been scarred by generations of talons. Shreds of bloody lamb meat and smears of raw egg had attracted a mass of flies.

"As the falcons grow older we give them small birds or rabbits, so they may learn to recognise prey. Every day for a month, at dawn and dusk, the food must be presented here. Punctuality is of the essence, Honored Guest, and the falcon must never be suffered to carry away the prey, only to pull at it on the board. A falcon that has twice missed feeding has undoubtedly started killing for herself. It is then that she is caught and hooded and the training may begin."

The hawk seemed unsettled by the sight of the board and began to flap its great wings. He handed it back to Tomoki who took it to its post.

"You must be very skilled, Tomoki."

"It is a long and difficult procedure, Honored Guest, to bring a bird like Ren-san through her education. But the fine, hot-tempered bird who shows fight and passion at first is the most easily tamed. All the while there must be no disturbance."

Yasuko looked at the bird with delight. "A single impatient action," she said, her voice becoming husky, "and the hasty falconer undoes the work of weeks. These birds love to be stroked with a feather, and whispered to with the utmost tenderness."

"They do?"

"Yes, Mister Straker. They are brought to obedience by love. And then they will kill on request for their master."

She moved away, towards the battlemented walls that overlooked the great paved square below. As he walked to join her he wondered about her desire. Nothing else mattered. She had unsettled him that day in the Star Garden. His nerves had jangled with each thought of her. And when next they had met, days later, it had been electric.

It had been amid the mosses and waterfalls of Sakuma Hidenaga's gardens. He had seen the marks on her neck, the bruises she would not speak about. His insistence had angered her. Her anger had outraged him.

"Lady, I'm asking you to tell me. How did it happen?"

"And I am telling you not to concern yourself."

"I am already concerned." He had almost checked himself, but then he had gone on recklessly. "Because I suspect it was your husband—why turn away from me like that, Yasuko-san?" She had set her face. "So, I'm right! It was Shingo-san who did this. Of course. No one but a monster with a love of cruelty would want to do such a thing. No one but a fool would dare claim the right!"

"No. You are wrong, Mister Straker. It was my own fault."

"I'll punch the devil out of him, so help me. I'll teach him to respect you!"

She had sighed, standing still. "I said the fault was mine."

He had faced her then, his voice almost drowned by the rushing of the water. "How could it be your fault? What right could he possibly have to do this to you?"

"Every right." She had daggered him with her eyes and walked on faster than before. "Every right in this universe."

Then she had lifted her mood falsely, and she had laughed at his pompous indignation to distance him, and he had been deflated, but a little later he had said to her, "Lady, you do not fool me with these antics."

She had stopped again. "You are a strange man, Mister Straker. A kind man in head and heart. A man of good thoughts and temperate emotions. You are impossibly direct, despite which I still appreciate your intended sympathy. But you madden me intensely! Now, please, the matter is closed!"

"Lady, I am concerned for you." He had placed himself in front of her. "Unless you forbid it expressly I will avenge you!"

"Then I forbid it expressly."

"In that case I shall protest to Shingo-san's ignorant face, in terms so direct he will have no option but to fight man to man."

She had huffed at him. "Oh? Now you want to fight with him? But that is not our tradition. If you threaten him he will simply have you killed. And in any case such a fistfight as you desire is beyond your own Amerikan code."

"How's that?"

"If I understand it correctly, you cannot demand to fight with a man who has lost the proper use of his arm, since you would then be at an intolerable advantage."

"Lady, that is not an insuperable obstacle. We may negotiate a solution to it. Have you heard the term 'monomachy' before? We may fight using fixed blasters!"

"Oh, no, Mister Straker. Not when your fame among us is as the foremost shootist of the Amerikan MeTraCor, or had you forgotten that? And when it is well known that Shingo-san detests beam weapons, and would not use one to save his life."

He had had no reply to that. After a moment he said, "Yes. You're quite right. Of course."

She had stared into his eyes. Then the laugh had been genuine, wistful this time. "It fascinates me the way you seem always to think and feel at the same time. Your thoughts appear always to be tempered with compassion, and your passion is always considered. It is not often so among our women, even less, I think, among our men—or any men. I think you are an admirably made person.''

''Lady, be careful or you'll embarrass me. And then I might do something I'd regret. That we both might regret.''

''You see? No matter what the circumstance, your mind is always working and working. You are never overwhelmed. You have a very clever knack of balance. On the soul of my mother, you are difficult to deter. But your rational logic should tell you that you cannot make correct conclusions from false beliefs.'' She broke off, considering, then she said, ''How, instead, if I tell you everything? Will you promise not to interfere?''

He stiffened. ''If it is your wish.''

''It is my wish. But you should promise first.''

He had hesitated, but then said, ''I promise.''

''You swear by your gods?''

''I swear on my honor.''

He walked with her for longer than an hour on the flame-lit ramparts. She talked freely, telling him how she had been charged by Hideki Ryuji with the task of controlling her husband. How it was now up to her, and himself also—if he would consent to be her ally—to use Shingo and the new amygdala to shape the future of Yamato. She had won him with her words. Astounded him with her revelations. She had also confirmed something else in his mind: Now he knew he would have to have her.

''The night sky is beautiful here, Lady.''

''Yes. Can you pick out the Four Masters of the Northern Bushel?''

''The what?''

''Perhaps you call them 'Big Dipper,' because from Old Earth they looked like a water vessel. Seen from Edo, they are difficult to associate. They do not form one constellation.

We have a children's game that involves finding the Four Masters in the skies of different systems.''

"A charming idea, Lady."

"You can see our seven little moons?"

"Yes. That, too, is a charming idea. I understand their periods and albedos and colors have been chosen to maximise their esthetic effect in the night sky as seen from the Shogun's palace."

"Yes."

He pointed overhead, at the brightest object in the sky, a violet-white point so bright it cast a shadow. "What star is that, Lady?"

She hesitated. "That is something you should not ask about, Mister Straker."

"Why not?"

"Because it is not a star." She seemed suddenly very tired. "Because the light you see is in fact the deaths of millions of people."

"What do you mean? A disaster? An ecology that failed for some reason?"

"No. It is Nagoya. A system that was deliberately destroyed by the government. Its primary mass was very special and so certain experiments with it were performed. It was provoked into a nova condition by the detonation of a nexus inside it. The aim was to secure Yamato's own source of superheavy elements."

"An inhabited system?"

She nodded. "Many millions of people. Only certain castes were permitted to leave the system."

As they stood at the battlement separated by a yard of air that seemed to him at once a thousand parsecs and nothing at all, he heard the music of distant drums on the wind. The sound was growing closer and there was twined in the beats another sound. A dreadful sound. Pitiful. Keening. It unnerved Ren-san on her perch. Yasuko pulled the corner of her mantle across her shoulder and leaned out to find where it was coming from. From these high walls they could see everything below.

They watched a curious crowd gather below, awaiting a procession that seemed to be leading into the outer precincts of the palace complex. The wailing was that of a young woman. They saw that she was distraught with terror as she came into view. She was led stumbling and crying, on a chain held by a Shinto priest; a body of a dozen guards in dark green surcoats and black helmets followed. They were led by two young drummers, thrashing their drums with curved sticks to give warning and to summon. An official came forward and the rhythm stopped suddenly; the wailing continued.

Yasuko watched, horrified, as a proclamation was read out.

"What is it?" he asked, unable to catch the words himself.

"*Seidotoku*," she breathed. She stared down at the milling crowd.

The word meant nothing to him. "Seidotoku? What's that?"

"Listen. The girl is having the sentence read for her crime."

He craned over to see better. They were tormenting the hysterical woman by reading out some kind of solemnity. The crowd swelled. There was muttering and indignation, then shouts from raucous women began.

"What's she supposed to have done?" he asked.

"They have invoked the law of *seidotoku* against her," she repeated, her voice heartsick. "It was his word against hers, and because she is a woman her testimony was deemed inferior."

"Do you mean she's been found guilty of perjury?"

"No, Hayden Straker. Not perjury."

"Is she samurai?"

"Yes. Of the First Rank. She has been very stupid. She has betrayed herself and her family and the rank she holds."

A clinking sound came up. The young woman's crying intensified. She was standing facing the crowd insensibly, her head uncovered, shoulders sagging, arms hanging. The noise that came from her was a howling sob, the same imploring noise a young child makes after breaking its parent's temper. Then a sudden yelp came from her, followed by louder crying, as if the parent had given another slap. But Hayden Straker saw that it was no slap that had made the howling change pitch.

He saw her robe torn aside while the official who had read the proclamation berated her ill discipline.

"Jeezus! They're stripping her!"

"It is part of the punishment for what she has done."

He stared, horrifically fascinated by the sight, until a large man appeared and knocked the woman to the ground. He flinched as if feeling the numbing pain of it himself. As she began to crawl, the shouting crowd encroached on her in a crescent of hate, until they had driven her back against the walls, cornering her like a baited animal.

I must do something, he thought. He shouted at them to stop. He shouted until he was hoarse. But his shouts were not heard, or if they were, they were ignored. There was no way to stop it. No way to get down from these inner citadel walls except by the main gates. A terrible hard knot formed in his stomach as he knew the impotence of his position.

For several minutes he remained paralysed by the sight as he watched her robes torn away. Blood was pouring from her nose now, matting her hair, staining her body, and spattering the gravel. There was no way out. The screaming began again. She fought hysterically to escape through her assailants, but was thrust back. She tried to dodge and fend off the

blows with her arms. Then she could no longer get away. A
huge guard came forward and drew an extra-long sword. Two
more guards held her arms outstretched, and the crowd came
so near that the magistrate had to order them back. The crowd
closed in a full circle, and she was lost to sight. Then the
sword came up briefly and flashed down, and a moan of
satisfaction came from the crowd.

When it was over Hayden Straker looked up at Yasuko
with a haggard face; his voice was almost gone. He wanted
to vomit. "It's barbaric!"

"It is the law. The punishment ordained for such cases."
Her voice was low, on the point of breaking.

"Then your law is barbaric! What in the name of Jeezus
did she do to deserve that?"

She touched his hand, squeezed it gently, her face full of
pity. There were tears in her eyes. "Her crime was adultery,
Hayden-san. The penalty for that is death."

Arkali's hopes fluctuated again as she walked with Luka
Rohan, the commander of Fort Baker, leaving the orbiter's
bridge for the ring. Behind them, light spilled from scanners
that were still manned by defenders, though the native Osumi
support staff had gone planetside long ago. She felt suddenly
astonished at her own strength. They had made it here against
the odds, but it had all been in vain. Hayden was not here.

Rohan was a strange man. In his mid-fifties, cadaverous in his features but unexpectedly tough; his stubbled cheeks dropped over a weak jawline that swiveled this way and that above a rooster neck that was tied with a sweat-soaked throat tie of once-white cotton. His battered cap was dirty and his jacket braid fraying. Everything seemed faded and grimy and worn out aboard this forgotten outpost, and Rohan himself was no exception.

"C'mon, c'mon, Miz Hawken. Thisaway. Show you the ring and our Park and the place I like to call home these days."

She followed, considering him. Had his behavior been the cause of his banishment to a bad post by the MeTraCor highups? Or did he get this way through having ridden shotgun on this crazies' rig for too long? She had collected a few facts about Rohan. He had been tried at a MeTraCor court-martial some years ago and shunted here. What had his crime been? The creepy way he acted, it could have been just about anything.

He led her along a transparent tube, a dizzyingly open space-frame corridor towards the ring and the Park. Here on the star-spangled walkway, the compensators were incorrectly balanced. They maintained one gee on the feet, three fourths of a gee on the waist, and half a gee on the head. As they walked, they passed through resonance fringes. It was sick-making.

She kept her eyes on the only horizon that made any sense. Outside was a crystal-clear tube, a bright-lit torus of bubble plex and green landscape, rotating slowly on a web of slender plex spokes. The ring was probably a half mile across, the living bed of the Park eighty, maybe ninety yards wide, with grass and trees and running water and even a crazy waterfall whose water bent like a rainbow as it fell. There seemed to be a couple of big white structures too, set across a diameter for balance, big places built like Greek temples or something. It was bizarre. Back the other way, Fort Baker proper was an ugly fat spider hanging off the delicate tracery.

It was possible, she had thought, that Rohan might see her point of view about Hayden, if she were to catch him at the right moment. She had tried to talk with him more than once about the situation, but he had wormed away from the subject every time. It was about time to pin him down.

"About Hayden—"

"Jeezus, wouldya look at that! Oooo-eee! My kingdom, Miz Hawken. My kingdom last four years. Two more to go, then I get the hell off this sonofabitch. Parole." He smiled tautly. "Li'l joke, is all."

Then he started explaining how important it was that the Kan ships be kept at a respectable distance from Fort Baker when suddenly he stopped, unclipped his blaster, and drew a bead on a small and hunched gray form at the end of the walkway a hundred yards on. It scurried forward, then stopped, and started to go back the way it had come. Rohan stuck out an arm to hold her back, squinted down the short sights of the Wesson, and whispered.

"It's the park, see, Miz—the rim with all the green stuff. If the Kan force us to jettison, we're on a countdown to suffocation. Our air courses communicate. We got very little canned air and no recirculators. I know it sounds fritzy, but see the fort was designed to function on eco only."

"That's crazy!"

"Nope. Officially it's to happy-up the shit-tour crew some: smooth rotation gravity, real-air, maybe do some home-growns, a place to play ball, swim, whatever. Real reason is built-in blackmail." He looked at her with red-rimmed eyes. "See, the idea is to make sure we run for the nexus within a day or so of jettisoning the ring."

"Why?"

"Follows. The only reason we jettison is if we're attacked. I think you should know I ain't much of a talent, and because of Aziza Pope and her cost-cutting I got no expensive astrogators here. See, MeTraCor Board back on Liberty wants to be kept informed about any trouble coming out of Osumi. Only way that can happen is if Baker carries news out through the nexus. Once the Kan make us jettison, we'd all be killing each other for canned air inside a week. We got no option but to hit the nexus."

"Without an astrogator?"

"Uh-huh."

She felt a sudden horror. "Can't you fix recirculators in?"

Rohan suddenly swiveled and hit the trigger. The shipney jumped a foot in the air, looked about itself stupidly, recovered its wits, and began to scramble away with a drunken weave.

"Sonofabitch is made of flexiplex! 'Scuse me, Miz. I get chest-tight over rats. 1000 series Wesson's none too accurate once it's run low."

He clipped the blaster into his belt and fished out a couple of small tubes to feed into the butt.

"Why can't you fix recirculators in?"

"Hmmm?" Rohan roused himself to her question. "Where'd we find them? Now look at that big bastard. What's the betting I can bring it down from the overheads?"

She sighed with frustration. The defense of Baker was deadlocked, she knew. Kan ships had been firing at them, off and on, since they'd stolen the lander. Whenever a Kan vessel orbited within a few hundred miles, they lined up, hoping to catch Baker unawares and shield down. Several lock-ons had kept up for a minute or more, but the powerful fields were still functioning, and no sustained surface fire had been seen. Without bigger ships in the Osumi system and troops and heavy beam weapons that could only be brought in by another battle squadron, the Kan could not harm Baker much, but equally no Amerikan could land from the fort either.

Barb Eastman had been gloomy about their prospects. "We don't have a choice," he had said. "No choice but to sit tight while the Kan watch us."

He had said that Yu Hsien would be waiting for Baker to decide to pull out. Without Kanoya City and without trade, Fort Baker looked like a waste of plex. Yu Hsien would probably be hoping Luka Rohan would decide to capitulate and evacuate to Seoul—which is where they should have gone in the first place.

Barb's a stubborn man who wants everything his own way, she thought, disliking the dominant flavor of Eastman's personality. And in this case he's wrong. Commander Rohan's told me an order to run Baker for the nexus could only come from the Board, the Council of Members on Liberty. That's months away down the shortest chain. Meanwhile he says he'll never surrender to the Kan, nor will he withdraw. Hardship or not. He's a real strange man.

"What's the point of keeping on up here, Commander?" she asked.

He put up his blaster and looked at her quizzically. "What's the point? That what you said?"

"Yes."

"Change of heart, Miz? Thought you were the one who persuaded a half-dozen MeTraCor staffers to come up here."

"Maybe I didn't know how bad the situation was. Maybe I've begun to think that we should surrender after all. Accept internment in Kanoya. Yu Hsien's virtually pledged to ship us all out to Seoul."

"That's what you think?"

"Yes. That's what I think."

He laughed a nervous laugh that stopped prematurely. "No way, Miz. Nooo way!"

"Think about it, Commander."

"I've thought. But, see, I didn't hock the last four years of my life to make the same mistake again. This time I do it by MeTraCor's rules, yeah? Right by the book. That's flat."

"There'll be hardship," she said. "The air supply problem will see to that. Already Dover catalyst is running low. When that's gone we can't eat."

"My problem. Not yours, Miz Hawken. I don't make mistakes twice. By the book this time. And the book says we stay put until we have to jettison, and when that happens— if that happens—then we take our chances on the nexus. Nobody's going planetside."

"Commander, you have no right to detain me. I brought the lander here. It's mine."

"MeTraCor property. Says so on the bulkhead."

"That was before the Kan captured it. And before Barb Eastman and I captured it back from them. It's ours. We took it."

"Barb Eastman's MeTraCor. An employee. The lander's impounded. Sorry."

"No, you're not. You're not sorry at all."

I'll never see Hayden again, she thought suddenly. I wonder why he wasn't here when I was so sure he would be. How much psi talent do I have? What if you're low on talent and you still put your faith in powerful hunches? Are you a risk-crazy chancer, then?

She began to feel a horrible emptiness inside her chest. The void that she felt each night between hitting the strap and falling asleep, the void that filled with panic if she allowed herself to dwell on it.

The thought of him lying dead somewhere on that ball of rock, without even a marked grave holo to memorialise him, made her stomach turn over. She banished the vision from her mind, thinking instead of the sacrifices she had already made for him and how they couldn't be allowed to fail now.

Their journey to Fort Baker had been accomplished in a tortuous way. Barb Eastman had masterminded it, getting the group of fugitives out of the city via the service ducts with astounding ingenuity. They had been six in total, Arkali herself and Eastman and Bosco Shadbolt and three other MeTra-Cor staffers she had persuaded to come—one man, Ildren Janski, with a trace of piloting experience.

They had jumped the lander guard and bloodied the crete, making a hell of a din. Then they had discovered that one engine was out. In the taut silence, with two Kan bodies in the aisle, and a death sentence waiting to fall on them, the "pilot" had told them the worst.

"Can't be done against one point one three gee, Barb."

"Don't tell me that!"

"Look at the figures. Root gee em on ar. Five point oh one miles per second is the magic figure. With one engine axed, best we can do is four point nine two. We don't have the power to reach escape velocity."

"We're only just short!"

"Well, hell, man! That's the end of it! We don't have the power! What you want? To walk the rest of the way?"

"Don't you know we're at latitude fifty north here, Janski?"

"So?"

"So, shitferbrains, every point on Osumi's equator rotates through two pi times her radius every twenty or so hours. Stand on the equator and you'd be slingshotting at a shade over point three miles per second without moving. Here we're only cosine fifty of that: say just under point one nine three. Lot of difference. All the difference, my figures say."

They agreed that they'd have to fix the motor or overland

it to the equator to give them the slingshot they needed to reach Fort Baker.

Eastman had decided: a ground break from the apron, skimming into wooded country and hiding out in the many caves of the "limestone" district of Shinju Horaana until the uproar died down. Then do the three-thousand-mile run to the equator.

That first night she had sat on the greasy winglet of the shuttle and looked into a measureless vault illuminated by the shadowed beams of the landing lights. She had wondered how carbonate rock could exist on a planet like Osumi, barely a century out of terraforming. Then Barb Eastman had told her that the entire network of caverns was a "false-lime" feature: a robot-made former built out of manufactured calcium carbonate substrate to a fractal design. From the overall plan right down to the smallest details of the lumps and bumps on the stalactites, the beauty of Pearl Caverns had been sculpted, then washed for eighty years in a mineral-rich spray of water to lay a few millimeters of real lime deposit on top. The result was hard to distinguish from the process of millions of years. In places, the designers had gone to the limit of their art, impressing the skeletal forms of early sea creatures into the substrate to mimic the fossil legacy of an ancient shallow ocean.

"You can't tell," he had said with an eerie pride in his voice. "Not even an expert petrologist with a microscope can tell."

One of the others had snorted. "Bullshit. Just listen to the echoes, man. Yaaaa-hooo!"

And Barb had grabbed the man by his jerkin edges and thrown him down, inexplicably enraged, whispering fiercely.

"You ever been in a real limestone cave, Janski?"

A whipped-cur look from Janski. Only Old Earth had real

limestone and nobody had been there since the catastrophe, except the Cloistermen.

"You know what real limestone echo sounds like?"

"Well . . . no, Barb. I just . . ."

"Then, zip it, Janski. Just. Zip. It. Okeh?"

They had left the caves after nightfall, as soon as the overcast had thickened up. There had been detours through the night to throw surveillance, and orbital observation to avoid when the cloud started to break up in the first rays of dawn.

Before they left, Eastman had explained how they could get help from some of the local people. He knew the villages to which Kanoya's native refugees had fled, the people who had once lived in the town now known as Charcoal City. But he also warned them that there would be many spies watching out, spies and sly wayfarers who would sell information to the Kan for a few bowls of rice.

Despite his words no one had thought about giving it up, or of challenging Eastman's plan to get them offplanet. They had skimmed and laid low, skimmed and laid low, for days, and soon they were in virgin wooded mountains a hundred miles from the broken dome of Kanoya City.

Once outside the Lease, a change had come over Barb Eastman. He had treated everything with great suspicion, disciplining them harshly when they failed to carry out his instructions, but Eastman knew the language and the ways of the people, and though all his staffer courtesies had fallen from him, he exuded a kind of strength that gave them confidence.

"Hey, Eastman, we're not in your army, you know," Shadbolt had complained at their first night camp in open country. Eastman had come back from a squat in the bushes and quenched their fire just as Shadbolt settled down to cook.

"C'mon. You're outside radio black. Inside the shuttle! Now!"

"Hey!"

Eastman's temper had worn thin. "Listen! This is dangerous stuff we're doing. More dangerous than you know. We can't afford to advertise ourselves."

Then he had robbed them all of sleep by describing in blood-clotting detail the power of ship scanners to pick out body-heat images from two thousand miles up and blip them out with a tight beam before they knew what was happening.

"They're professionals. Kan crews ain't stupid. Lie out under the stars and they'll pick you out with a needle beam in the dark and fry your brains through your eye socket as you sleep."

"I don't believe I've ever heard of that," Shadbolt had commented mildly.

"That's because you go around in a dream and you don't give shit for tek manuals."

"It's not fair to frighten Arkali with—"

"Are you sure it's Arkali you're thinking of? Or your own squatting peace of mind?" His eyes had gleamed in the darkness, white in his dirt-smudged face, then he had looked right at her and laughed. "Better a frightened Arkali than a dead one, eh?"

The following day Eastman had insisted they track way off their southerly course, and they had tried to vote him down, seeing no reason for his obsessive caution.

"This is not a matter for squatting votes," he had hissed at Shadbolt. "I only want to know if you're coming with me or not. If you're not, then get out of the lander here. Arkali and I can easily go on alone. But if you want my leadership, then you'll squatting well obey me. Understood?"

For the sake of security, they had all pledged themselves

to him, some more sullenly than the rest. But he had won them to him firmly later that day when they learned from their scanners that a Kan air sweep had carved up the place they had just detoured out of.

"How did you know there was going to be a hit there?" she had asked, but Eastman had only shrugged and said that he had not known, he had just felt that they should take a wide excursion around the peninsula.

She had watched him since, stamping the nodes of the equipment consoles with his big blunt fingers, hushing them to listen to distant talkback of others. His natural caution had come to seem like good sense as the days and nights elapsed and they delved deeper into unknown territory. They also grew attuned to the primitive dangers of Osumi's unexplored ranges whenever he led them into deep jungle, and they began to respect his leadership instead of resenting it.

At every stop Eastman negotiated with the wide-eyed local people. Despite his own advice on walking outside the lander's ground-cone of radio black, he took to sitting in their villages, taking tea with the headmen. On these occasions his knife came out, and he whittled on a stick, making nothing but a heap of shavings it seemed. Eventually she had begun to see in him a weird light, a light that shone out at certain times of the day like a psi aura around him, and she fancied that any Kan beam that tried to kill him would have to pass through that light first, and such a thing seemed impossible. She had stayed close to him after that, seeking his protection as if he were a talisman.

Eastman had expected the lift-off to Baker to be the most dangerous phase. It was a carefully calculated window, after dark and dead on the Osumi equator. He had held them back and made them wait on the mud bank of a rice field, naked and open to the sky.

"What's happening?" she asked him.

"There's plenty of Kan up there. Y'know, if I were Hu Tsung, I'd have had the place taken by now."

The awful terror of that thought had lodged in her throat like a fish hook. "What do you want to do?"

"Take a chance. We ought to take a chance and run for Baker direct. Just do it. No messing."

She had been astounded at the suggestion, coming from him. "Can we do that?"

"It's important we're not seen."

"So you're waiting for all their ships to set?" another had said.

"Yeah."

They had dumped their water and shed as much of the innards of the lander as was compatible with safety. Minutes later they had lit out of their mud bank and followed the optimum line into the eastern sky. The tantalising orbital turn that had separated them from their goal had been their biggest problem. Once offplanet they would be meat to any Kan ship that spotted them.

"What'll we do now? Wait 'til they pick us up?" Shadbolt had asked them all.

"Don't you believe in radio black, Bo?"

"We'll be blown to bits!"

"C'mon, Shadbolt, there's nothing else we can do, man."

"What then? Sit here like a lump of silex?"

"We'll never make it. I'm not talking about the Kan, I mean Baker. We got no datachord and no ID to give the interrogators, and unless they want conversation—"

"Fuck it all. We're Kan to them! They'll burn us and then ask questions."

Eastman had silenced them. "There's another way."

"What?"

He had taken a sound module from his pack and patched the player into all hailing. "A recording of the Adventer

Philharmonic on Utah II playing 'Liberty Bell.' They won't
fire on us if the interrogators hear that.''

"You're star-crazed!"

"What then, Mister Blackmore? Do you have an alternative?"

They had looked at the grim nutshell of Fort Baker, at the
gaping hole of the dock port and the huge beam weapon
emplacements standing out on each side of it. With its ring
of green light Baker looked like a Kansas sea oyster that had
acquired a halo.

It had been nerve-fraying, knowing that the still blackness
that invited them must be, in reality, one gigantic ambush.
Then there had been sporadic firing from the Kan, and they
had watched Baker's shields flare with hits as they closed on
the dock, even more sure they were already plasma.

Arkali's terror had blended with high excitement as they
crossed the last horrendous miles to the shield. The critical
moment had come at last when they had abandoned the radio
black they needed to escape the Kan, and began instead to
make loud advertisements that they were Amerikan. The hull
motes had blared out every symbol of Amerikan sovereignty
they could program, from stars and bars, through Hercules
of the North and Aquarius of the South to the Eagle of Aquila.
At the same time they had begun to fall into that inevitable
sequence of tractor seizure, weapons lock-on, interrogation
that on a hi-alert fort could easily mean unthinking vaporisa-
tion. Measures meant to face down a suicide attack using holo
deception were not going to take too kindly to John Philip
Sousa on hailing.

But a fortside operator had been hunch-struck by the Adventer music coming over talkback, and had rushed an override on Baker's automatic systems without any understanding
of who they were or what they were trying to do.

All Arkali had known about it was that she was still alive.

She had seen the burning red ends of the weapons towers slide by as the fort's gut-grabbing tractors reeled them in. The sight of that evil ruby point wavering through the gloom towards them as they came on stopped her heart. It was like being an insect held in the claws of a scorpion with the tail poised to jab down and kill. She had been told by Eastman that those red lights that looked so much like the fort's scorpion eyes would be probing them with everything they had.

This was the sort of nightmare that was frequently set by Navy schools to catch half-trained fort console ops unawares, the moral of the exercise every time: Don't trust your own gray-haired granny. But this was no exercise and they must have had the authentic feel of Greeks just loaded down with gifts. The invitation offered to approach the dock was not real. Couldn't be real. At this range Baker's weapons could easily blow a big battle wagon to hell fire in one firing.

Then, BANG.

The duty op aboard Baker must have run shouting from his niche in which he had doubtless been praying and slamming every override in sight. His scratchy, breathless tones had come over the hailing like the Voice of God.

"By Jeezus, you'd better be real or I'm dust! Which is it?"

Sweat had dripped—literally dripped—from Eastman's chin too. "You just saved our lives, John."

"Console matches your voice as MeTraCor #198529 O/KC, Eastman B.T. That you?"

"In the flesh."

"Well, Mister Eastman, you are one psi-touched muvva. I ought to burn you anyway for what you just put me through. Who else you got on board?"

He told them, and then asked cool-as-you-like, "You wouldn't be an Adventer, would you, John?"

"How'd you guess, Mister Eastman?"

"Peraize the Lawd."

"Either that's some talent or you is one icy muvva when it come to lateral thinking."

"Nothin' to it. Just added usa to So and got Sousa."

"What's that you say?" Rohan asked, squinting at the halo of trees.

"I was speaking about the reason I came here."

"Well, you certainly did a crazy thing bringing a lander here," Rohan told her again. He patted her back in a friendly way. "We had real need of six extra mouths, and your boys—"

"They're not my boys, Commander Rohan," she said, irritated by his way of not listening to anyone but himself. Despite the lapse of time, her disappointment at not finding Hayden here had not diminished, and she had raised it with Rohan at every opportunity.

"Oh, yeah. But, anyway, you know Eastman's good for morale. Real charisma, and he's interested in tek. Got to be the only person who ever liked it here. Says he's happy as a flea. I recommended him for a full commission."

"Mister Eastman wanted to run off to Seoul like all the rest," she said, piqued by the praise that was being showered on Eastman suddenly. She knew what the real attraction was in being stuck on Baker. The man had not left her alone for a single day in the time they had been here, and his company was becoming a real pressure. "Before I dissuaded him he was all for going to Seoul in an old Kan thousand tonner."

"That so?"

Rohan said it with that maddening faintness that told her he did not believe half of what she said. She was sure he knew plenty he had not thought fit to tell her, and it burned her up to be kept deliberately ignorant.

"It's quite true, Commander. Eastman thought Admiral Hu Tsung would be disposed to giving them a ship to make the journey. I didn't think so. If it hadn't been for me, they'd still be in Kanoya City now, locked in like my father.''

"Oh, yeah. Jos Hawken. Ex-Navy big cheese. Independent trader now. I've known him must be twenty years. Twenty-five, if it comes to that. Sharpest poker player I ever saw without a rating.''

She stopped walking, cut in on him, knowing there had never been much goodwill to be lost between Rohan and her father, but Ellis Straker was another matter. Straker had supported Rohan at his MeTraCor trial by standing as a character witness. As a result Commander Rohan had not been busted and dismissed from the Corp, he had been reprimanded and moved to Baker.

"I know you know my father, Commander. You know Ellis Straker too.''

He tried to throw her off. "Something I didn't tell you, Miz Hawken. Straker made a run for Two-Eight some time ago. He's cut his ship out—repossessed her, if you like—and he's gone from this system.''

She tried to absorb the new information without getting phased. "I'm surprised you couldn't arrange some kind of search for his son. After what he did for you when your career was on the line.''

Rohan stopped also, sighed, his eyes avoiding her. "Cannot be done. Wouldn't be practical.''

"Why not?''

He shrugged. "Not enough probability of success to warrant spying that minutely. And the Kan''—he waved a hand vaguely at the disk of Osumi—"they'd be too interested in what we'd scan.''

"I didn't mean an orbital scan. I mean going down. I brought five men here who all got up safe on one engine, surely three could get down again on two. Let the lander go down. You could allow that. Volunteers to find Hayden Straker.'' She raised an eyebrow, going for the trump. ''You need to find him. He's an accredited ship's master—if I could bring him up, he could help astrogate you through the nexus when you had to jettison. Let me go down to Miyakonojo.''

''Cannot be done.''

''Why do you keep saying that?''

Rohan became peppery back. ''In the first place, Miyakonojo's under full military alert. Domed and shielded, with eight times the field strength of Kanoya City's shields. And who can blame them? If the Kan bring that singularity gun out, the Prefect's got to keep it at least a mile away or end up with a holey city. That's a joke, Miz.''

''I'm sure I can get to Miyako—''

''Hey—I said Miyakonojo's locked up and silent on all frequencies. They're not talking to anybody, friend or foe.''

''Let me worry about getting in. Just let me off Baker.''

''It's not in my power to issue passports to allow Amerikans to drop in on Osumi whenever they please. Especially not the capital. That requires permission from the Prefect's Court.''

Her fists balled with frustration. ''But how can you get permission from Miyakonojo if you can't raise them?''

''Now you see the problem.''

''Just let me do it!''

''MeTraCor rules say no, Miz Hawken.''

Her temper broke. ''But we're at war! You can't treat the normal rules as sacred under these circumstances. The Kan are breaking the Prefect of Kyushu's rules by dropping whole regiments on his soil! They've attacked and driven off Hideki Ryuji's forces! Your ops say they're firing beam weapons at us from our own Lease. For God's sake, wake up!''

''Please don't raise your voice to me, Miz Hawken.''

She shook her head desperately. ''Okeh, not me, then. I'll

stay here. Say someone else wanted to go. It's no different than the journey up.''

" 'Fraid I can't help you, because in the second place—''

"You're just being deliberately obstructive!''

Rohan's face clouded. "Because, in the second place, it's too dangerous. I can't let anyone attempt Osumi. They'd burn ten seconds after they got outside our shields.''

"Hell, the trip's no different than the ride up here. Please, Commander. Let Barb Eastman go if he volunteers.''

"He's not that crazy.''

"But if he does?''

"Cannot be done.''

She gave him a freezing stare. "I'm sure you'd say yes if Ellis Straker were asking in person.''

He shrugged, and she fell silent, thinking angrily of Hayden and why she had wanted to come to Fort Baker in the first place. *I won't give up. I refuse to give up! Rohan's full of guile, and his reasons are hollow. The journey up was dangerous, yes, but we completed it. I'm sure that Eastman could make his way down to Miyakonojo. I don't like him here. His presence bothers me. If only Rohan can be made to order it, I might kill two rats with one shot—get Eastman off my tail and find out if Hayden is at Miyakonojo . . .*

There was a sudden alert over the talkback. A signal from the bridge and one of the ops' voices distorting.

Rohan's narrow face looked up at the interruption. "What the fuck—?''

"Teth-Two-Nine. A ship in transit, Commander.''

"Which way?''

"Inbound.''

He pursed his lips. "She'd better not be Kan.''

"Is that likely?'' Arkali asked.

"Satsuma's one of the few systems that knows what's going on here."

"But so's Seoul, by now," she said peevishly. "If Ellis Straker's gone like you say."

"Yeah, I'd've expected the Kan to come in first." He looked stonily at her, then quickly away. "I didn't tell you this either, but Hu Tsung's fleet transited out the system just before you came up here. That's why you're alive. When he comes back, or when any new ship enters without Amerikan ID, it'll mean we're on countdown to a run."

The information winded her, but she kept up with Rohan all the same. He called for status and within seconds his hip unit was going code-happy with all kinds of ID tones. He peered at the data, and listened at the run, heading back along the walkway to the fort proper until she yelled at him.

"I said, no need to worry, Commander!" she shouted with cold anger. "This one's Amerikan."

"She sounds Kan to me," he said, unconvinced, waiting for the lock to cycle.

"No. Listen to it again."

"Shit! All ships in the Zone get along by trying to appear to be something they're not. Some Amerikan traders' ships are built in Yamato. Some try to make their ID mimic Navy vessels to avoid pirates. Some pirate traps are patterned after traders for the opposite reason." He stared again at the blue image in the hip unit. "Even some of the Navy's ships are Kan-built, captured as prizes—"

"I know that much about my father's trade," she said cuttingly. Her anger simmered as they waited between the lock doors. It was not so much Rohan's patronising attitude, nor even his secrecy, but at what was now to come. She knew that what she had tell them should make everyone aboard Fort Baker jump for joy—everyone except herself. "Fact is, I know that vessel is the *Chance*. Ellis Straker's ship."

He ran ahead again, heading for the bridge. "You can't possibly tell that from what's coming over—"

"Commander, when I was at Kanoya City I spent hours listening to that ship's signature! I know what she is!"

"Don't shout at me, Lady."

"Then don't treat me as if I were a child, Commander! And please have the good manners not to call me 'Lady' again! You can't believe how irritating that is."

He avoided her eyes. She heard him give the order to ready the beam weapons, and immediately Baker's ops and almost everyone else whose duties were not elsewhere began to gather on the bridge.

"If Hu Tsung's ships are gone, then who is it who's been firing at us?"

"Admiral Hu lit out, but another big Kan ship came in not long after. Yu Hsien. Big boss of China Products on Satsuma."

"Why didn't you tell me?"

"Lady, you didn't ask."

They waited. Bets were laid and opinions passed from desk to desk. Then Eastman came to stand beside her, nodding a greeting.

"Arkali. Commander."

Rohan was bloodless and flaky back. "G'day, Lieutenant Eastman. We've got ourselves a visitor."

Arkali immediately felt the impulse to ask Eastman for confirmation of her opinion, but she also felt disinclined to open conversation with him—give him the time of day and he would be like a barnacle, attaching himself until forcibly removed.

Rohan said, "Miz Hawken thinks it's Ellis Straker's ship."

"I reckon Miz Hawken is right. That is the *Chance*. Why don't you attempt to copy-copy from her?"

When an answering signal was received from the ship

and familiar handshakes convinced Baker's cautious systems, caps were thrown into the air all along the bridge, and winners and losers alike were happy to settle up their bets.

10

The *Chance* had hit orbit, and the first shuttle was already docked with Fort Baker. A huge, dominating figure was striding down the umbilicus.

"By God, Lu Rohan, you're a sight for sore eyes!"

"Good to see you again, Ellis."

Ellis stepped into the fort and came up to grip the Commander's forearm. "And I've come with all kinds of gear to help your fight, and great news from Seoul!"

Arkali pushed forward, her hair zigged out like she was holding on to a static generator. "You sonofabitch!"

"Ah, now what's this? Somebody talking to me? Arkali Hawken? That you under all that hair? So, you came up to Fort Baker after all, did you?"

"Yes, sir—one aurium-thieving sonofabitch!"

He looked perplexed. "That an accusation or what?"

"Hayden's not here!"

He stood back on his heels and sucked on his cheroot. "That a fact."

"He never was here! And you knew it! You lied to me!"

"Steady."

"You lied to me! To get your hands on that aurium!" She

slapped his face and pulled back to strike again, but he caught her arm.

"Don't you want to hear about your daddy?"

One of Ellis's men took her around the waist at a nod from him.

"Put me down!"

"Yep, put her down."

The *suifu* dumped her on a pile of lubey paper waste that one of the overworked drones had collected nearby. She got to her feet, lube sliming her garb. Ellis turned to her smiling, his eyes big and innocent. "Your father's affairs are proceeding on Seoul, and I'm keeping the old outfit alive while poor old Jos is stuck on Osumi. You should be thanking me."

"You left him there deliberately! To the mercy of the Kan. You—"

"Ah, now! You can't say that. He put his shirt on Hu Tsung giving him an old tub so's he could get himself and all them weasels on the MeTraCor Council over to Seoul. It was his mistake, not mine."

Two Oriental women appeared from the umbilicus. One of them kowtowed to Arkali while the other just watched uninterestedly.

"Suzi? Is that you?"

"Yep. I brought your maid," Ellis said generously. "How about that? Straighten up, gel. She came with us when we left Kanoya City. Wouldn't think she'd distract a shuttle guard, let alone two, but she did. Looked pretty good in Eriko's silk teasies."

The other woman, who was Eriko, grinned lasciviously. Suzi blushed, then squeaked.

Arkali shouted, "You dirty scheming bastard!"

Eastman came up beside her protectively, but she was too incensed to register him.

"You double-crossed my father!" she said. "The reason

Hu Tsung changed his mind about that nexus ship is because you stole the *Chance*.''

''Stole it back, you mean. And good thing I did, because now you can dine on succulent real-food and vintage fizz tonight, not Lu's hobby-grown root veg wine and the hug-matee you have to drink up here. If you'll accept my invitation.''

''Dine with you, you shamming huckster? I'd rather eat lander rations and drink Minnesota mine lube!''

''No problem. I'll tell my people to oblige you in whatever you choose.''

Ellis's men laughed as he strode away, Eriko following. He cast a glance back at Arkali and saw the humiliation burning in her. By psi, but she's growing up all right, he thought. Last time I saw her she was sick in the head, and the time before that she was a stuck-up little madam. A shame she's still got a swinging arm on her that leaves some way to go, but she wasn't afraid to use it, and that's something!

He patted Eriko on the rump, and wondered whether it was time to tell her what had really happened to Hayden.

Maybe.

Maybe not.

Have to wait and see what goes off first.

He set his crews the task of trans-shipping a flask of Dover cat and a couple of recirculators. There would be enough food to last the garrison for two months, he thought. If they can survive that long. I have it that Hideki Sadamasa, who still commands a remnant of his father's army near Miyakonojo, has been bought off by Yu Hsien. That the Kan are preparing to launch a serious attack on Baker can't be denied. God willing these provisions'll put better spirit in the defenders. That and Rohan's stubbornness might just be enough to keep this smudgy place ours for a while.

He stared around Baker's bridge loftily, his chin jutting, his sumac cheroot ground in his jaw, brass-knuckled stick in his hand like the rod of office of a Europan legate. They're MeTraCor men, sure, but okeh despite that—exiles of the Kanoya City Council mostly, men whose faces didn't fit with Aziza Pope's establishment. That's a good enough excuse in itself to have saved them—but they'll still have to treat me with gratitude, by psi!

"Well, then, gentlemen!" he said. "Let's get down to business!"

The officers went immediately to Luka Rohan's private quarters, following him and the Commander like a gaggle of black-jacketed geese. Normally they avoided Rohan's private paradise. Luka was from the equatorial belt of Oklahoma and only suffered the stuffy, lube-smelling air of the fort to be set for low temperature and humidity so long as the Park made him feel at home.

"Willa's favorite spot when she was here," Rohan said. Ellis knew that he bitterly regretted his wife's death two years ago, but being a private man he had grieved alone. "I keep the place up in her memory. Especially the champak tree."

"And very pretty it is too."

"Do you smell it? Isn't that a special scent?"

"Uh-huh."

"My wife wanted to be buried here. Her dying wish. But MeTraCor thought better of a grave in the Fort Baker recreation area."

Ellis grunted, choked up at the idea, but damned if he would show it. Once he settled to the microclimate it was very pleasant here. To be in rare Coriolis gravity again was a nostalgic pleasure and he luxuriated in it like a connoisseur. It was unlike the compensator gravity of most shipboard places, and unlike the real-gravity that stuck a man to a planet.

There were still some Coriolis craft around, like the small orbital pleasure ships they had circling Disney World, or the research ships they sent out to systems of special scientific interest.

Rohan steered him aside a little way, out of earshot of his subordinates.

"She was a romantic woman by nature," he said distractedly. "She enjoyed music and played wonderful piano. Had one shipped out for her fortieth birthday. Unique here. In the drawing room." Rohan rippled a hand over the lawn. "Sounds were like port wine, Ellis, carrying out over this here garden. She knew she was dying even then. Damn place holds far too many memories for me. Far too many."

"At least you nailed the sonofabitch responsible."

"Yes. And his friends would have nailed me, if it hadn't been for you. I haven't forgotten that."

"Good. I haven't forgotten it, either."

Rohan digested that visibly. He opened the double front doors, and showed them in. Inside, the mansion was fifty percent taken up by a big machinery housing, but that still left the other half. There was a dining room and a drawing room and the Commander's private apartment, there was even a small library, but where the banqueting hall should have opened there was only Regency striped wallpaper and rococo plex moldings and a pair of twentieth-century Louis Quatorze-style electric filament candelabra. Pity, Ellis thought. A little fun is what's wanted. Something to lift morale. Yep, a party.

They retired to the dining room with some of Baker's officers; Rohan got some good fivestar uncorked, then he laid out the situation as he saw it: that the Kan were going to have to attack in great force. Ellis listened in silence. He lit up another mellow sumac cheroot, then it was his wish to speak.

"Okeh. This is the size of it. There's a small squadron of Navy ships heading downchain towards Two-Eight under

Admiral Griffin. He's no John Oujuku, so I heard, but he's no Shrinking Violet either. I don't believe his force is big enough to retake Kanoya City, but at least it gives some hope the Kan might be kept out of Baker indefinitely. If it arrives.''

He sucked on his teeth and went on. ''Now. If Hu Tsung stays out of the system, and if Yu Hsien doesn't get reinforced from Satsuma, and if Liberty has sent the right orders, and if Griffin's a brighter man than some at Seoul give him credit for being, then there might just be a chance of kicking ass at Satsuma while Yu is busy here.''

They showed delight at that, but he quelled them.

''That's a lot of ifs. But it's your task to keep Baker functioning and keep Yu distracted.''

''Rest assured it's our aim to stay alive, Mister Straker,'' Rohan said formally.

''That's why I brought those recirculators.''

Later, Rohan ''ahemmed'' privately and said something watery about sending a search party down for Hayden.

''My son? My son, you say?'' He arched his eyebrows at Rohan. ''I don't have a son, Commander Rohan.''

The Commander stared back blankly, embarrassed in front of his officers. ''Mister Straker, Ellis, I meant your son, Hayden. I'm told he's not . . . dead, as you might have thought. Miss Hawken believes he's at Miyakonojo on some kind of diplomatic mission. Do you know anything about that?''

''I used to have a son, but he betrayed me. I don't know where he is, or what he's doing now.''

''I'm sad to hear that.'' Rohan's narrow face looked suddenly mournful. ''Seems I've picked up a garbled story from somebody. So you've disowned him? It's a blood tie nevertheless. Can't it be repaired?''

''I'll thank you to mind your own business, Mister Rohan,'' Ellis said dangerously. ''If I set eyes on the bastard again, I'll likely cut his gizzard out for his crimes against me. Trouble here's mostly his fault.''

Sure, he's disowned, he thought as Rohan tactfully steered his conversation away, but it's true I've changed my mind a fraction on him. I've listened to gossip, by psi, and there's no doubt he brought the Prefect's forces down on Kanoya City like he said he would, and that's something. Now they say he's winkled himself a berth aboard Ryuji-sama's embassy to go see the Shogun. He's lit out for Edo to talk with Sakuma Hidenaga himself! He's sticking to his task better than I thought he would, but then he's my—

He resettled himself in his chair joltingly as he caught himself thinking sloppy thoughts. Ah, you're going soft on him! Soft! He'll have to do a great lot more to get his account straight with me! And that's the truth!

So, Yu Hsien's in town, he thought. That lone White Tiger ship he came on soon made a scoot for the outer planets when Griffin's retinue appeared, and I don't blame her captain. Hanging out on the black side of some low-gravity moon would seem to be the better part of valor. And I don't doubt that Grand Heavenly Wizard Yu thinks it might be the wisest course to have somebody carry away news of what happens here to Xanadu. Only it isn't going to happen like that. Won't he be surprised when he finds out the Navy nailed Satsuma instead? Eye for an eye—yep, always liked the ring of that!

Suddenly the scope of his thoughts widened to Mutsuhito's death, and the shock waves reverberating out from that event. There's going to be a new reign era, probably a new Shogun, the Kan have got the singularity gun, and suddenly things are getting way out of control. I hate these break points of history. It's like some bastard's blown a whistle and everybody's suddenly got to find a new balance. Maybe they should name this new reign the "Era of Pissing Blood," because that's what we'll all be doing before long if we're not careful.

Later, Ellis hung in a big strap that had been thoughtfully provided by Rohan. His shaved head glistened in the semi-darkness. The Hainanese girl beat on him and scratched at the mat of hairs. Eriko loved his big daddy chest and his dead-secret drunk's-regret tattoo. She was his little 'cutie, his sparrow, come with him from Seoul. Her real name was Fu pao—"Luck and Fortune," but she'd called herself by a Yamato name to give herself a little more class.

Broke my own rules, he thought, bringing her with me on the ship, but five years with her is a long time, and she begged to come with me one day, and I plan to be on Baker awhile this time. What made me do it? He mussed her hair fondly. Ah, but she says in her spicy way, "Any old gwailo woman slapping your face. Don't like! Insulting to your person very much. Don't like! 'Cept fo me, yes!"

Ah, you little beauty, Eriko. You look after me right loyally, don't you? Trusty as a 216i Wesson! But now ol' Arkali's well disgusted at me, innocent as she is. She thought you were my maid, until somebody whispered the truth to her: "No, she his honey pot. He been going with a whole gang of native women only half his age, for years. Everybody knows that."

But I'll not be put down by an apron gossipmonger, nor her mistress. Still, it was fun to see. Arkali's Adventer eyes nearly dropped to the deck and rolled into the runnels when she caught sight of Suzi hopping out of the umbilicus. And I think Eriko really blew her mind. Can't take the notion of a man adapting himself to his place of residence—taking himself a concubine or three. Ha! My girls get their food and lodging paid, don't they? And all of that rich self-respect among their sisters and cousins for being a great man's choice? I'm not a bad personality neither. Poor casteless flowers'd be locked up in a Yamato cathouse if it weren't for me, and that's a fact.

"Aiee!"

She dug her fingers into him hard, just as he liked. I'll have to have a word with young Eastman. Point him at Arkali more definite. Egg him on some. That's what I'll have to do. Yep! There's enough women on Baker—maybe three dozen— we'll have a hair-down and I'll ship in some booze from my own private stock, and some of that Lao Shan vodka that's supposed to be an aphrodisiac. I'll mix up a bowl of booze that'll loosen both their collars and put Arkali into an amorous frame of mind. That'll be good all round. Don't Eastman have prospects? A full commission's coming to him, so Luka said, none of this brevet-rank stuff. And by all that's real that boy needs a woman. As for her, she's in need of a solid man, not some flake like my—like Hayden, with his head stuffed full of frivolous notions like going off to be a poetaster on Liberty!

He laid a big arm all along his pretty beauty's bare back. Ah, the boy'll be having his fill of poetry at the Shogun's palace right now. They'll wrap his poetry three times around their Golden Palace if I know samurai diplomats, then they'll do exactly nothing for him. And when this is all over and the Kan are kicked away over the Three Thirty Degree Plane where they belong by force of Amerikan arms, then back he'll trot! Yes, I can picture it just as nice as you please— the boy coming back down to Kanoya, full of noble ideas about wedding Arkali Hawken, and what a valiant and indispensable part he played in the upheaval. And it'll be "Surely, Father" this, and "Sweet Jeezus, where's your forgiveness" that, and . . . the selfish little bastard'll try everything on!

No way! Because he'll find Arkali married already, by psi, and that'll make sure her creditless father won't be hanging around my neck while I'm getting myself straight with Ei Bank on Seoul!

Eriko pummeled at him. "Turn over now! You bad temper man. I got beat devils out of you."

By psi, I'll still have to kick the shit out of Hayden for this mess if we're fated to meet again.

"Turn over! Very good! Thisaway!"

"Ah, knock off that screeching, Eriko!"

"You want me massaging for you, don't you?"

"All right, then, but no mocking the nexus, now! No tee-hee-hee!" He wagged a finger at her.

"Oh, that naughty Chinee needle-man he joke you up real good, Elly Straker. If only everybody know that!"

"You'll say nothing to anybody!"

"Oh, Elly Straker big pride secret!"

"Promise me, Eriko!"

"I am promising!"

"And you won't laugh."

"I no laff."

So he turned himself over and she sniggered. He growled and thumped the strap. "No tee-hee! I told you—it was done years ago, after a few drinks, when I wasn't quite myself."

"Yes, yes. No tee-hee-hee. I hear." She sniggered once more. "Your nexus ship he escape me again, Elly! He gone transit in his nexus again! And you such a dignify personage! Ha! Ha Ha!"

His back was as solidly fleshed as a bull's, rising up through a thick neck to a shaved head. His arms were strong with well-defined muscles, as were his legs, and his waist was without fat, about all of which he was justly proud. But there was that infernal thing he did not like to admit. Disappearing into the cleft between Ellis Straker's buttocks, looping out across his right cheek, was tattooed an unmistakable nexus ship fin.

11

Eastman was watching the screens when Admiral Griffin's squadron transited into the Osumi system some days later, just as Ellis Straker had said it would.

Griffin wasn't prepared to play diplomatic footsie over crew composition. Five hundred Navy personnel, and male and female were in natural proportion, and if Yamato wasn't happy with two hundred fifty-five women, then tough.

One hundred fifty crack Marine troopers staged over on Fort Baker, and with them came full MeTraCor commissions for #198529 O/KC Eastman, B.T., and #199440 O/KC Shadbolt, L.B. Now he had the official sanction to command staffers in MeTraCor's pay, or Navy rankers on MeTraCor territory, and the prospect delighted him. On the military front it was real comforting to feel part of a big muscular outfit, and things didn't come much more muscular than the Amerikan Navy. It couldn't be long now before they set about taking the "Kan" out of Kanoya City.

Eastman had been genuinely proud. Proud enough for him to forget who he was for a few minutes. His eyes had wetted up looking at that commission notice. Sure it was only MeTra-

Cor, but it meant acceptance, official confirmation that he had made the grade. Hard work and persistence had won the day for him, just as it would win everything he had dreamed about. One day.

But what if they found out? What if the big, ugly, terrifying secret that had hung over him all his life was to leak out? One day, somebody would discover the truth. About him. About what he was. It was bound to happen. And when it did, everything he had worked for would disappear in a puff of smoke. They'll trash me for sure, he thought. They don't bother with fair trials and justice and benefit of the doubt for your kind, they just trash you. So you'd better be careful, Barb. And you'd better go for what you want now, because tomorrow might be too late.

By the night of the big party, he had received his dress uniform, a handsomely cut thing of red and white and black and gold, though the jacket was a little tight under the arms and the floating rib hem was cut in new-style scallops he didn't like as much as the old bat's wing back panel. He noted Arkali with Shadbolt as he arrived at the Park lock. Her party garb was rumored to be cut down from one of the late Willa Rohan's, but although that might be the case, she was unquestionably the most attractive-looking woman present. Her hair was elfed up high, and her pale blue garb made her locks all the more coppery.

Eastman's stomach turned over at the sight of her.

How dare Bosco turn up with her after what I said to him? he thought moodily. As soon as I heard about the party, I made my intentions quite clear, then I went and asked her particularly to accept me as her official escort.

Arkali had seemed taken aback.

"I'm flattered, of course," she had said unsmilingly. "And I would—if it wasn't for a prior request."

"Prior?" The disappointment had sickened him, turned the party from a potential paradise into Jigoku. "Who? May I ask?"

She had turned those shoulders past him. "Your friend Bosco."

Lyonel Boscone Shadbolt.

Bosco, I'll beat the squat out of you, he had thought. I told you what I wanted. I told you that!

Eastman eyed the host stiffly. Here was Commander Rohan himself, with the Admiral and Mister Straker, all toting glittering chrome dress Wessons in their belts, and in their best jackets with their collars turned up and caps set jauntily forward, all ignoring the tropical-style heat manfully. He saw the way Arkali looked pointedly away as Straker made a little bow at her and kissed her hand. She was more steamed up at that than the plex torus walling.

The service women were making quite a show. Their garbs were Navy, and some Marine, but all in severe dress uniforms. All were simple by necessity. Under the circumstances they made a gut-squeezing sight, all those tight waistbands and gorgets. Some were in open-backed suits with mesh-mail epaulettes, others wore jackets that pushed their shoulders up. Most of them with anything to say favored skin-tites below the belt and Baker's ops were already looking beam-shocked. Hair was in every shape, style, and color imaginable. Under a blaze of bright floods and listening to the latest music, they were coming up now for the formal introductions on Rohan's lawn.

Most of the Navy women, Eastman knew, would be unattached, and he had already had a taste of the group predation behavior they seemed to slip into as soon as they got outside of their own hulls. But Eastman had no wish to join the eager lines of red and blue uniformed MeTraCor staffers who competed for their attention.

Eastman could not take his eyes off Arkali. With growing jealousy he watched officer after officer from Griffin's squadron present their compliments to her. She declined everyone's attentions, and stood with the embarrassed Shadbolt who seemed lost and forlorn beside her. Eastman willed him to move away so he could waylay him discreetly and take him down the Park rim a way for a thump in the mouth. Then Straker cruised in under full power and took them both to the punch bowl.

He summoned Eastman with a hooked finger.

"Have a dip of this, boy. You too, Shadbolt. Ah, but excuse my manners, a bulb for the lady first, isn't that right, Arkali?"

"I don't think so."

"Nonsense, Arkali. You'll drop in this heat unless you drink something, and this here's a delicious fruit beverage designed specially for the silly sex."

"Did I hear you right?" she asked frostily, holding her brimming glass of ruby liquid so that it dripped clear of her garb. "The silly sex?"

"What else would you call the sex that got the work side of procreation instead of the fun side?" Straker nudged her escort and winked at his glass. "Get it down your throat, Shadbolt."

"Sir!"

"What's your opinion, Eastman?"

Eastman came out of the shadows. He sipped and recognised the strength of spirits that underlay the fruity camouflage. "It's . . . good . . . God."

"Remember now, it's a recommendation to the women that we're after from you! Did you hear him say 'good'? Ah, what a judge!"

Ellis hooked Rohan to his side. "You see, like I told you, Miss Hawken and me are best of friends again. The misunderstanding the other day was just that. A misunderstanding. I'm told she apologised for being so damn rude. I hope you forgave her.''

Rohan nodded his head as if disposing of a trifle. His narrow arch of front teeth were like a horse's in mid-whinny. "Hey. We've all been under a good deal of strain here. None more than Miz Hawken.''

Arkali's eyes flashed at Ellis, then she forced a momentary smile for Rohan, but Ellis was not finished. He said, "Now, Commander. We're at war, ain't we?"

"Last time I checked."

"And we're in the presence of the enemy, ain't we?"

"I guess."

"And in any case you're the whole law aboard this vessel? With total powers under martial law?"

"Technically."

"Well, why don't you give us some of your legislation, right now? A special ruling to cover this state of emergency?"

Rohan took the bulb of booze that was thrust at him. "What did you have in mind?"

Ellis made a play of thinking it over. "Oh, say, a law that everybody we ask has to put down at least one bulb of punch. To prevent dehydration.''

"Okeh! Fooh! . . . This stuff's . . . delicious.'' He drew off another bulb of it. "Okeh, you got yourself a new law, Ellis.''

"C'mon, Arkali, you don't want to embarrass your escort by defying the law and the Commander to his face, do you?"

"If you think that I'm going to—"

Ellis leaned over and whispered conspiratorially on Rohan's blind side. "You want to get permission to go to Miyakonojo, don't you, Arkali?"

He fixed her with a beady eye until she nodded tightly,

then he leaned forward again, this time winking at Rohan as he said in her ear, ''Get Rohan drunk and he'll promise you anything. He likes you.''

She drank a sip if only to show Rohan that she wanted to undo the unpleasant scene she had been blamed for causing at the umbilicus.

''Down the tubes, Miz Hawken.''

The solemnity of her face was unbroken. ''It's . . . a pleasant enough mixture, don't you think, Commander?''

''Drink up, then!''

As Ellis badgered Arkali to finish her bulb with Rohan grinning on, Eastman took Shadbolt aside.

''What's the squatting game, slug?'' he whispered fiercely.

''Eastman, I'm sorry. I had no idea!''

''I told you.''

''She came and asked me. Just like that. What could I do?''

There was pleading in Shadbolt's eyes, but Eastman trampled it underfoot. ''You'll retire hurt—one way or another. Through drink, or through me. Go and make an excuse to her, and then get the hell out of here. Understand me?''

''But I'll miss the party.''

''You'll miss having a pair of balls a lot more.''

Shadbolt's brow furrowed. ''Barb, I don't like your tone.''

He felt Eastman's will focus on him frighteningly. ''Get, Bosco, or I'll cut you. I swear it!''

Shadbolt sighed and folded his arms across his chest. ''If that's what you want. But you should know you're not going about her the right way, Barb.''

''I'm going to have her tonight!''

Shadbolt sighed and shook his head. ''No.''

''What do you mean, no?'' Eastman's eyes were full of defenses. ''There's nothing wrong with me. I'm a fully commissioned officer. See that braid? These buttons? I'm recognised as a man of standing now, and I've got good prospects. Good prospects. Nobody looks down on me ever again. Okeh?''

"Barb, it's not that—"

"Okeh, so I've got no plutocratic blood in my veins, but neither does she. Her father's a bankrupt, insolvent and discredited, and a prisoner of the Kan. She ought to jump at the chance of—''

Shadbolt was shaking his head. "It's not a question of blood or rank. Or even prospects."

"Then what?"

"I know you, Barb." Shadbolt's tact was a creeping, slimy thing and he hated it. "I know what sort of woman you need, and she's nothing like Arkali Hawken. Arkali's a thoroughbred; high-strung and flighty. You need someone like my sister, Marley, back on Jersey, a country pony by comparison, true, but loyal and calm in her mind, the sort that'll stick with you through thick and thin, a woman who'll accommodate a compromise, who's good with credit and will fit in with MeTraCor. A woman content to have a solid man to father her children."

"I don't need your whining advice! I know what sort of woman I want! You don't understand ambition!"

"I'm just trying to help out."

"Well, butt out! Or I'll cut you up bad! Hear me?"

Shadbolt pursed his lips and unfolded his arms. "Well, then. You might as well know what she told me."

His eyes were on Shadbolt again like a flash.

"She thinks you're an asshole, Barb, and she wants nothing to do with you. And you know what? I can't say I blame her."

Eastman watched him walk away, his shiny little dress

pistol neat at his side. If this moment was not so poised, he thought, infuriated, I'd kick you from here to the squatting bridge. Fuck you, Shadbolt, you just want her for yourself! Well, you're not going to get her!

He strode back to Arkali and took the empty bulb from her hand. She was momentarily so shocked that she allowed him to steer her away from Straker and Rohan with a brusque "'Scuse."

"What? You want to dance?" she asked dubiously, then when she got no direct answer, "Where's Bosco gone?"

They approached the big curving wall of plex and it struck him oddly how the turf grew right up to it, a millimeter away from hard vacuum.

"Please, Miss Hawken—Arkali—I've got to talk to you. I know . . . I know you've been avoiding me, but I have something important I need to tell you."

As he steered her past the flowering shrubs a bird flitted from the branches of a tree, startling her. Perhaps Eastman's heard something about Hayden from one of Straker's crew, she thought. Something Straker wouldn't bother to tell me.

She followed him deeper into the thickening foliage to a small clearing where a bench stood, overhung by leafy branches. Here, the condensation on the plex had been dried off by one of the hot-air blowers and they could clearly see the sinister form of the fort and the brilliant blue-green-brown disc of Osumi, gibbous and filling twenty-plus degrees of the sky. Her hopes rose and fell as he faced her, a strange light in his eyes, waiting, as if calming himself. Then he sat her down on the bench beneath the tree and sat down beside her, his seriousness starting to unnerve her.

"Do you know what sort of tree this is?" he asked at last.

She looked up and saw the tracery of branches against what felt like a gigantic moon.

"This is what the locals call *sakura no ki*—cherry tree," he said. "It's very special in Yamato. Smell the sweetness its blossom gives to the air. Here. For your hair."

He reached up suddenly into the long branches that were laden with dense blossoms and snapped one with a shimmering sound. The flowers were pink and fragile, ripe to fall apart.

She took it from him to prevent him trying to put it in her hair. The music from the party was distant. She felt suddenly trapped. "Listen, Barb . . ."

"Have you heard the phrase, 'kamikaze'?" he asked as if it were a matter of life or death to him also. "It means 'divine wind.' In the Pacific War of the twentieth century there were young Japanese pilots who wore cherry blossom embossed on their buttons. They were prepared to die for what they believed in."

"Suicide pilots?"

"Just as I'm prepared to die."

"I don't see . . ."

"Now I'm commissioned, my prospects are excellent. I can get out of MeTraCor in two years' time, but I'll still have my trade license. I'll be empowered to trade through Kanoya City as an independent if I want. And when this war is over I can guarantee I'll amass a great deal of credit on Seoul."

"That's good, Barb, but . . ."

"I'm saying that I want to do it all for you!" His sudden and intense agitation shocked her. "These flowers are tokens of that wish. Arkali: I want you to marry me."

She stared back at him, dumbfounded. Sickened by the saccharine sweetness of the genetically engineered flowers. Revolted by his assumptions and his ham-fisted declaration. "Say yes to me, Arkali. I'll be richer than any man alive if you'll agree to be my wife."

"I . . ."

She got up and began to hurry away, but he rose and caught her.

"You must say yes. It's your destiny. As I've always told you. Don't you see?"

"Let me go! I'm going to be married to somebody else. You know that!"

"Hayden Straker's dead!" he blurted out.

It was more in exasperation than anger, but his face set hard and that stopped her.

"What?"

He had spoken hotly and suicidally, and nothing now would recover what he had let go. More words came tumbling out. "He's dead. Of course he's dead. It stands to all calculable reason."

"How?"

"He was with the samurai forces that attacked Kanoya City. He was in one of the saucers brought down by the singularity gun in the battle. You saw. It was a massacre. A bloodbath. Thousands died. Hayden died, too."

She stood gaping at him as if he were a ghost. "How do you know? It's from Ellis Straker, isn't it? Another lie from his scheming brain?"

"No! It's not from Straker. It's from my own spies among the Lease people," he said. "I paid them to tell me things. The Kan brought down a vehicle with a *gaijin* aboard that day. It must have been Hayden. It's inconceivable he survived."

She shook her head in disbelief. How could anyone who knew how much Hayden meant to me have kept so vital a piece of information back? "You knew all along! You've known ever since the battle!"

"No."

"Yes! You knew even before we left Kanoya City to come here. You must have. And yet you allowed me to go on believing until the moment was right for you to make your move. I can see it all now. I can see what you had in mind right from that night we met on the roof in Kanoya City.''

"Arkali, no! I swear. I learned just two days ago. Thousands of men left the battle in disorder, most returned to their own *han*. One of them, a lord's son, is a spy. MeTraCor has been running him for years, to keep an eye on the samurai civil power at Miyakonojo. I got through to him on microwave forty-eight hours ago. Please believe me, I've tried hard to find out what I could about Hayden Straker—for your sake.''

"For your own sake! What if you'd heard he was alive? Would you have told me then?''

He was wounded. "I told you exactly what I've heard. The report was of a *gaijin* traveling in the *sora-sensha* of Hideki Shingo-sama. Who else could it have been?''

"You say you knew all this forty-eight hours ago?''

"By all that's real, I couldn't tell you before, with the party coming and all. I wouldn't have told you tonight even, except that . . .''

"Except that your pathetic proposal failed.'' She looked at him directly, her anger cold now, but her face still bloodless from the shock of his words.

"Arkali . . .''

Her words were flat and eerie. "And when I turned you down you lost your temper and found spite enough inside you to invent a vicious lie. Well, I don't believe you, Barb Eastman. I think you're deliberately lying to me in the hope that I'll change my mind over you.''

"Why do you cling to him?'' he demanded. "I can't understand you! He's a thief and a ship-jumper, disowned by his own father. A notorious coward. But I saved your life. You owe me something.''

"I owe you nothing. Yes, you saved my life, and for that I've thanked you.'' She took several paces from him. "I wouldn't marry you if you were the last man in Known Space.''

She turned away, leaving him in hell. He watched her silhouette recross the lawn and disappear into a crowd of milling people. The suffocatingly sweet smell of cherry blossom sickened him as he threw his head into his hands. Then the rage inside him began to burn white-hot and he felt it begin shaking him.

12

The gloomy shell of Fort Baker stood darkly haunted by eclipse as the station wheeled into Osumi's shadow. The flat clam shape was hard to see now that the green halo had been sent spinning into an orbit of its own. Though radio black and active camouflage scintillation were both prohibited under the terms of the Lease, the full-spectrum matt surfacing was the next best thing. The shape that blotted out the bright nebulosities of the Milky Way as it orbited suggested heavy slumbering fortification. Close inspection revealed surfaces on which neither drones nor men labored. Nothing gave it away as being anything other than an abandoned facility except the sallow lights that pulsed here and there in the infrared, and a winking beacon showing the location of the dock-lock on the recessed equator. Heavy conical projections on each side of the lock suggested two psi-almighty huge Dahlgrens, weapons big enough to afford big cover for an escaping lander.

Bosco Shadbolt nipped at his flask and felt the fivestar warm his throat fiercely as it went down. The Park had been jettisoned two days ago, when it had become clear that Yu Hsien was preparing to fight. Now he stood ready to inspect his scanner team.

They were keeping a close watch on developments inside the Lease. For the entire time since the night of Commander Rohan's R&R session, the Kan had been moving troops and weapons up from the apron to three or four ships in orbit, and concentrating on building a weapons cluster complex south of Kanoya City that could cover the Osumi-centric celestial equator. Since Fort Baker was now occupying the prime standing orbit for Kanoya—on the Kanoya City meridian— she would appear at an elevation of ninety degrees minus the latitude of Kanoya, or eighty-two degrees. Any Kan weapon on the Lease aligned on azimuth 180 and altitude 82 meant that the station was looking down a barrel. And any ground cluster deployed to focus at a range of 20,075 miles spelled trouble.

Great vigilance had been necessary, especially at night or when it was cloudy and surveillance of the Lease was impossible. Never, he thought uneasily, had the atmosphere inside any orbiting fortress he had gone aboard been so tense.

On a shift like this, sweating over the visualisers and inter- preters, it was possible for the imagination to run riot. The situation had deepened intolerably; a new Kan force of four ships had transited and was now braking, looking for Osumi orbit. Yu's ship had started in from the outer reaches of the system. Two small vessels had come up from the apron and lay in parking orbits, unseen just round the planetary limb. For all Baker's officers there was the sense that psi forces were molding events beyond the control of ordinary people, the fear that the situation on Osumi was coming unstoppably to a bloody and final crisis.

If it's not prescience, then what is it that's making my back prickle so much? he wondered. He took out the flask once again and gave himself another belt of fivestar. Perhaps it's the sudden way the Colonel started showing a lot of interest in the shields this afternoon. What's in his mind? There's no doubt something important is about to happen. Perhaps Eastman got to know. But if he did, would he tell me?

He straightened his cap and considered the sequence of events.

An experienced ex-Army colonel, Zev Lawton, had arrived. Originally posted to Kanoya City by the MeTraCor Directors in Lincoln, this onetime regular officer had taken more than enough schlock from MeTraCor sinecurists. His transport had entered the Zeta CrA system after a long-hop voyage via the Sculptor cusp, and he had got in unbriefed on developments since the Kan invasion. His ship had docked at Fort Baker, and within an hour he had announced himself, assumed command of all MeTraCor station personnel, and declared martial law. He had begun furiously to take the defenses of the orbiter in hand, organizing Baker's makeshift crew into seven squads. The draconian military code that punished indiscipline had meant that the very necessary reorganization had gone ahead without a hitch.

Then, some days ago, Ellis Straker had disappeared again, taking the *Chance* away to Seoul and leaving loud warnings that a new Kan squadron was imminent in the system from the Chain of the Lotus Flowers. It terminated on a nexus the Tao mathenauts named "Lian Hua 1327"—in other words Teth-Two-Nine. Griffin had taken note and taken station on the exit tracks of Teth-Two-Nine, unwilling to be surprised while lying in orbit around the frigid gas giant of Dosei. The Kan ships had showed the next day but they had veered off to the outer circuits of the Zeta CrA system, no doubt to defreezee Yu Hsien's looked-for reinforcements unmolested.

Now, some days ago, there had come the news that yet another Amerikan Navy squadron was on its way, from Idaho—a fleet of six big warships and five smaller vessels, carrying two thousand Marines. It was thought to be commanded by no less a man than Admiral Edd Maskull, Admiral of the Union, the man who had distinguished himself in 'forty-one aboard the *New Jersey*, at the taking of Ulsan, then later in the *James Decatur* when he had captured the *Shan Xi*, then yet again by running the *Ning Xia* into Admiral Lewis's fleet.

I'd heard that Maskull was killed by a flash-over in an action in Paracelle, Shadbolt thought, *but it seems not. If these new rumors are true, and Maskull's coming here with a substantial force, then the Kan will want to be in possession of Fort Baker by the time he transits.*

Shadbolt felt a hot turbulence in his belly as he looked over the scanners once more. *Damn the differences I've had with Eastman,* he thought. *I'm still rattled by that offhand remark he made half an hour ago, a stupid argument about real-food, wasn't it? How can he get so worked up over the merits of the Dover process? Why do I let him get to me? We've had nothing but differences since the night of the party. That was the turning point. That was the moment he ceased to be the Barb Eastman I used to know. That night I saw something terrible in his eyes. Something I'd rather forget, but can't.*

He looked around suddenly. *But I'm sure it's not him that's prickling the hairs of my neck, it's something else. I feel as though someone's watching me—it's exactly as if a weapon were trained on me.*

He shivered. His hand strayed to the pocket that concealed the fivestar flask again, but this time he checked himself. He thought he heard a faint click in his earpiece, like the interference that gives away false-image jamming on an interpreter. He controlled his urge to stop and retrack the scan, and pushed it on to the almost-completed weapons cluster, checking to see that his predictions were still holding.

Nothing had changed down there.

He stood up. Went to peer over the shoulders of his subordinates. They were good people, familiar with their decks; they looked up from their visualisers at his approach. If there was anything down there in that morass of black shadows, his sharp-eyed squad surely would have seen it. Colonel Lawton told them all to be especially attentive this shift.

He admonished the third man, a Korean, for having the chin strap of his cap set too loose.

"*Ki o tsukete kudasai*," Shadbolt told him mildly. Take care. The man snapped upright in his seat and Shadbolt moved on.

According to Eastman, Colonel Zevaniah Lawton was an Army veteran who had risen from the ranks to become an officer in record time. At the age of twenty he had been commissioned into General Clayton's 512th Tactical Regiment whose live-by was the sinister motto "Death or Glory." He had served on Solomon II and Hiva Oa and risen to acting Colonel; then MeTraCor had appointed him to the post of Kanoya City Garrison Commander on the death of Major Quincy at two hundred fifty thousand in personal credit per annum. Astonishing, Shadbolt thought, that MeTraCor should have gained the services of so dedicated and able a soldier when its efforts in the past had bought it a lamentable line of Macau-Kalifornian drunkards and destitutes and the dishonorably discharged dregs of every sweat canyon in the home Sector. They must have known something political was building out here.

Eastman's got a fellow thinker in Lawton. He seems determined to give responsibility to anyone who deserves and wants it, and Eastman certainly does both. If the Colonel had seen what I saw the night of the party—perhaps he might have thought twice . . . uh-oh, talk of the devil . . .

Shadbolt saw Eastman coming in his direction along the walkway. He cast his mind back to the black passion that had engulfed Barb Eastman after the party: He had come back alone from his stroll with Arkali and drunk down several bulbs of Ellis Straker's pole-ax punch one after another before stalking away to find suitable company for his state of mind.

He had begun by taking on a tableful of notorious aristo Navy officers in a few dozen hands of "sham." They had seen him coming, a drunken sonofabitch, ripe for the fleecing. Then, after the last smart card down, the time had come to settle.

"I said we'll double the credit on another hand! Or aren't you sporting in the Navy?"

The officers had resented the remark, but one had had the capacity to sweet him along.

"C'mon, it's a fritzy amount," she had said. "What's thirteen hundred? Pay up, MeTraCor, and let's get on!"

"The amount is not fritzy to me."

"Pay up, I toleya. Square. What's a few rattling creds to a man in a red jacket? We're all 'merkn officers of one sort or another here."

"You may be officers," Eastman had said pugnaciously, "but you're far from being Amerikan."

There had been a general loss of humor at that, but Eastman had spoken into the silence, quite deliberately tensioning things. He had gunned a finger at the most obvious one of them.

"You can go straight to hell, Lady."

"Listen, hobby trooper, you pay your debts now, 'keh?"

"I say she cheated me."

The lieutenant from the *Isaac Hull* had taken it up, her words cold and precise. "You realise that if you do not withdraw that word, there is only one course open to me?"

Eastman had lounged back until the challenge had come. Then he had been stubborn. "Outside then. Here and now."

I had to step in, Shadbolt thought, reliving the moment. If I hadn't stepped in, I could never have forgiven myself. After all, he was three-fourths drunk. Even at that point there was something in his eyes that scared the shit out of me. A frightening void.

"Barb! For psi's sake, man! Let me settle up for you."

"Keep out of this."

How could I say it? Sure they'd been cheating! It was understood. These particular officers were known for it. Their notoriety as dangerous bad-risk chancers was widely put about, and it was a reputation they delighted in. He had brought himself deliberately into their game, knowing full well what their mode of entertainment was. Eastman had upset everything quite deliberately. Alone and in the midst of their territory he had as good as smacked their leader's face. And therefore they had been obliged to rise to him. Yes, it was a matter of form—in a strange way of honor, too. A challenge had been absolutely inevitable.

But even so, the way these things always went was generally a matter of bluster and bravado, coming to nothing in the end. Bluff, just bluff, and bluff back again until they settled in some grudging way. But here Eastman was calling the bluff. He was calling Lieutenant Keene from the *Isaac Hull* out—immediately—and no two ways about that.

They had left Rohan's private tropics in orderly fashion and found a quiet place in conduit fourteen. No seconds. And no way out. This was dirty play now. A squalid dispute. Hard as iron. A deadly clash of wills. The white-faced lieutenant, hooked like a trout on her inflexible pride and the honor of her service, handling blasters in a dark, throbbing space deep in the belly of the station. Eastman, strutting, utterly bent on either self-destruction or murder to discharge the pain of passion inside him. Did it matter to him which it was to be? By his expression, not at all. Oh, they had mistakenly picked on a quiet maniac to insist with in this MeTraCor boy. What a mistake. I'd never seen eyes like that before. Empty, they were. Unholy radio black.

Shadbolt wiped at his forehead, remembering that sickening failure. No doubt it's the memory of it working my pores open, he thought. He felt salt in the corners of his eyes. But it shows you how quickly alcohol and bristling pride can make dead meat of a man. Two hours before and he was fluttering like a butterfly over Arkali Hawken. And there I was enjoying the Commander's party as well as I could after his dumb threats. Then, inside a few minutes, the party had turned to bile. It had come to a psi duel in a dark conduit.

He had gone down into that cold hole, knowing he must, for Eastman's sake, still looking to conciliate. But there had been none of that. No Monomachy Code. No Queensberry Ethical Procedure.

It had been a brisk business. The plaintiff and accused had opened their weapons and pulled the wholly illegal but very common modification pin that made the Wesson into a dueling gun. They had marched apart, then Eastman had turned at the appointed place and fired one ragged point-one-second burst with his selector cranked up to overload.

No doubt that psi dueling gave the victor a vast sense of justice. No doubt it settled things beyond argument. To survive an ordeal that had an equal chance of killing either participant was a matter of blind luck, and what human truly thought there was no justice at the roots of destiny? "Psi tells!" Adventer children would say when any little crime or misdemeanor came unexpectedly to light. And they were right. Psi did tell. Most times.

A severely overloaded blaster put out a lashing snake of energy, ill-controlled, poorly directed, and with a fifty percent chance of blowing back and turning everything from trigger finger to elbow into ash. Eastman had understood that. As plaintiff his was the ''privilege'' of firing first.

He had chosen his moment as psi dicers do, tasting the local index, and fired on the upswing. A bright flash and a hellish reverb as the argentium tube delivered one percent of its total power. No blow-back. But the Lieutenant had remained upright, unhit. A miracle, really. The beam had grazed her chalk-white cheek and melted a weld hole in the steel grating behind her.

Suddenly the woman had realised and rocked back on her heels: now the entire opportunity was hers! Free and clear to do with as she liked. A flush had risen through her face like red wine. She had leveled her Wesson with relish and directed it towards Eastman's heart. They had stood watching like a pack of lunatics, silenced by the awesomeness of it, willing something to happen. But Keene had neglected to fire.

It was an unheard of breach of etiquette, a Naval Lieutenant walking back up to Eastman slowly like the bitch she was, a petty tyrant versed and schooled in the cruelties of a junior officer's life. To her, like the rest of the Navy, there was no such thing as a draw.

Keene had put the weapon to Eastman's head. To his left eye to be exact.

''You said I cheated.''

Eastman had stared on in that inhuman way, one eye eclipsed by the blackness of the muzzle as Agni Keene prepared to make him beg.

''Now, MeTraCor boy, you will retract your accusation.''

But Eastman had stood there still, as if calculating in the

freezing cold, an overloaded Wesson just a light squeeze away from blowing his brains into ash, whatever happened. Suddenly all the psi had gone out of it. His chance of proving justice was gone. This was a dead end.

"I will not retract."

"I'm telling you! Retract!"

"And I'm telling you: Pull the trigger if you want. I say you cheated. You did, and you know you did. I'll never pay you."

Eastman's will had locked against the other's.

The pistol had quivered, steadied . . . then it had been put up.

Maybe Eastman had read something in Keene's face, heard her heart thumping with relief and triumph, so he had decided to gamble again. Or maybe he had decided to tempt death. Maybe that had been it. But whatever it was he had accomplished it with the look from a single terrifying eye.

Keene had almost slumped. There had been some striding around as the Navy people had anxiously tried to cover the shame of their officer. Then they had found a formula, insulting Eastman between them.

"He's crazy! Stark staring!"

"Yeh. Insane. Been out too long."

"Shit! Not worth getting cashiered over!"

"Let's get out of here. Ozone stinks! C'mon."

There had been detectable fear in their voices. They had slunk away, a little like curs whose barking into a cave had brought out an unexpectedly large bear—but more like ordinary human beings who had witnessed something incomprehensible as well as powerful, something almost terrifying.

The next day had seen inquiries made MeTraCor style: tentative at first, feeling out the truth of the matter, and looming with monstrous consequences. There was a telltale hole in the gratings of conduit fourteen. The penalties for dueling were severe. Eastman had been called to account but he had refused to blame anyone. Finally he had told both Rohan and Lawton flatly that his unnamed opponent had granted him life, and he therefore owed her her liberty. He would neither associate with her nor testify against her. At a word from Lawton, Rohan had agreed to drop it, and Straker had placated Admiral Griffin for them with a case of fivestar.

That kind of spirit in the inquiry won Eastman the admiration of all MeTraCor's officers on Fort Baker, Shadbolt reflected. The men liked courage, and the straight account of it was good enough currency for everyone to spend. Morale had rocketed. But the admiration and the fame haven't helped to heal Eastman's heart. There's a worm eating at the soul of that man, souring him, embittering him. It has taken me long enough to realise what it was.

Shadbolt took a last nip of fivestar. One for courage. No good saving a good label when it might be orbiting vapor tomorrow. When Eastman was twenty feet away he made a gesture of recognition.

Jeezus, Shadbolt thought, returning the greeting with a twinge of guilt. I wish we could turn UT back to the day before Arkali Hawken made planetfall. I never imagined until the night of the party what she'd come to mean to you. It was stupid of you to've proposed to her. And thoughtless of her to have let you down the way she did. And pretty tactless of me to have explained her true feelings towards you. And now you're in the black pit of the soul, with a broken heart beyond the reach of everyone, and you act as if your life means nothing much at all to you. Barb, you chance yourself against death, and volunteer for dangerous duty. Huh. No wonder the Colonel thinks you're such a find.

Eastman stretched luxuriously in front of the console, and

told the op to take it easy before he spoke to Shadbolt. Incredibly, he was in a very buoyant mood, completely turned around from the blackness that had been in him three hours ago.

"Jeez, smell the squatting air! It's like wine! This is the moment we've all been waiting for. And about time, eh?"

"You seem very certain of that," Shadbolt said cautiously. "You've come from the Colonel?"

"Yeah. I just found out the good news. Monitors have picked up leaky comms planetside. Guess whose bugs were in Yu's war room?"

"Whose?"

"Ellis Straker. Had Pope's staterooms wired for over two years, the sonofabitch."

"Jeezus."

"Likes to keep up with MeTraCor decisions. When he told Rohan he nearly fell in a fit. The Colonel couldn't sit down for laughing. Apparently, Straker blamed the whole thing on Jos Hawken's ass. Can't help but admire the man, can you?"

"So what's going to happen?"

"No point in us slugging it out with ship beam weapons. It would take too long. It'll be a boarding hit. Kan forces are preparing to jet across to give us hell. Eight hundred regulars and a thousand freezee troops are descending on us with cutters and whatever else."

"When?"

"Very soon. I hope. And why not?" He rubbed his palms together in anticipation.

"It's good to know the Kan are doing what's expected," Shadbolt said flippantly. "Has it occurred to anyone they might know about the bugs?"

"Zev's no fool."

"Zev, is it?" Shadbolt paused, then found himself willing to venture a little more with Eastman alight like this. It was a fire very different from the blue flame of alcohol burning inside this man now. "Well, if 'Zev' is so capable, why did he choose to unman the upper stern quarters? Any fool can see that's the way in. They have a reasonable chance of reaching the conduits and blowing our shields away. And if Admiral Maskull could be here soon—"

"That's why I'm here now."

Shadbolt was perplexed. "Why?"

"Orders from Colonel Lawton. You're to get your unit suited up, and back into sections nine through thirteen with as much camouflage as you can adopt and await instructions."

"What?" Shadbolt's irritation surfaced. He sighed, hands on hips. "But that's exactly the section we withdrew from six hours ago."

"Not precisely. You were manning eight through eleven. Now you're to dispose your people along the conduit entrances."

"Jeez, Barb! It took us three hours to get pulled out. I understand that the Colonel likes us to be kept busy for the sake of morale, but shifting people back and forth and back again like this doesn't make any sense!"

"Bosco, it makes perfect sense."

"I don't see how."

Eastman eyed him with something like pity. "You don't. And that's why you'll never be a Colonel."

Shadbolt sighed. "Whereas you're capable of explaining the whole deal to me?"

"Easy as light and dark, Bosco." He waved his hand in the air. "Squatting day and night. The Kan have powerful probes watching us. Of course they do. Their big ships are no more than two hours away from injection and they've been snooping on us from the ground, putting dipole footprints all over the hull. Their scanners saw us jettison the ring, and they saw our men withdraw from the upper stern quarters with no holos. They saw us register back on station just like ops would be if they suspected an attack. The Kan saw us pull out of the upper stern, Bosco. They'll believe the evidence of their sensors.'' A lopsided smile broke over Eastman's mouth. ''They won't as readily believe we've remanned it under radio black.''

''You mean we're going to ambush them?'' Shadbolt said, taken by the brilliance of the ruse despite himself.

''Yep. We'll reman upper stern in absolute stealth. In secret, and under cover of holo. So far as their scanners are concerned we'll all be sitting at the consoles, or at regular station, or in the blisters waiting to shoot them out. Yu Hsien's force'll be here come 02.30 UT, thousands of them falling in on us, too many for the blisters to cope with. They'll think they've got us cold and start cutting in.'' Eastman's eyes smiled. ''But with our units waiting right under them they'll have no time to get in and disperse. They're dead already. Maybe now the Shogun'll decide which side he ought to choose.''

''I hope you're right.''

''Sure I'm right. You'll do me a favor, Bosco.'' He took out a document pouch. Shadbolt had seen it before: it was an old diplomat wallet, used to contain orders. But instead of orders there was a neat paper envelope inside. It was addressed to Arkali Hawken.

''Supposing I get killed in the action and you survive, I expect you'll pass it on for me.''

Shadbolt took the envelope reluctantly. ''What makes you think you'll die and I won't?''

Eastman's characteristic half grin passed briefly over his face. ''Let's just say that now fate has to kill two men to prevent me saying what I want to Arkali.''

A faint stirring in his belly prompted Shadbolt to pull out his flask and sip. The fierceness of the juice made him shiver.

"What's the matter, Bosco? Somebody walk over your grave?"

Shadbolt passed the flask over and Eastman took a swallow.

"You got a nasty talent for phraseology, Barb."

They leaned against the console and talked a little more, and Shadbolt saw that the prospect of action had lifted Eastman's spirits more than any amount of fivestar was capable of lifting his own. It was peculiar how the deadly moments took a man: like the moment when he learned of the declaration of war, when he received his first rumor of the enemy's strength, when he heard the order to suit up and go wait for them. It made a man's guts feel like they were falling out of his ass. But in this circumstance Eastman was different from anyone he had ever met. He actually seemed cheered by the onset of conflict, and in this expansive mood he was as lucid as he had ever been. He talked of his hopes as if they were intentions, and his intentions as if they were certainties. And in Eastman's mind, clear as star-shine, was the hope, the intention—the certainty—that today would see him demonstrate his courage. And so brilliantly would he show it, and so incontrovertibly, that Arkali Hawken would have no choice but to see him in an entirely different light.

The whole idea's doomed, he thought as Eastman left him. How can there be a man who understands women so little? Does he really think she'll magically begin to love him because he may succeed in killing several Kan with his bare hands? Does he really imagine that she, of all women, concerns herself about the quality of a man's courage? Does he still think she'll ever forget about Hayden Straker? And what the devil did he mean about the Shogun taking sides?

13

Eastman monitored Shadbolt's suited platoon as it crept back into sections nine through fourteen under total radio black. His own unit did the same, troopers picking their way through the darkness to their cubbyholes and hidden positions among the narrow corridors and abandoned chambers of the upper stern quarters. Each man carried a good rifle blaster and a grenade and thirty tubes of power. Each found a comfortable hiding place a little way back from the compensator bulkhead in the jumble of machine housings and conduit inspection hatches.

There was no air in this section, no life-support at all. When the violet flame of the meson cutters began, and star-light started to show through, they didn't need any rushing of air and debris to complicate matters.

As they waited, Eastman's optimism grew huge. He began to calculate again. By listening carefully to the Colonel's comments he had learned much, and he had stored the information away carefully in his mind for later use. Admiral Griffin's arrival had allowed reinforcements to be landed, but the total at Baker was now still only four hundred seventy-three Marine regulars and three hundred seventy-one MeTraCor militia—the same kind of trustless Macau-Kalifornian scum who had failed at Kanoya City—and one thousand Navy people.

On the other hand, Griffin's departure for Satsuma had

allowed the Kan Admiral, Huang Mien, to land more troops at Kanoya City and ready them. According to the sightings, these ships had transited out of Satsuma under a commander called Wu Shen. They had moved in-system ten astronomical units in five and a half days, and tracked along an intercept that took them wide of the Amerikan fleet while Yu's lone ship burned for a standard day at five gee, then came in cold for seventy-two hours to rendezvous near Osumi.

An even fight, he thought, settling himself inside the softly suspiring suit. Without a doubt there'd be a Kan attempt to cut in through the upper surface of Baker, and aft of the big batteries, where the vital systems were closest to the skin. That's what I'd do, and that's why I asked for these positions for my unit, why I asked Colonel Lawton to swap mine with Shadbolt's. That's where the hottest fighting'll be. That's where I'll cover myself in glory—or a squatting freezee lid. Either way it'll be an end to this hell. And if I take a few real mother's sons with me, that's just too bad.

Someone lumbered past, an ill-defined ghost, gray on gray, even in the hi-def faceplate, but there was something about the way the suit moved.

He selected Shadbolt's channel. "Bosco, that you?"

"Always been me. Who's that?"

The figure seemed to slew round, then disappeared again.

"Are your people all set?"

"Set as they'll ever be."

"Better get into position."

Hesitation. "Barb, I need a word. Off air."

They clashed lids.

"What's on your mind?"

After a little while he said, "Barb, what if they've got singularity guns?"

There was wheezy laughing. "Only just think of that, did you, Bosco? Fact is, they haven't."

"How do you know?"

"Keep it to yourself?"

"C'mon."

"Ellis Straker told me."

"Barb . . ."

"Heh-heh, listen. Turns out was his half brother helped RISC develop the technology thirty years ago. He lives on one of the Aleutians now with a Yambo wife. That's one of the places Straker went when he lit out. He asked his brother about it. Seems that Almighty Dai Yamato never had the capacity for building them at all. Seems Duval Straker was personally involved in the manufacture of all singularity guns outside of Stanton Inc., sole suppliers to the Amerikan Navy, before the ban."

"So the theory that a Yamato scientist took the secret to Xanadu is way out?"

Eastman nodded. "Has to be. They don't believe anyone in the Sector could've developed a working prototype, 'cept Ganesh Ramakrishnan, and nobody knows where he went when he left Amerika."

"So, where does the Kan gun come from?"

"Seems the security services never did account for all the models that were made before the ban. Pharis Cassabian— you know, ex-head of spooks?—seems he tried to track them down. But a half dozen or so had disappeared."

"Jeezus! You're saying that thing the Kan had at Kanoya was a leftover? Some relic from before the pre-ban days?"

"The gun the Kan've got ain't a new type, for definite."

"What about the scatter effect? Nobody's ever seen that before?"

"They think it's a regular old number that's all whacked out of alignment. The scatter effect is just instability. Better pray to psi that's the truth of it."

He settled down in the quiet dark, absorbing the freezing

blackness, giving occasional whispered encouragement to his people. There they waited, together in spirit, and Eastman's mind drifted into fantasies of himself driving down the skids of Kanoya in an open dish-top to a big city reception, with a commendation in the Plaza and—yes, why not?—promotion to Captain in MeTraCor's militia. And there would be Arkali to see him, and she would apologise for not having recognised the true Barb Eastman sooner.

How can she resist, when everyone will be contrasting the notorious cowardice of Hayden Straker with my own amply demonstrated bravery? Impossible!

At 02.30 UT there came the unmistakable sound of their own batteries opening up, then of troopers raining in through the shields. Some collided heavily with Baker, probably pressure-frozen cooked meat already. Some, the momentarily fortunate ones, adhered to the hull. He heard them making their way along the dorsal strake. They appeared to be carrying heavy equipment, and landing automatic cutting drones, and everybody prayed they hadn't got through the shield with a singularity gun.

A small lander seemed to have made it onto the skin somehow, by the noise of engines. A detachment worked furiously on the other side of Baker's plex armor, just four inches away, an advance team tripping off the antipersonnel devices that peppered the fort's skin. Huge chemical explosions scoured off the first wave of attackers, but without generating shock waves, and used against plex-armored suits, straight explosives were pretty ineffective. Sometimes a jag of shrapnel would hit something vital with enough inertia to smash it, but even that wouldn't work beyond the slowing tensor of the defense shields. There was no substitute for the burning power of beam weapons in vacuum, but here again no system of big guns could hope to track a mass assault by thousands of troops whose own personal shields made them as slippery as frogspawn in free space, and who only presented a targetable image when they were too close to lock on to.

The Kan deployed on a wide front, got almost twenty percent of their force through. They climbed along the hull and started attaching the cutters.

Eastman put his head down, and he supposed his men did likewise. He heard the boots of the Kan crunching on the frozen plex of the sun shadow. As the cutter team struck up their jets an intense lilac light burst in a hundred tuned-up faceplates. There was a shower of sparks and shadows dancing riotously everywhere in the orange light, as shards of hull just parted and fell in. Then the sound of Kan breathing and speech suddenly came in over the open channel, a sergeant counting his men in, loud in the silence.

The men in the unfamiliar suits were the enemy. They spread out a little way along the corridor looking for the way to get down to the service conduits. They were men preparing to take over what they presumed to be a totally deserted sector.

Eastman heard the amplified gasping breath of his own men, and he wanted to speak to them, infusing them with confidence, willing them to be still and quiet in these last, critical moments.

The heavy hatches that barred the conduits were opened, and the doors swung back and secured in their niches. Then orders came from the outside, and the Kan began to pour in in response to shouted orders.

They came on in hundreds, having found a place where there was no resistance. Jaunty as thieves. Officers with their men in tow. A picture of hubris.

When two or three hundred soldiers had swung in through the holes and followed their pathfinders down to Green Assembly, a cavernous quarters area, then a raucous Amerikan order was yelled out and men and guns appeared from their cubbyholes.

A tremendous roar blasted the darkness, flashing fire into the frozen gloom. A totally unexpected crossfire of beams and arcs poured down into the rec area, beam after beam scything into the occupying force. The surprise was absolute as their ranks were cut down. Screams and yells began to escape the churning stew of trapped men, all control broke down and the Kan began to scatter in panic for the exits.

Eastman could hold himself in check no longer. He stepped out from his recessed doorway with his blaster in his hand, and physically barred the retreat. His men sprang out after him.

By all that's real, I'll show them what it means to be a man, he told himself, his thoughts clear as ice crystals. Kill or be killed. I'll lead them, and we'll see if any of them are better than me! Pity she's not here to see me do it.

He raised his gun.

"Aaaagh!" he shouted, his heart thumping inhumanly, the battle shout raw in his throat. Then, ahead of his men, he bolted forward into the melee and threw his tortured self bodily into the killing fray.

BOOK 2

Material excerpted from
"A Manuscript Found in Space,"
by A. Hacker
Ozma Vault Transmission Package KVFG #0222,
Copyright Synthetic Educator Corp., Orenburg, VIR.,
By Permission of the Central Authority, Old Earth
A.D. 2451
[Ref. Module MCMIV-437.957620 /Engl.]
[Cross-reference to other SEC modules in CAPS.]

SYNTHETICS

The compilers would like to express their thanks to J. W. Olenfurth of Custom Personality Labs Inc., and to the Halide Corporation of Slaughter Beach, DEL II.

Begins: #casioned by the need for reliable specialist workers able to undertake tasks too hazardous for human beings to undertake. The original solution to this problem was the nonbiosystem approach, giving rise to multitasking electromechanical ROBOTS. Ruggedly constructed from plex and metals, and using TDH matrix sentience technology, these highly mobile and autonomous devices began to pose a seriou

. . . HACK INTERRUPTED . . .

#Projections (made by SKELTON, O. J.; HARDY, R., Princeton, ARI. A.D. 2433) show that synthetics will outnumber genetic humans in Amerika by the year A.D. 2500. This will undoubtedly bring with it complic#

. . . HACK INTERRUPTED . . .

#in response. The question of psi-activity was settled by the Supreme Court in SECTOR v. PATTERSON (Proc. Lib. Law, A.D. 2339, Vols 432–511) when it was shown that so long as a stated upper limit of intellectual capacity was not exceeded, a minimal risk would be posed, only slightly higher than that generated by domestic pets. After the FKG range of Halide biotechnical units (the first synthetically engineered species grown in human form) were tested successfully, an ethical ruling was made by the Adventer Synod. In effect, this influential ruling made it clear that all forms of life where the genotase boundary did not overlap the human genotase by more than ninety-six percent were deemed to be nonhuman, and therefore without immortal souls in the generally accepted sense of#

. . . HACK INTERRUPTED . . .

#ivilege of the rich. Key developments made during the last fifty years have brought down the unit price to the point where low-grade synths have become a mass commodity. The dream of developing a universal labor-saving device app#

. . . HACK INTERRUPTED . . .

#low I.Q. limit. But the major problem facing legislators i#

. . . LINE ABORTED

14

It was night when they came to the deserted tower.

The Tower of Jade was built at the eastern extremity of the Shogun's palace, a pleasure pavilion of commanding height and breathtaking views, yet with a seclusion so precious on Edo where so much was seen or overheard.

Since the death of Baron Harumi, it had been abandoned by the *bakufu*, and stood empty and neglected.

"Doesn't anyone come here anymore, Yasuko-san?" Hayden Straker asked.

"I am afraid not, Hayden-san. The *bakufu* meets elsewhere, out of respect for Baron Harumi's memory. He was a great warrior, and this is the place he came to meditate on his campaigns."

It was built out over the precipice on a network of thick timbers that reminded Hayden Straker of the piers of an early railroad bridge. On closer inspection he had found the carpentry to be superbly precise, each joint embellished with a bronze boss depicting the mon of the Harumi. Atop it was a deck of rosewood on which a large shallow pool an acre in extent stood. It was lead-lined and ornamented by dragons, and retained rainwater no more than a foot deep. The water was crossed by a wooden arch bridge, and the platform where they stood now was surrounded by a low fence, navel high, protecting the drop that fell dizzyingly into the wooded valley far below. On the far side of the pool rose a pagoda of seven tiers, a neat replica of one of Old Japan's most revered buildings.

Overhead, Ama-no-Gawa, the Milky Way, was a luminous band that stood reflected in the glassy water below. She was dressed in a kimono of Roko brown. He stood beside her at the rail. Then a faint stirring breeze rippled the surface, destroying the illusion of standing in command of all Creation.

They heard the temple bell, the echoes carrying from the distant cliffs, sounds reflecting from the capital's huge fortress walls, reverberating, layer upon layer, until it was dreamlike. He fell prey to the awe of the moment. She counted the beads of her Buddhist rosary, enumerating the one hundred eight sufferings that were born of worldly passion. Then she spoke the poetry in her heart to him:

> *"To this world, farewell.*
> *To the night, too, farewell.*
> *He who goes to his death*
> *is as frost on the path*
> *to the burial ground.*
>
> *With every step melting away.*
> *This dream of a dream is sad.*
> *Now count the chimes—*

Seven mark the dawn,
and six have tolled.

The one that remains—
last fading echo in this life,
the bell echoing joy to come
beyond our death.
Not to the bell alone,
to grass, to trees,
to sky, too, farewell.

For the last time, they look up—
Clouds, too, are heedless;
On the water's surface,
the seven stars reflected bright,
wife and husband stars,
In the river of Heaven. . . ."

"Lady, that's beautiful."

"It is from Chikamatsu and tells of a love suicide at Sonez-
aki."

The Tower of Jade was lightly built and not meant to be
entered, but they climbed the tiers together, he pursuing her
up the creaking timber staircase that rose higher through ob-
long apertures in the levels, and from the topmost tier of the
pagoda they watched the clouds coming.

Vast expanses of opaque blackness stole over the sky from
the northwest, blotting out all the primaries and all the
homeworlds of Known Space, making the heavens darker
than the land.

He stared in wonder, mesmerised by the scope and scale
of that heavenly wilderness. "Look at it, Yasuko! Isn't that
the most fantastic sight?"

"Truly!"

"I wonder what it's like down on the coast, in the fishing villages."

"Very bad, I think."

"Yes. I think so, too. And here, soon." He felt the low rail give a little under his leaning weight, and when he over-balanced, it gave, and a slat of wood came away, its joint rotted. He gasped at the sudden pang in his stomach. A momentary fear of falling, but it passed quickly. He had to say something to cover his anxiety. "It's strange to be on a world so traditional and so old that wooden things have been built but have also had time to decay."

"Hayden-san, perhaps we should go down while the air is still calm."

He seized her arm. "No. Let's stay. Whatever the danger, I will stay—if you will."

She hesitated. "I think this pagoda is too delicately built."

"It is old. But by that fact it must have stood through many storms." He looked at her penetratingly, regret in his eyes. "But perhaps we should go down."

She did not move. "As a child I used to come to a place very quiet like this to seek solitude." Her voice was tiny with piquant memories. "When there is no one here, like now, I can imagine I am back among the hills of my ancestral home, the place where the spirits of my bloodline reside."

"You make it sound a great and mysterious place."

"It is. For me there can be nothing in the universe to compare with it."

He watched her eyes, met them as she looked up.

She said:

> *"And now they hear the song.*
> *'Why will you not take me as your wife?*
> *You may think of me as one you can do without.'*

Oh, we may love, and we may grieve,
But fortune and the world are not as we would have
  them.

Every day it is thus:
Until today never was there a day, a night,
  when my heart rested.
I am tortured by a love I should not feel.
'Why, oh, why, is that so? Not for an instant can I
  forget.

If you wish to leave me and go on your way,
  it cannot be so.
Lay your hand on me, kill me, then leave.
Only thus shall I leave you free.'
Thus she sobbed through her tears.''

They were alone. Close. And seized by the moment. Together. Wordless. They embraced.

Fine airborne dust gritted the timbers where they sank
down. The needles of starlight sheened brightly against a
ghastly half sky of impenetrable gray. Silent forks of brilliance stabbed from the thunderheads rising over the distant
Zempukuji Mountains, astonishing and delighting him, but
frightening her.

"Listen," he whispered. "Do you hear it?"

She put her hand to her mouth suddenly.

"You're not scared, are you?"

She hid her head in his shoulder. "The common people
say it is the gods warring in the sky. Thunder is the weapon
of Kami-nari, the Thunder God. Thunder is sent to kill! When
Kami-nari finds those who are wicked the Goddess of Lightning shines her mirror on them and the thunderbolt destroys
them."

"But you don't believe that. Why are you trembling?"

"It is dangerous! The common people say that savage thunder animals fall from the sky in storms. Have you never seen a tree split and burned by the Thunder God's bolts? It is foolish to stay here in this high place, Hayden-san, insolent and tempting to the gods, and such disrespect will be punished."

"You do not believe that, Yasuko-san. You are samurai. If that lightning is made for us, how can we run from it? You said only wicked people are hit. We are not wicked. Let's glory in it!"

To him, electrical storms were magnificent. They filled him with feelings of elation.

"There is nothing to fear. Let's stand out here on the open balcony and dare fate. Trust me."

As she looked up at him a huge flash lit up the east and again she stiffened. The words of the Old Earth poet Dryden came to him—the electric flash, that from the fond eye darts the melting question . . .

See how she must love you!

"Quickly now, count the seconds! Count with me, Yasuko-san. There now, you hear it!"

"Why do you count, Hayden-san? Is it a talisman? An Amerikan charm to protect you?"

"No! To measure the distance. Every two seconds is one *ri*. The last strike was more than five *ri* away. It can't harm you."

Another flash huge and violet and lingering, and still there was no rain, but the leaves swirled on the deck fifty feet below in wild eddies. "The power of such storms!" he said, full of wonder. "Incredible! Do you know that a big storm releases as much energy as a nexus ship?"

She listened to him, pressing closer to his chest. "Please hold me."

There was gooseflesh on her arms, he felt it under the silk that covered her. He squeezed the obi that hugged her ribs, and looked at her.

"Why are you trembling? When you were so brave in the battle?"

"Do you know, Hayden-san, that in Nihongo Japanese *'haiden'* means 'electricity,' but also it can mean 'sanctuary.' "

Her voice was urgent, and he enfolded her with his arms when she flinched at the next cascading crack of thunder. He had never seen her like this, revealed as she seemed to be in this unholy, unworldly illumination. It was her struggle with shame. The shame she must feel so strongly.

He looked into her eyes once more and he saw her head tilt and her lips part, and he leaned forward and then he kissed her. Hungrily, meltingly, and in certainty that it was very wrong, but in certainty also that it was very right.

And the rain began. Big drops like the gods' tears falling in coronet splashes on the dusty wood around them. More and more, and soughing louder off the tile roof, so suddenly a drenching downpour, forcing a haze of spray that wetted their hair, wetted the planks, wetted their naked bodies as they moved as one, as he did what he had desired to do from the moment he had first seen her, as she received him as she had ached to receive him from that moment also.

15

The sun was closing the lotus flowers of the carp pond when Hideki Shingo stirred.

He knelt alone on an island of shingle in the middle of the Garden of Kudan Gyoen in the last dying hour of the day. His eyes were closed as he wrestled with the problem. He was daring at last to face it, as his mother had told him he must.

He occupied the center of the small island. A little bridge of stepping stones connected the island to the shore. The surface of the waters between reflected the waning blue of the sky, and on them three kinds of lotus flowers floated, their cups of rose-tipped flowers rising on slender stalks above huge leaves. Under those dark green pads, old golden carp— a onetime present sent from the Kan Dowager—breathed torpidly in the shadows, brooding.

Shingo's breathing was slow. His seminaked body was warming in the slanting rays of the late sun, his skin still glistened with the oils of the masseur who had recently completed another session of palpation on his arm. His shoulder was almost healed now, and meditation was focusing his mind once more on the difficult choice he had to make.

He roused himself with a deep inhalation of breath and stirred, breaking the reverie. A few experimental sword cuts and he smiled. There was no pain; the feel of grinding gristle in the joint of his shoulder was almost gone. On Edo, the fast cloning techniques existed whereby a temporary arm could be removed and a new arm, grown from his own tissue, reattached. This had been done. The feeling of contamination, the pain of his spirit, the heartache he had suffered for so long, was now at an end.

Yes, he thought. Now I can make the answer yes.

The day had been unusually languid and deliquescent, a day made for tigers. And like a tiger he had lain with Myobu, and then with her maid, then he had drowsed and taken a little food. But there had come a cool breeze before midday. The atmosphere had subtly changed. His mother had come to him, hissing with her undeniable words and her ultimatum.

"What are you going to do about her? If you don't move, I shall be forced to, my son. It's over. Something else is coming. There is no more time!"

Now that something was even more palpably in the air. There was a smell, a definite quickening of the pulse of the Shogun's palace. The signs were discreet, but definite. Messengers trying not to appear urgent. A change of guards to older, more trusted men. And whispering everywhere.

Last night there had been other portents: in the bathhouse an old woman seer wailing, then quickly hushed by a chamberlain; four gray-headed crows disputing above the pagoda of Baron Harumi until one fell to the ground; one of the younger princes falling in a fit at prayers, four body servants bearing him away . . .

Four was an exceptionally ill-omened number.

Last night he had ridden down to the Kudan Gate—the four torii of Omura Masujiro. And so strong had been his feeling that something was turning that he had checked the sky for comets very carefully on his way back. They were ethereal things that shivered in the waves of psi disturbance emanating from an unquiet nexus.

He stood up and crossed the stepping-stones, going to find his mother.

The Lady Isako was in the screened balcony of a reception room next to the Hideki quarters of the residence. She was awaiting his return impatiently. A complex network of niches and folding screens decorated with a dozen or more complete armor suits occupied one wall of the long and classically dimensioned room. The opposite wall was fashioned in rosewood, elegantly curved, like nothing she had seen before. Early light flooded it with cool shadows. There was something undefined about the room that bothered her. It was not the Shogun's war trophies and their camphor smell, but another scent.

"My son, have you now thought upon it?" she asked him formally.

"Mother, I have."

"And will you do as I suggest?"

"I will so do."

"And you will take me completely into your confidence at last?"

"Yes."

"With a clear conscience concerning your father, I hope."

"Yes. You alone shall be my councillor."

Her eyes widened. "Good. Very good. You will not regret that decision."

Isako felt a wave of triumph flood her. As an instrument of his father's policy, Shingo-san was constrained to act with tremendous circumspection while on Edo. He had not been able to move against Yasuko-san for fear of the insult to his host, and for fear of setting off an explosion of gossip and scandal that must ultimately sweep him away.

She realised suddenly that there was a very faint smell of jasmine on the air. That was what was bothering her. It was a fabulously expensive perfume Yasuko-san sometimes used, a scent that remained. So! She had been in the room. When? Overnight sometime? Why?

"Yasuko-san is still the heart of your problem."

"Yes."

"Then tell me what that wolf-bitch advised."

"She said I should offer the *gaijin* jewel to Honda Yukio."

"On the grounds that he will relinquish his claim to the Kyushu Quadrant if he succeeds Sakuma Hidenaga as Shogun?"

"That's what she said."

"Oh, she was lying to you again!" She brushed at her lap as if disposing of his first problem with ease. "Obviously she was hoping to sway you against Yukio-sama by making him her choice. She believed you would automatically go against her advice, and that you would therefore choose Sakuma Kiyohide. Don't you see?"

He looked back at her, bewildered by her intuition.

"How do you know that?"

"Because I know the devious way the she-wolf thinks, and because I know your father's mind. Now, what has the Amerikan been doing?"

"Why do you speak of him?"

Patiently, she told him, "Straker-san's part in this matter is not insignificant."

Shingo's lip curled moodily. "He is still attempting to persuade Yukio-sama to petition the Shogun to move on behalf of the Amerikan trading company. He has tried to make contact with Kiyohide-sama also, but so far he has had no response. Nor shall he have one. What business do samurai of the First Rank have with mongrels?"

Isako smiled. "That, as you shall see, is the kernel of the matter. Your father's plan—"

"My father's plan is a desperation plan believed in by fools," he interrupted.

"No! It is far from that." She regarded him momentarily, her eyebrows arched, ensuring that he gave her his full attention. "It is a beautifully crafted web spun to hold all his possibilities in place until he can move on them one by one."

"I don't see—"

"In the first place, Ryuji-sama knows that you must try your best to secure confirmation of his position. You are forced to do so. We must assume that Sakuma Hidenaga has read the reports of indiscipline among the foreigners who have been so unwisely allowed into the Kyushu Quadrant. If he should interpret those reports amiss, and take it into his head to replace Ryuji-sama as Prefect of Kyushu, then you, Shingo-san, will never succeed as you hope. You will become merely the second son of a displaced and disgraced general who once lost a battle against foreigners, and your claims to Miyakonojo will be as worthless as dog droppings. Your father knows that. And he knows that you know that. So, you are forced—no matter what you think of him—to do your best on his behalf."

Shingo nodded slowly. "That's why he entrusted the Amerikan amygdala to me. To present to Sakuma Hidenaga, and to no one else. And that's what I would have done were not Sakuma Hidenaga hidden away in the depths of his own palace. His *fudai* are weak and scared men, and everyone else in his government is in the pay of either Sakuma Kiyohide or Honda Yukio. I cannot get near the Shogun—any more than the Amerikan can. My patience is at an end."

Isako waited for him to finish, and resumed her instruction. "Something more than patience is needed in this, my son. I know you are a proud man, but you must realise that Ryuji-sama is only seeking to neutralise you by sending you here on this ultimately futile embassy while his power is in disarray. Your injury was heaven sent: it permitted you to be conveniently packed away to Edo while the real work is happening in Kyushu. While you are here, your brother is marshaling your father's forces, ready to punish the Kan and drive them from the systems of Osumi and Satsuma. And all this without him having to worry about what is happening behind his back in his own capital.''

Hideki Shingo's jaw clenched. ''My father is siding with dogs, helping the Amerikan Merchant Traders Corporation!''

''Please listen! In the third place he has sent Yasuko-san here to choose who shall have the new amygdala. Here she is in the one place where she can accomplish the dual ends of protecting herself from you while still remaining close enough to you to monitor and influence you.''

''I hold the amygdala! I, Osumi no Hideki Shingo! It is locked in a safe in my apartments and guarded day and night.''

''You hold it, yes. But Ryuji-sama knows he can depend on Yasuko-san to dispose of it correctly. She must also be under orders to manipulate the Amerikan, for there is a more essential business here that has nothing to do with the new amygdala. She has been told to steer you to the correct choice, but even so she is here on a much higher mission.''

He looked at her, astounded. ''What higher mission?''

''Do you know that Yasuko-san is gathering intelligence on behalf of your father about Kan intentions?''

''She is the daughter of deceit!''

''Thank the gods that your eyes have been opened to her at this last possible moment.''

He looked at her without understanding. ''Why do you say that?''

''Do you not feel the breezes that blow through the terraces of the Shogun's capital? They are winds that portend a great change. Hasn't that ever been the case in high politics? So much waiting, so much raising and dashing of hopes, and when the real crisis comes, everyone but the most astute is found unprepared. You must make your choices now in these last hours.''

"Last hours before what?"

She gestured at the lightly swaying stalks of flowers growing outside the balcony. ''Don't you know what that breeze is? It is the breath of heaven. Power is passing out of the hands of Sakuma Hidenaga. His spirit is preparing to leave his body and begin its final journey. His body is going to the fire, and his name into the histories.''

"What do you want me to do?" he said, unable to see the answer. "Who should have the Jewel of Power? The Shogun's son, or his grandson? The uncle, or the nephew? Kiyohide-sama or Yukio-sama?"

"You must offer the amygdala where it commands the highest price. Consider the nephew. For him it is vital. That is why he has been so much more open to you than Kiyohide-sama who holds himself aloof. Unless Honda Yukio gets your father's jewel he will lose the power struggle here, and Sakuma Kiyohide will become Shogun. With the new amygdala in his possession, Yukio-sama may just succeed.''

He looked back at her, utterly at a loss to understand how she could know so much.

The Lady Isako smiled. You unfortunate boy, she thought. How you let your prejudices cloud your judgment. How your mind seems blocked to high understanding. If only you knew how much politics is conducted through the gossip of Court. Few men feel the shocks reverberating through Edo as clearly as we women. They don't understand what it means. So how can I make you understand that the battle in which you were almost killed was certainly the most important battle of recent times? That it might conceivably be the most important event in Yamato for seven generations! How can I, a woman, explain that to you, a proud warrior? And how can I tell you that the *gaijin* whom you hate is the pivot on which the destiny of all Yamato now turns?

"I chose well when I bought Myobu-san for you," she told him. "She spent her learning years here and she is a rich fount of information. She says that Yasuko-san really wants you to present Kiyohide-sama with the jewel because he is the most likely of the two probable successors to entertain the idea of continuing Amerikan trade with Yamato. That is so because Honda Yukio-sama has been in secret communication with the Kan."

"What importance can that have?"

"Just this: By supporting the Amerikans against those who destroyed your father's army, Kiyohide-sama will have been seen to reestablish Yamato pride of arms. He will desire to help the Amerikans crush the despicable Kan, and Ryuji-sama, whose forces are already aiding the Amerikans in their struggle, will be too valuable and strategically placed an ally to replace as Prefect of Kyushu."

"I told you: My father is siding with dogs! Kiyohide-sama will never do that. No bearer of the Shogun's sacred sword would descend to involving himself in a petty squabble between *gaijin* and Kan. And nor should my father."

"He has no choice. You must allow yourself to understand—to fully understand—that everything is changed. Everything! The Kan broke your father's army with a singularity weapon. Since then, our spies tell us that thousands more Kan and Amerikan troops have arrived in the Osumi system, in dozens of warships, to continue their feud. Millions of peasants have been driven from their fields by both sides using beams indiscriminately. This adversely affects our economy. Osumi has become a casualty of a war between outsider and outsider. It must have occurred to many to ask how many more of Yamato's sacred worlds must be despoiled before the foreigners are finished. Many must even now be asking: How big an army will the next Shogun have to send to throw the *gaijin* and the Kan out of Yamato now? Or, indeed, if he still can . . .''

She saw that her son was in turmoil. Every fiber of him was repelled by the idea of admitting the truth, but at last he nodded, knowing in his heart that his mother spoke wisely.

"Therefore," she said softly, "Sakuma Kiyohide needs an ally at Miyakonojo. Moreover he needs one whom the Amerikans already know and trust as a friend. Besides that, of course, Kiyohide-sama wants to be seen as the legitimate successor to his father. If he succeeds, he will be naturally inclined to endorse Ryuji-sama as Daimyo of Osumi since your father was his father's choice. Kiyohide-sama could not very well depose your father, even if he wanted to."

"Yes."

She opened out a folding paper *ogi* and began fanning herself. "Now, my son. We must talk about Yasuko-san."

"I understand." He said it so tightly his mouth seemed full of bitter bile.

Isako told him what he must do to solve the problem of his wife, then she sat back. The stirred air brought another whiff of jasmine to her sensitive nose. It was an Imperial essence, said to be used by the women of the Emperor's Court.

"*So desu ka*," Isako said, pleased with herself. "I think statecraft is your father's greatest strength. His policy is artful, and it is also sound."

"So you think Yasuko-san is right? That I should offer the powerful crystal to Kiyohide-sama after all?"

She put her hands flat on the low table before her. "On the contrary, I have a much better idea. Myobu-san says that though Honda Yukio-sama's aim is to become Shogun, he is nevertheless terrified of the sword. I think he will remember and reward the one who made the amygdala his.''

He looked wonderingly at her. ''Why do you want Yukio-sama to succeed?''

She said darkly, ''Because I think he is a dirtier fighter than Kiyohide-sama. I believe that once he has gained the shogunate he will set the Kan and the Amerikans on one another wherever he can, and encourage them to rip out each other's throats. Then he will turn on the victors while they are still reeling and destroy them utterly.''

Shingo could not contain his zeal. ''Then I will give the jewel to Honda Yukio!''

''No, my son. You must not give it to him.'' She smiled. ''You must sell it to him.''

''How?''

''Go now, and tell him this: that you came from your father who since his defeat is raving and insane. Say he is going about Osumi kissing foreigners' bottoms with disgusting servility. Tell Yukio-sama that it was you who chose to bring him the new amygdala, against the wishes of your only surviving brother, Sadamasa-san. Tell Yukio-sama that you see him as the only leader who has the correct attitude towards the *gaijin*. Say: Yukio-sama, I will give you the key to Edo, if only you will give me my heart's desire. Make me Prefect of Kyushu in my father's place! You will not regret it.''

''Oh, yes. Yes!''

''Soon we can be gone from here. Soon we can be in Miyakonojo once more, then all your other scores can be settled.''

Yes, she thought, and after you play your part you can leave the wolf-bitch to me. The laxity of Edo has been her downfall. By spending so much time with the Amerikan she has all but sealed her fate. So far she has been clever enough to avoid leaving evidence of her secret trysts with him. But no longer. Tomorrow we shall have witnesses enough to her infidelity.

Shingo got to his feet, fired with the idea of shedding the burden of the strange psi-active jewel, and returning at last to Osumi and the capital that would soon be his.

No wonder the Hideki's fortunes have been so terrible. Ever since the *gaikokujin* first appeared nothing has gone right for us. Oh, truly a curse is on the man who has anything to do with these disgusting crystals. It stands to reason we have all had bad luck, the way they warp psi in so artless a way, it must overcome any good luck a person may naturally carry. I wonder if it is true that this one will cancel the evil of the other when they are put together. It seems to me the owner will have twice psi warping, but maybe it's like a magnet. Oh, but I don't understand these technical matters . . .

As Shingo rose to leave, Isako caught a half glimpse of something moving on the very fringe of her vision behind the dangerous forms of the Shogun's war trophies.

Her heart missed a beat.

Behind the lacquer screens the dark shape froze.

A spy!

Oh! How stupid of you to have posted a guard yet not to have checked the room! What have you said? Think! What have you let slip? But first get hold of yourself!

Her eyes widened but she checked herself and stepped forward smoothly to bow to her son as he departed, keeping everything from her face.

Shingo noticed nothing, and as he went past the guard she took stock of herself.

At first she was aghast. Then she was angry. Angry that anyone in the embassy of Kyushu would dare to listen in on her private conversations. Then her mind began to explore the possibilities ravenously.

Who is it? You must know! What have you said and who may come to know it? It's so delicate. Isako, you must take care!

As Shingo's footfalls echoed away, she moved close to the screens, paused deliberately, and depressed the panel that summoned her servants. Whoever was concealed in the niche was trapped; she could not rise and flee without giving away her identity. Her only choice would be to sit and hope.

Isako was careful to show by her actions that she suspected nothing. But she remained standing close to the eavesdropper as Uchimaro, her chief steward, arrived. The excitement was almost intolerable. What might have been overheard was immense and explosive. There had to be immediate action.

"Have Myobu-san attend me presently."

"Yes, Lady," he said solemnly, and departed.

Isako savored the moment despite the way the whole future was balanced on a sword edge. First it had occurred to her that the eavesdropper was completely trapped for the moment, and that made it a delightful torture. Who was it behind the screen? Whoever it was would have to be silenced—one way or another—and Myobu-san was the best ally to have here. *I could deliberately drop many more secrets while talking with her. Secrets that are wildly untrue, or perhaps just truths that are a little distorted, though distorted enough to entrap the listener. Or if that failed, Myobu-san's poisoner could do me a service.*

A feeling of power crept over Isako. Then one of keen anticipation. Moments later, the courtesan appeared.

"My Lady."

"Ah, Myobu-san."

"Come. Sit down here. Will you take tea? Or perhaps a little soup?"

They exchanged pleasantries, Myobu-san refusing all that was offered with courteous finesse.

Isako watched her, smiling towards her. Together we are a force to be reckoned with, you and I, Isako thought. By going along with my plans and allowing Honda Yukio to have his will with you in that disgusting way—which must have been a painful experience—you have gained, if not his trust, most certainly his gratitude. Your organix powders have loosened the *gaijin*'s tongue, and we have discovered what he really wants here. We have also found out just how much Honda Yukio is depending on our amygdala. What we have not yet got from him is where he stands with the Kan and what precisely he intends.

She sighed with disappointment. How tiresome! I was so looking forward to playing a marvelous game with the eavesdropper, but how can I signal my intentions to Myobu-san? I'll risk arousing suspicion from the listener if I try.

Then she thought again, severely. This is too important to jeopardise with games. Best just to silence the spy, whoever it is.

She whispered to her servant, who moved away silently, then she steered the courtesan to the far end of the room and said in a low voice, "Myobu-san, can you find out what Honda Yukio-sama is planning?"

"In what respect, Honorable Lady?"

"In respect of the Kan, of course."

"He is guarded in this matter."

"You said he showed you the antique timepiece he was given by the Kan general."

"Only because he was planning to score a point over our *gaijin*."

"Can we know anything of Honda Yukio's mind on the Kan?"

"He will never willingly tell us." Myobu-san's eyes turned to the pierced balcony screens, then flicked back. "But, then, that would be an artless approach."

"What do you mean?"

"My Lady, why go to the trouble of squeezing drops of blood from him when we know one who has already amassed all there is to know about my lord Honda Yukio's dealings with the Kan?"

Isako nodded, pleased with the suggestion. Yasuko's guard included one very unlikely samurai. Unlikely because he was no samurai at all, but a man in disguise. He was one of the elite messengers Ryuji-sama retained. Yasuko-san herself had brought aurium *koban* with her—no doubt for use as bribes. On at least two occasions she had been seen letting down something on a line from the city ramparts in the dead of night. Strange fishing. But there have been even stranger eels in the foliage below.

Isako thought about it carefully. The faint scent of jasmine came to her again, throwing her mind into sudden panic.

"Yasuko-san," she breathed as if she had been stabbed.

Of course, Yasuko-san! That's her fragrance I can smell! She's behind the screen! Oh, hell of hells. I could have easily silenced a servant. I could have terrified or bought off anyone else. But not her! Not her! What can I do now?

"That's right, my Lady. Yasuko-san." Myobu-san nodded, unaware of the eavesdropper and the double play in Isako's mind. She looked quizzically at her contract-holder and asked, "My Lady? Do you feel quite well?"

"Yes. Yes, quite all right, thank you."

Myobu-san was going on. "It has to be assumed that Yasuko-san's lines of communication with Osumi are good, and that Honda Yukio's message ships are probably being tracked, maybe even intercepted. And more, I know that she has made friends with the nasty little Korean who oversees the Lord Shogun's private apron. Even if Honda Yukio-sama is using message probes to communicate with Osumi . . ."

Isako stayed her with a raised hand. "Are you sure you will not take tea, my dear?"

"Thank you again, Lady. But no."

Where's my steward? she thought, almost frantic. I can't very well confront Yasuko and berate her for eavesdropping. She will easily be able to face me down after all I've revealed. It's too difficult to feed her false information, now, and nothing I could say would recover what I've already said. What can I do?

Suddenly her mind became very still.

There is only one solution now. A strike that will simplify the whole situation. What a gift! Why did I fail to see it sooner. It is so perfect I can hardly believe it. There must be a terrible accident . . .

When Uchimaro reappeared she told him to bring the room guard before her. He came, bowing low, his eyes averted, his long assault blaster held tight across his chest.

"The suits of armor in this room bring many memories back to me." She turned to Myobu and moved her towards the door. Well out of earshot. "My dear, have you ever seen what a direct hit from a beam rifle can do to a man?" she asked.

The question startled the courtesan. "No, Lady. Never."

"Let me show you how it's done." She tossed back her sleeve and spoke softly to the guard. "You. Soldier. I want you to fire your rifle at that suit. That one there. Aim to hit the middle of the face mask. I will have your name removed if you miss."

16

Hayden Straker watched Hideki Shingo as he approached across the deserted boardwalk, hating him. It was the first time they had locked eyes since Yasuko's beating.

This is our place, he thought. Yasuko's and mine. You're not welcome here. You despoil it, and that makes me sad and angry.

Long shadows fell across the planking now—bronze dragons, the arch of a bridge, and the tall, sculptured form of the Tower of Jade. In daylight, the artificial ponds had lost all their magic, stagnant pools sullied by constant refilling and evaporation. Bitter water, low now after the heat wave. Water in which fish no longer swam, but the larvae of mosquitoes hung in their millions. Edo's astonishingly changeable weather made life unpredictable. Ten days ago there had been hail rattling off the roof tiles of the Shogun's Court, but at midday on each cloudless day this week, the fierce sun-star had grown hot enough to bake bread. He could still feel today's heat seeping up through the soles of his socks from the timbers, and he wondered how Shingo was habitually able to stand such extremes on his body during his daily outdoor meditations when he wore nothing but a *fundoshi* to preserve his decency.

Hayden Straker had come here to meet Yasuko. They had arranged the tryst two days ago, and since then he had been unable to stop himself from wishing the slow moments away. He had waited and waited, since before the appointed hour, but she had not come, and now Shingo had appeared in her place.

"*Shibaraku desu, ne?*" It's been a long time since we last met, hasn't it?

He did not expect a greeting from Shingo, but returned the automatic formula thanking him for their last meeting.

"*Kono mae wa arigato gozaimashita.*"

"That is well," Shingo said. "You have learned to express yourself properly. When we first met you would always say '*Ikaga desu ka*,' which is not appropriate. I think *gaijin* inquire after the state of each other's health far too often, and I think that most of the time it is of no concern to the inquirer." He paused, his eyes betraying something of the deep rage that he had buried in calm. "You seem to have learned much about us. Perhaps too much."

"Perhaps," he replied acidly, wishing that the verbal combat in which they would now inevitably become entangled could turn to actual violence. The impulse came as a shock, upsetting his view of himself as a man of principally intellectual reactions. If only he would take the swords off, he thought. Then we would see!

"What was it Gama-san taught me about your excellent form of government? That the Emperor, who is a god, rules all Yamato from his Imperial throne on Kyoto."

Shingo was motionless, fire encased in ice. Merely making mention of the Emperor was apt to be lethal. "That is correct."

"Yet it is the Shogun, a mere mortal, who does the controlling."

"Unlike your President, who is, I believe, a woman."

"Ah, yes, women. You have no legal powers over them

as they do in the Sector of Izlam, instead all your women are bound to their stations in life by chains of tradition.''

''Perhaps you have not understood us after all. Naturally, the Way is not remotely comprehensible to *gaijin*.''

''I've learned something of it. That your ruling classes outwardly scorn the idea of credit and commerce, but inwardly covet the wealth and power it brings. Yes, Shingo-san. I've learned some things in my time here.''

The other turned proudly, staring out at the mother-of-pearl ribbon of the Hanegawa River, far below. ''Outside Yamato, in the Gaikai, there is only turbulent barbarism. Inside Yamato, the ideal is refinement to perfection. See! What appears to be a wilderness below is in fact a minutely tended park. The ideal has come full circle. As in *ikebana*, the finest arrangements appear to be wild.''

''How right you are, Shingo-san. It does look like a wilderness to me. To me, if something is exactly the same as another thing in all respects, then it is identical. It is irrelevant by which route that state was arrived at. But there is something that makes that land a wilderness much more. Ownership. In Amerika a man does not buy a plot of land, he buys a slice of the planet right through to its molten core, substance, surface, and structures. In Yamato no one can buy or sell land at all. Only rights to it are granted, rights to use the land. You must excuse me for saying so, but I believe this denies your people self-respect and full status as humans.''

''Why should this abstraction of ownership seem important? Here rights are granted for peasant cultivation, for grazing or building, for mining or wood cutting—and lease rights for foreigners to buy: rights to carry out their poisonous business.''

''And when the samurai decide to tax those foreigners?'' he said crisply, also looking away. ''What then? Isn't your system compromised? Credit changes hands. Isn't everything suddenly too interconnected to allow a ruling elite the luxury of noninvolvement?"

"What tenants do within the law is their business. It should not concern those who rule. As for myself, I believe there is a better way. This is why we maintained our boundaries against foreign incursion for many years. We are refined. We do not want contamination."

"Or development. Maintain the status quo is your motto. So sorry, but you seek to keep Yamato pure, and to dominate and despoil everywhere else. Otherwise, why does Yamato maintain so many soldiers?"

"Every level of our society has its separate function. I am samurai, therefore it is my function to follow the Way of the Warrior."

"Yes, Shingo-san. I've seen your Way . . ." His words trailed off. Suddenly it seemed to him that his spirit had leapt from his body. It seemed that he was seeing himself and Shingo standing at the rail, two men burning with the implacable fires of hatred. Warring. It was hard to see how they prevented themselves from tearing each other to pieces.

To bring himself back to his senses, he clapped his hands at a mosquito, killing it, so that a smear of blood dirtied his palm. "I dislike sucking insects. They're adapted to do nothing for themselves except draw a living off the blood of others. To me, they are the lowest form of life, and I despise them."

Shingo's voice remained level. The remark was obviously designed to insult outrageously, to curtail the conversation, to make him stomp away, but he did not rise to it. He only indicated the forested land below. "Like our esthetic ideal, the samurai way of life is probably impossible for a foreigner to comprehend. The Emperor gave all the worlds of Yamato into the keeping of his Shogun. Each Quadrant has a Prefect.

Each Prefect hands power down to his planetary Daimyo, his deputies. Below them there are lesser Daimyo who rule continents and subdivisions of continents that we call *han*. It is their sons and underlings who tax the land, and even these lowly samurai stand far above peasants or merchants. My father, as you know, is Prefect of Kyushu. His thinking is of a very high order. His decisions should never be questioned—by such as the son of a silk peddler. This is our law.''

Alarm bells rang louder in Hayden Straker's head. What was Shingo's intention? Why was he lingering to be insulted? Why wasn't it possible to pick up the duplicitous under-thread to the samurai's words this time? Did Shingo know that Yasuko was due to come here? He must do. Of course he must. I'm not scared of your bloody swords, he thought. You can't afford to kill me on Edo. That would give your enemies exactly the opportunity they require. I've learned more about you than you think. That my father was right about a lot of things. That he was completely right about you. You're a fool if you think Yamato power and samurai honor are anything other than shabby ruins. A stinking sham. Like late twentieth-century communism, or twenty-first-century Japanese tech-nocracy: the rotting corpse of former glory . . .

He brushed back his hair, again deliberately affronting Hideki Shingo with his directness, at the same time his own spirit rising. ''As I've said before, Shingo-san, I think that to be the son of a silk peddler is a greater thing than to be a bud on a corrupt and failing dynasty. Despite what you think, commerce is the most powerful force in Known Space. We peddlers' sons know that. We mind our businesses and build up our credit a step at a time. But one day we shall buy and sell the likes of you, Hideki Shingo-san. You may count on that.''

The Prefect's son heard him out without reaction. ''I see that to call you the son of a silk peddler—which is avowedly what you are—insults you. If that is so, then I apologise. I would never be deliberately rude to an ignorant outsider. *Gaijin* sensibilities are so hard to predict. I wonder. I wonder what, truly, is your idea of honor?''

"Let's make a comparison," he said, locking mental swords with his adversary immediately. "Whom do you say is the most honorable, Honda Yukio-sama or Sakura Kiyohide-sama?"

The blow carried Shingo back. "Both are equal in honor."

"When one treats with the Kan, whom you call dogs. And the other, soon, will treat with me. Yes, indeed. Equal."

Shingo's eyes were half-lidded. "I say both are honorable men."

"And which would you have as Shogun?"

"Either one would uphold the Way if he were supreme military ruler. But, as you know, Sakuma Hidenaga-sama is Shogun."

He faced Shingo squarely now. "If you had the intelligence of your father, you'd choose to work with me, not against me. Who are you going to offer the crystal to, Shingo-san?"

Shingo stood motionlessly, then he raised his eyes and presented the palms of his hands in the way an Amerikan might shrug. Somewhere in the shogunal palace a beam rifle arced and the noise sent multicolored doves scattering from the roofs of the pagoda.

"Who may know the will of the gods?"

That was no answer to any question.

He turned angrily on his heel, but Shingo called to him. "Why do you leave, Mister Straker? I have sent word to my wife to join us here. She will arrive presently. In the meantime, you will take tea. Kaneharu-san!"

A big retainer stepped out from behind one of the bronze dragons. Sweet Jeezus, he thought. He does know what Yasuko-san and I feel for each other. He knows we're lovers.

"No, thank you."

"Please, I insist."

He sat down, and they waited for Kaneharu, the servant, to bring the pale, fragrant cup that still left the glow of tranquillity an hour after the first taste.

"The Way is a concept with which you have great difficulty, Mister Straker."

"Our beliefs are incompatible. Our brains are formed too differently." His reply was savagely offhand, and for a moment he thought he had pushed the Prefect's son too far.

Shingo regarded him distantly, but still the inhuman exercise of control kept his rage in check. "Ours is a Way that, to outsiders, is hard to understand. The rules are built on rock. These are the principles of Jocho's wisdom that support us: First, we say, 'Self-attainment is indispensable!'—the pursuit for Buddhahood is false. Even if I were to die and be reborn seven times I would not want to be anything other than myself. It is essential for a samurai to know who he is. It is essential for a man to contemplate the Void and the nature of the universe. In Amerika no one knows who they are."

"We know enough to know we're all important people. And that's sufficient."

"We say, 'The Way of the samurai is death!'—in a choice between death and life, it is correct to be able to choose death. In the same way that a man who cannot make decisions is not truly a man, so a samurai who cannot decide when to die is not a true samurai. In Amerika everyone wants to live forever."

"We think there are more important subjects to contemplate than death. We find it comparatively easy to forgive. We hold that the only really intolerable human fault is malice."

"The third item of our code is 'delicacy.' A man must be delicate in his social behavior. Someone who does not know how to behave in public is a disgrace. In Amerika, no one has delicacy.''

''We have far less appetite to impress one another.''

Suddenly Yasuko appeared on the Castle Path, dressed in a striking ice-blue kimono. As she came up she bowed to her husband. It was clear that she had been ordered here at this time. Shingo stared at her as he went on speaking.

''Samurai training is suffering, Mister Straker. Often we go without food or drink from dawn to dusk. We learn the pain of need, and the self-discipline of commanding the complaints of our bodies to be silent. Samurai indulge in no form of sex for the duration of the ninth month. This is to honor the Way and to prove ourselves able to ignore weakness.''

He felt the brooding power of Shingo's will flare up. The turmoil inside him, and the slashing cut of his words. There was an unexpectedly deep and gritty quality to his voice, as if his words had been forced up from his belly, and chopped into staccato syllables in his mouth.

Then Yasuko spoke, soothingly, lightly, delicate as rose petals. ''But in the samurai code there is also forgiving. Jocho himself said that sometimes it is better not to hear or to see.''

Shingo turned to her as if looking through her. ''Yes. As she says, Mister Straker. There is a way samurai can forgive. But there is a difference between forgiveness and pretending not to notice.''

She said nothing in reply, feeling the incredible tension between husband and lover. Not knowing how to resolve the conflict was agony for her. The spirits of the two men seemed to circle around each other like twin stars, one bright, fast-spinning, intense with white fire, the other a black and infinite appetite that stripped the substance from the other. Shingo turned back to Hayden Straker. Their eyes contending. His cool blue eyes unblinking. The dark, burnished eyes of her husband expressionless.

"I give you the services of my wife, Mister Straker. Let her show you what she will. Ask of her whatever you will—to help you to understand us better. You have my permission."

He turned and walked away, leaving them, leaving Yasuko clutching the sleeves of her kimono, leaving Hayden Straker watching her.

17

After a moment alone she fell against his chest, hugging him, trying to reignite a spirit that had been suffocated as if by a hard vacuum.

"Oh, Hayden-san!"

He was stiff and unresponsive.

"I feel bad." He shook his head.

She said, "You must not allow my husband to intimidate you."

He shook his head again, as if shedding a perplexing dream. "Yasuko, he wants you so much. What are we doing? This is crazy. I don't know anymore . . ."

Suddenly her voice had an edge of desperation in it. "You know what he meant. You did see what he was doing?"

"Yes . . . he was trying deliberately to shame us."

"To shame you, Hayden-san. He knows he cannot say or do anything that can touch me."

"I have nothing to feel shame about," he said.

She looked at him another long moment, wounded. "Oh,

you say that too quickly, Hayden-san. Too hot and too sharp. As if you believe I am guilty of a crime. I love you, Hayden-san. And I know that you love me. We are what we are now. We must live for this moment. What else can matter?''

He made no reply, feeling extraordinarily transparent to her, yet feeling the burden of Shingo's words even so. Her great, dark eyes looked at him; they were depths that were calm, and without threat. He wanted to talk. To open out to her. To shake off the gloom and watch the swallows and huge fruit bats wheeling over the trees below as the dusk gathered.

She sat down. ''You once told me you were a nexus rat who belonged to no world and knew no family.''

''That's true, Yasuko-san. There's only my father. And now that I have declared war on him I am utterly alone.''

''You have no mother?''

''My mother died years ago,'' he said. He saw her sympathetic expression, and he smiled inwardly at the pang of love that came into his belly. Yasuko-san is what she is now, and I am what I am now. That much I agree is true, because what is past is gone forever, and cannot be recovered. Why not trust your instincts? Trust Yasuko-san in a way you've never allowed yourself to trust before.

''My mother was called Reba,'' he said slowly. ''She was young when she met my father, but even then she was promised to another. My father must have been very difficult to ignore. They met and fell in love at my grandfather's house in Lincoln, and that spoiled everything for her family.''

''Samurai marriages are always arranged. Did her father not talk first with your father's father?''

''They never met. My mother's father was Conroy Lubbock, at that time the principal political power in Amerika except Alia Kane herself. My father's father was already dead. He died fighting against oppression in the days of Lucia

Henry's government. He was executed. My father was just a boy then.''

''Oh!'' She said it significantly. ''That is why your father has the talent so strongly.''

He smiled. ''Maybe!''

''And your father's mother?''

''A wild-tempered woman who followed her husband's political stand. She had Mohawk blood, and was related to''—he paused—''to the wife of Jos Hawken, founder of Hawken Inc.''

''Ah. So after the execution of your grandfather, your father's family was left destitute?''

''There was just my father and his brother, Duval. They were very close.''

''Did they run away?''

He looked surprised and she rushed to explain her meaning. ''I meant that your grandfather was . . . disgraced. In Yamato, the custom is for the *kempei* to kill all the dependents of a rebel Daimyo, so that further problems do not arise.'' She poured a little of the tea that Kaneharu had left. ''Your father was not obliged to beg? He was too young to commit *junshi*?''

He knew the word meant a particularly spectacular form of mass suicide on the death of a family head. The horrifying ritual was frequently enacted in Yamato, whenever a grief-stricken retainer wanted nothing more of life and demanded the right not to outlive his or her lord.

''It is impossible to commit *junshi* on the cold clay of a Liberty graveside, Yasuko-san. It is not our custom.'' He paused, somewhat unsettled now. ''In any case, that side of my family were not Daimyo, not aristocrats. This was before Alia Kane's time, when Amerika was run by a pack of gangsters. My father's folks were just ordinary people who decided they weren't going to put up with a turncoat government. They stood up to be counted—and got caught in the cross fire.''

"What did happen to your father?''

"Billy Hawken was a few years older than Jos, and by this time the two brothers had started nexus trading in the Zone. They signed my father on. He worked hard for them. Eventually got to be an astrogator, then a captain.''

"He is a great talent. A legendary talent.''

"They say it runs in the family.'' He sighed. "But I don't see much evidence of that in me.''

"Who can say, Hayden-san? It may be that your story will turn out to be greater than his. Here we believe talent is mostly the result of childhood or adolescent trauma,'' she said. "Most of our astrogators are of high rank. The Court of the Shogun, and every other Daimyo in Yamato, is smothered with childhood trauma. When a lord has twenty, fifty, a hundred consorts, there is plenty of chance for children to be caught in jealousy struggles, and a samurai becomes a man at the age of thirteen when cruelties can be at their most intense.'' She inclined her head, interested again. "What became of your mother when she refused marriage to the man her father had chosen?''

"She didn't refuse. She was married to Kurt Reiner, heir to the Halide Corporation. But she was pregnant with me at the time.''

"Oh!''

"Reiner was a capricious and unstable man. My mother told me that he and my father had had a knife fight the very first night she met him. Right there in the middle of a Lincoln political soiree! Can you imagine that?''

He laughed, and whistled softly. "Reiner left her. She raised me alone, believing my father was dead. You have to understand the situation wasn't at all to the liking of the people who ran things in Lincoln. My grandfather was a man in high office, but he was also in political jeopardy. A scandal could have broken him.''

''But your father was banished?''

''Something like that. He'd gone off to trade in the Zone. And to find his brother. Dad came back when I was five. I remember this huge man coming to the house one day and giving me a love bear.''

She smiled. ''He left a strong impression on you.''

''He leaves strong impressions on everyone. In more ways than one sometimes. I guess that's one of my earliest memories. My father was in his prime then, a privateer warring in the Zone.''

''A hero?''

''A pirate stealing Yamato aurium is the way your official chronicles will probably describe him when the history is written. What the chronicles will probably not mention is that my uncle Duval was responsible for developing the singularity gun for Yamato. Even my father rarely speaks of that, and the story of Duval is hard to wring from him.''

''That is not surprising, Hayden-san.''

''I know that my uncle came back to Amerika just after the Invasion failed. He settled down with his Yamato-born wife, but he's a reclusive man. An academic. I've not seen him for years and years. Nor my cousin, Kenichi.''

She clapped her hands delightedly. ''This is how it should be between our Sectors. So, your aunt went to Amerika also? She must have been very brave to face such a life.''

''Oh, she's quite a woman, by all accounts. Her father was of the clan Hasegawa. They'd settled on Sado, the aurium world—the same one my father found so attractive.''

''Many men have died for aurium,'' she said sadly, her eyes flashing. ''It is too important.''

He laughed. ''That's always been the way. Strategic goods,

resources and 'interests' are at the root of all wars. And the scarcer they are, the dirtier it gets. That's why I laugh to hear your mighty samurai talk of their warrior honor and the lowliness of merchants. Your government oppresses the people in order to maintain power, but samurai rule is not divine. One day the injustices will be recognised in Yamato. People—all people—have particular rights, rights that are"— he hunted for an apt word—"inalienable."

She digested that silently and seemed unsure whether to believe so outrageous a pack of ideas. Then he feared he had said too much, because she said, "I think we were made to believe very differently as children."

"Only psi."

"Yes. Always only psi."

Hayden Straker thought of himself then, and was suddenly overwhelmed by the immensity of odds against his existence. He was the product of such an unlikely combination of circumstances that it was impossible to understand the reason of it. "Yes," he mused. "Just unfathomable."

She smiled. "Your father is passionate. I think he married for love."

"Of that there's no doubt. Yes, he loved my mother very much."

"He is a great man with undeniable charm underneath. I often see him in you."

"God forbid!"

"You should not despise him so much! Be dutiful to your parents—as even your Christian religions say."

He pursed his lips and his brows knitted. "My father believes in trade and nexus ships and commerce and the amassing of a fortune . . . I don't want any part of these things."

"That is not what you once told my husband," she said,

her eyes sliding up to meet his. "You have said that trade is of the greatest importance. I wonder: What do you really believe?"

He sighed, torn by her probing, unsure now about anything. "I was speaking as my father's son when I told Shingo-san that. To you, I speak only as myself. Don't you see, Yasuko-san? Nexus ships mean nothing to me. I don't care about trade and profit and getting ahead. I have a different dream."

"You must tell me your dream."

"I dream of going back to Liberty. To Lincoln. Just as Kyoto is the Imperial center of Yamato, so Lincoln is the center of Amerika." He sat up, excited, his hands describing for her his conception. "It's a place of great houses and . . . and refinement, where literature is written, and where fine architecture is designed, and there are artists and scientists and musicians and thinkers of all kinds. Do you know of the great psience foundation they call RISC? Or the Museum of Known Space?" She shook her head, fascinated at his sudden excitement. "Oh, there are wonders! Houses of learning where brilliant minds from a thousand different disciplines explore the universe and investigate its nature. There are institutes in Lincoln where anyone can attend and have serious conversation with great men of ideas. Where anyone can meet and talk with guest philosophers from other open Sectors. I want to go there."

"All that, and only fifty parsecs away from here."

"Yes."

His voice was soft now, almost ashamed. She saw that he was lost in his dream of Liberty, a world he only dimly remembered, a world he would surely never go to, this Lincoln of the mind. Her gentle mockery went unnoticed and he sighed.

"A voyage of fifty parsecs."

"For that voyage you need a nexus ship—and credit."

He looked up at her honestly. "Yes."

"Costly."

"Very."

"Then your father is not entirely wrong to respect the amassing of wealth?"

He rubbed at his chin, irritated at the way her words had come full circle on him again. "No, you don't understand. Credit's all my father's interested in. He doesn't realise it's just a means to an end. You saw him. You saw the way he behaves. What he believes."

"He is a strong man. And his beliefs are his own concern."

Suddenly she sat up, listening to the crying of a young girl. The girl was sobbing her name as she staggered across the open space towards them.

He recognised the youngster as one of Yasuko's personal maids.

"Sukeko!" she said, and was on her feet instantly.

The girl was in a delirium of distress. Her face was shocked, ravaged by crying, and there was blood on her hands, masked at first by the red and white she wore. As she clung to Yasuko's kimono, the blood stained her.

"What is it?" Yasuko asked, hugging her and wiping her face. "Tell me. Whatever is the matter?"

"It's Niso-san! Niso-san!" she cried, almost unable to get her words out. "They've killed her!"

"What?"

Sukeko broke down into sobs again.

Hayden Straker looked from one to the other anxiously.

"Where are you going?" he asked. "What's happened to upset her? Is there anything I can do?"

Yasuko faced him. "It's my other maid—Niso-san. She's been injured. I must go to her at once. Stay here, Hayden-san. In this you cannot help."

With that she rushed away, rapid steps carrying her deep into the shadow of the maple trees.

18

What she saw when she arrived in the garden outside her own quarters stabbed her to the heart. There were easily twenty women milling there.

The wooden curfew shutters were open, and the *shoji* were slid aside, opening one full side of her twelve-mat room to the garden terrace. The inner space was shafted by bloody dusk light. The air was mint fragrant from the growing herbs, cool as melt water, and laced with the noise of a tumbling stream, but Niso was lying on the floor, her kimono red with blood across the right breast, a blackened patch on her neck and shoulder above. Her eyes were closed and her face was a ghastly gray, and set as if made from wax. The blisters were horrifying, and she was trembling.

At her side Isako knelt, watching unmoved as Myobu's masseuse poured a little water from a jug into a bowl. She lifted Niso's head and tried to induce her to sip from a bowl while everyone else down to the lowest ladies' maid crowded around in a semicircle and watched. Instantly Yasuko burst through them and dashed the bowl to the floor, smashing it. "Get away from her!"

The masseuse looked up, astonished. "My Lady?"

"Get away from her! All of you!"

They had never seen her outwardly angry before, and the semicircle drew back. Only Isako remained where she was. Yasuko whirled on her.

"You!"

"A most regrettable accident, my dear. One of the guards fired his weapon and the arc touched her. It was a terrible mistake."

"No! This was your work, Isako-san. It carries the mark of your despicable scheming. May the demons of hell choke you!"

Isako's patina of concern dissolved, her voice rising now so that everyone could hear. "Yasuko-san, how dare you speak to me like that?"

Yasuko's fury threatened to overwhelm her. "Get out of my way!" She snatched up the china flask, the one decorated with a hand-painted bamboo frond, and held it out to Isako. "What's this?"

Isako contained her own anger; her husky voice was reverberant in the closed terrace. "A little lemon water, to ease her pain. Please do not raise your voice. You can see she is dying. Give her her dignity, at least, Yasuko-san. Give her the peace of her last moments. Have you no shame?"

Yasuko thrust the jug at the masseuse. "Make her drink from it," she told Isako.

The masseuse's eyes widened; she stared at Isako, willing her to say something.

"I cannot ask her to drink from it." Isako tossed her hand so that the folded fan jumped in her sleeve pocket. "It is a special preparation. A herbal medicine to ease her pain."

"Then you drink it."

"I told you! It is a medicine! No one but the patient may drink it. A well person may be harmed by it."

"She will not drink it because she knows it is poisoned!" Yasuko's accusation rang out. "And you yourself will not drink because you know what I say is true. Why, Isako-san?

Why did you have her shot, and why are you trying to finish your murderous business with poison, you loathsome spirit of the hells?''

Isako was on her feet. "Don't speak to me of the hells. You're the one who's bound straight for Jigoku and the judgment of the sister of Emma-O. You brought this bad luck on your maid yourself with your disgusting behavior.''

"Poisoner! Murderer!''

"Yasuko-san, you will pay for these slanders. I have two dozen witnesses. Everyone has heard your filthy mouth. When we return to Osumi they will all report how you have slandered the number-one wife of our Lord. The Daimyo shall know how you have disobeyed and reviled your own mother-in-law, and the Court shall order you punished!''

Yasuko looked around defiantly. These were women of Isako's establishment, allies of low rank and her expeditors for the most part, Isako's personal women and the embassy's lesser courtesans and their servants. They would testify just exactly as Isako told them to testify. Despite the rage she felt, she knew she must do something to protect herself.

"Then let them report this also,'' she said, offering the flask to all who watched in turn. "Let them report the depth of their own conviction. Which one of you will drink? Which one? And who among you will lie to our Lord when he asks you directly which of you was offered to drink—and why you refused?''

The women began to melt away from the open room, their shame clear.

"Now leave my quarters!'' she told Isako. "Leave, or will you refuse to take your leave? Will you prove that you cannot rest until you have seen Niso-san dead with your own eyes?''

Isako retreated and took her retinue away. Yasuko turned to Niso and knelt now beside her where Sukeko shivered and sobbed.

She took Niso's hand. It was cold and pale. "Niso? Can you hear me?"

Her breathing was shallow. She was in shock, but she made a supreme effort, and her eyes flickered open dully.

"Yasuko-san," she whispered, "I am so sorry to be a burden."

Niso's eyes closed again. There was something she had to do. Something important that couldn't wait. But what was it? She drifted, fighting the black sleep that would close her eyes forever. She made another effort, but still she drifted . . .

Oh, yes, that was it. That was what had happened. She had been listening to Isako-san. Behind the screens, she had held herself rigidly still, not daring to breathe, but what she had heard more than compensated for the terrifying situation she had found herself in.

"Niso . . ."

She heard her name and stirred, opening her eyes against the weight of tiredness. And there was a vision of Yasuko before her. But the mistress's face was misty, as if in a dream. Was it, then, a dream? And why was Yasuko-san crying so many tears?

The memory drifted away. Aeii! Yasuko must be close to breaking under this intolerable strain, she thought faintly, regretting the way worry gnawed at her mistress. Our Lord, her honored father-in-law, has put too much on her this time. She is a most remarkably strong woman—though she thinks she is weak—but I think even she cannot endure much longer. And spending time with that *gaijin* is making her lose her mind. He's to blame for everything. He, with his blue, Burma cat eyes. It's as if the top of his skull were missing when you look at him, like seeing the sky. No wonder that every time she meets him she returns ill at ease with her soul. It's like a disease, or a madness. But whatever it is I must help her.

The gods be thanked that I have heard what I have heard!
Now I must tell Yasuko-san. I must warn her!

But Niso was drifting again, back behind the folding
screen, to the fear she had felt. She had almost gasped, as
beyond the screen, Myobu-san had appeared. The courtesan
had paused on the steps of the room, rippling with deceits.
Her carriage was as graceful as she was beautiful; her poise
as exquisite as her heart was false. She had slid aside the
shoji, got up, stepped into the room, knelt again, slid the *shoji*
closed, and approached her contract-holder with a deferential
bow. The despicable tigress, she had thought, and then she
had listened again, praying that she would not be discovered.
But the electric arc had burned a hole in her, and shattered
the world . . .

Yasuko felt the hand she was holding change as the spirit
went out of it. Sukeko stared at Niso's immobile face expectantly, then she looked up at Yasuko, swallowed, and looked
back. It seemed to Yasuko that the young one would keep vigil
for Niso's next breath all night unless she signaled an end. She
put out her hands to Sukeko who refused for a moment, but
then flew to her mistress to have her grief cradled away.

19

"So, *gaijin*, tell me: How did you come by it?"

Sakuma Kiyohide watched him gravely as he set down his
tea bowl. He was a slim, neatly bearded man, son of the great

Sakuma Hidenaga, but very much younger, in his forties, Hayden Straker judged. His bearing was regal, aristocratic, and intensely mannered. He had officiated as deputy for the Shogun for many years, and had assumed the full mantle of responsibility during Sakuma Hidenaga's long illness—every responsibility but one: until the Shogun died, he could not formally become bearer of Shori, the Sword of State. Strangely, he wore a tiny ion key around his neck on a fine metal chain. It was the only thing about him that looked out of place.

Hayden Straker felt the sweat prickle his temples as he laid the Chinese box down on the tatami. He could hear his father's tough voice telling him to get hold of himself. "There's no such thing as an 'equal' to a samurai, son. They're warriors. You know what that means? It means you're not one of them, so you're either worthy of their respect, or you're dirt beneath their feet. They'll take one look at you and make up their minds forever. Never let them take you for dirt, son. Never."

The box contained the chrysoid. Yasuko had thrust it into his hands an hour ago, telling him that Sakuma Kiyohide had granted him an audience. Then she had gone, terrified that she would be seen.

The *fudai* watched him impassively. He regarded his adversary's coterie of retainers with equal care, noticing that they would not look at the box in which the chrysoid lay. Their guards had run their detection machines over it, looking for any sign of danger. They had understood what must be inside and what was its import. They had all understood, these ministers and lackeys and nobles of the blood, but still none would admit so much before their master.

"It is said Amerikans enjoy specifics," Sakuma Kiyohide said, as if encouraging a shy youth. "Please, speak therefore in specifics. Tell me every detail."

"Where should I start?" he said, clearing his throat. "My own father came into the Osumi system from the Neutral Zone with it in his cargo. I myself brought it to planetfall on that world when it was threatened by the Kan."

"Threatened?" Sakuma Kiyohide looked to his advisers as if he had uncovered a significant point. "How may any stone, except a go stone, be safe or unsafe? Though I see how this object occupies a pivotal point in your game. But perhaps you mean 'ownership'—that its ownership was threatened by the Kan?"

"Quite so, Excellency."

"Yes, please be more precise in your speech. I see it would have been unfortunate for you had the Kan taken it—would it not?" He looked up again at his silent coterie and back. "But you took it to Hideki Ryuji. For what purpose?"

He feigned surprise. "Can it be you are as yet unaware of the singular nature of the item, Excellency?"

Sakuma Kiyohide inclined his head and waved his hand in the way that equated to an Amerikan shrug. "We have heard talk of a thing supposed by some to possess a certain degree of psi-activity."

He pursed his lips, remembering the seller of blades and sword furniture who had haggled with Hideki Ryuji so artfully. He knew he must sell the amygdala by not selling the amygdala. But how? How to begin? Perhaps by selling the amygdala's past. He swallowed and looked up, praying he was ready to reveal the myth he had so recently created.

"Such power as it possesses, Excellency, some may say is no great thing today, when so few believe in the power of pure psi, but once it was the terror of its makers.

"It was created many years before the disaster of Old Earth on Wolf, one of the systems now used by the Cloistermen, a dim M-type system that was within the Exclusion Zone, a world somewhere inside the ten-light-year limit that once existed, where no free man could legally go.''

''Ah, the disaster of Old Earth.'' The samurai blew on the surface of his tea and sipped at it. ''Yes. You know we prize our heritage very highly in Yamato. There was a time, when I was a child, when we would stand for an hour's absolute silence in all the worlds of the Imperial domain, everyone, at the seventh minute of the seventh hour of the seventh day of the seventh month, every year. Everyone. No matter what. In commemoration of the terrible event that destroyed Old Japan forever. How unimaginably terrifying it must have been when the final moment came for all those who could not escape. But you were saying—the item?''

''Yes, Excellency. At the time of its creation it was known to be a power crystal, just as your father's great sword's *menuki* is a power crystal, psychologically active and reactive, talking into the mind and listening to human thoughts. What a creation! What a powerful and wonderful technology, Excellency!'' He paused, looking around at Sakuma Kiyohide's advisers challengingly. ''But your father's crystal was badly faulted. It was believed that if it could be reprogrammed, then it might become a great power for good, and so a mind was sought that could maintain contact and accomplish the reprogram.

''The Hindu psientist who finally investigated it wore it as a pendant around his neck for four standard years, never once leaving the aura of its field. And though this man was an accomplished psientist, a savant and an expert in high-level meditation, talented and rigorous in his approach, still the psi power of the amygdala was stronger. It drained his mind and soon he became difficult and unwell.'' He kept his eyes on Sakuma Kiyohide's face, and dropped his voice, desperately hoping that his inflection and gestures would be enough to hold the heir's interest. ''Using the crystal he escaped from the Wolf system and took up as a saddhu—a wandering holy man—on his homeworld of Rae Bareli. At night, this psientist would roam the poor districts near the capital and buy children and take their minds to experiment. They would be found weeks later, without any physical injury to their bodies, but dead. And still the psi-savant went unsuspected, as he grew more insane. He would cause those who displeased him to be killed in freak accidents. He would make women he desired lie for him—then with him—and he indulged in other crimes too horrible for me to describe.''

Sakuma Kiyohide frowned and sipped. ''You say he had his enemies killed by freak accidents? How was this done?''

''With the crystal in his possession, Excellency, this man became a demon, manipulating psi and controlling people as if by hypnosis.''

''What kind of freak accidents?''

''Every kind imaginable. Remember that his mind was stripped out and beyond his control by this time. There was no way he could stop—''

''What was the name of this psientist?''

The direct question slammed into him. ''His name? Ah . . . He was known as . . . Krishna, Excellency.''

Sakuma Kiyohide considered, then grunted, signaling him to go on.

''As his insanity increased, his wickedness increased also, and it was noticed that the jewel hanging around his neck began to cloud with blood, and the original name of it meant in the language of Hindostan the Jewel of Blood . . .''

The heir stifled a yawn. There was a space of silence as Hayden could not go on, then Sakuma Kiyohide said, ''You are a foreigner. Perhaps that is why the point of your legend is unclear to me. I want to know how the jewel came into your father's possession.''

''Ah, but this is a history, not a legend,'' he said, quickly trying to cover his anxiousness. "The history begins long ago when Known Space was much smaller, and the forces of psi were much stronger, more concentrated, than today. May I ask: Has it occurred to you that the dispersion of mankind throughout our galaxy is following a similar form as the expansion of the universe itself? According to our understanding, this is significant. As the value of Big G and all the physical constants have been found to vary with the radius of the universe over cosmological time, so the physical dispersion of psi-active entities—human brains—affects the—"

"Yes, yes. Please continue with your description of events."

"It happened that one day the Governor of Oudh, the world where the psientist had gone to live, was called on by his people who could no longer endure the excesses of their holy man. Despite the fear they had of him, one man of great courage reported him to his Daimyo. Krishna was called to the palace and murdered by priests. He died clutching the crystal, like this, to the node of his forehead. And it is said that the priest who cut the crystal out of the dead man's hand screamed until he died.

"Wiser men devised a plan to prevent such a monstrous power from ever falling into the hands of anyone else. Instead of locking it away in a deep vault, they chose to do the opposite. The temple made it known that the psi-savant had died while communicating with the crystal. That some sectors of the device had been under program control by the mind of a murdered man. Therefore the crystal had experienced and stored the conditions of brain death, and was now too dangerous to make contact with."

"Why was it not destroyed?"

"These priests, Shaivites, did not believe in the destruction of self-aware entities, only in preservation."

"Continue."

"To the common people it was as if a spell had been laid on the crystal that henceforth anyone who touched it would die. For many decades no one dared to claim it; it hung in the marketplace of the capital, a fabulous wealth, yet untouched on its chain for seven generations."

He saw Sakuma Kiyohide's retainers look to one another at that, and he realised suddenly that his invention was growing beyond his control, and perhaps straying uncomfortably near to the legend of the crystal in the Shogun's sword itself. How close to the nexus can I afford to fly? he wondered. Perhaps it's no bad thing that the point is driven home in terms they can understand directly, but I can't afford any mistakes now.

"Perhaps," Sakuma Kiyohide said darkly, stroking his moustache, "it is your intention to mislead me."

Hayden Straker's heart fell to his boots. "I beg your pardon, Excellency?"

"You say that this crystal hung for seven generations where any man could take it. Yet no one had the will to attempt contact? I cannot believe that. Surely every samurai would find such a challenge irresistible?"

He damned himself for overelaborating unnecessarily, then he saw the way out. "I apologise, Excellency, for not making myself clear. We do not talk of a world like the worlds of Yamato. In Hindostan there are no samurai. But that is not the point, Excellency—"

"Do you understand the importance of this crystal to me?"

"Yes, Excellency. I believe I do."

"Then, take care to speak the exact truth." The Shogun's son motioned for the history of the crystal to continue again.

Hayden Straker began to sweat, completely forgetting the tale he had rehearsed. He began to extemporise. Thrills of fear assailed him that what he invented would fail to be convincing to Sakuma Kiyohide, or that he would stumble in his language, or destroy his purpose in some other way.

"So, Excellency." He shrugged, sadness in his voice. "A search was made until, on Mogok, a certain sect of monks were found who could destroy the fault in the crystal. He gave the amygdala into the keeping of these monks, men with shaven heads and robes of saffron yellow. Buddhist mendicants, men who relied on the charity of others to fill their bellies each day, men who had renounced all property to link their minds sixteen hours out of every twenty-four in a meditation ring."

Noises of satisfaction were made.

"Yes," Hayden Straker told them, astonished that he had succeeded in telling the tale, wondering where these strange ideas came from. "These monks were charged with the task of creating an instrument of good from the crystal. It was to become a weapon against evil, a defense against the very fault this crystal had developed. But that, they said, was a difficult and lengthy task.

"Permission was given. The crystal was taken to their temple and built into the forehead of their idol as an evil eye. They told the common people it contained so much madness that henceforth only members of their meditation circle were to stray inside its aura. But that when the name of god had been spoken ten thousand times ten thousand times, then . . ."

"Then?"

"Then the reprogramming would be complete. It would no longer seek to overpower and use human mentalities with which it communicated. It would be purified and filled with the power to do good. It would be able to reprogram other faulted crystals, if it was brought close enough. And in that way, if any other faulted amygdala came into their world, the repaired crystal could be used to render it harmless."

"*Domo.*" Thank you.

He was about to continue again when Sakuma Kiyohide nodded in dismissal. As one, his retainers rocked forward on their haunches and shifted the weight of their bodies onto their feet, standing up all around. Then they made formal obeisance, and backed away to the far end of the audience chamber. He motioned for Hayden Straker to stay.

When they were alone, Sakuma Kiyohide put his finger to his lips and said, "Do you really understand the nature of my power, Mister Straker?" He flicked a hand towards the men he had just dismissed. "Officially, they are still my father's vassals—but see how they obey me. In fact, a year ago, not one of them would have crossed a garden path to save my life, because then I did not have power over them. Not one of them would have hesitated to kill me if he thought it would advantage him to do so. And yet now they follow me like ducklings."

Hayden Straker said nothing, and Sakuma Kiyohide sighed wearily. Then his voice hardened. "Now, to specifics. How did you come by your story?"

"It was told to my father," he lied. "And my father told it to me."

"Please allow me to congratulate you. It was . . . amusing, and pleasantly told, and what more can we ask of a tale? However, all talk is mere words, and words are as rain falling on the sea. Do you not agree?"

"No, Excellency. I believe words are tools. And words are weapons. They may shape events as builders do, or as warriors do, if you will let them."

"We are a sophisticated people in Edo. We cannot afford the luxury of credulous belief, no matter what our yearnings for the glorious days of the past. Events are moving fast, and I must soon address myself to matters of state." He coughed delicately against his hand. "Now, was it not your intention to offer the crystal to my father's vassal, Hideki Ryuji, the Prefect of Kyushu, so that he would be able to overthrow my father and gain the shogunate himself?''

The temptation to accept Sakuma Kiyohide's words was almost irresistible. It was as if a brilliant shaft of light had been directed onto him, and he felt foolish and exposed, but he had enough wariness to cling to his story. He said, ''It was offered to Hideki Ryuji-sama, but only so he could offer it to you.''

''And you gave it to him? It became his property?''

''I gave it to him.''

''In that case, why did he not offer it to me through his son? I will tell you freely: I expected Shingo-san to approach me with this offer. Why are you selected as the Hideki intermediary?''

He licked his dry lips and plunged into danger. ''It's true that Shingo-san was charged with the task of bringing the crystal to bear as a lever. He was ordered to bargain it against Miyakonojo: Edo for the price of his father's continuing daimyoship of Osumi.''

''Then you stole the crystal back?''

He paused, then said deliberately, ''Yes. Because it was never Hideki Shingo-san's intention to offer the crystal to you. Only I would do that—''

Sakuma Kiyohide snorted. ''So. It was you who sent me the ion key?''

''Excellency?''

Now Sakuma Kiyohide sounded uncertain. He lifted the tiny cylinder on its chain. ''This key is for your box. No?''

Hayden Straker stared, looked down at the solid, decorative box of lacquered plex, and back at the ion key. ''Yes. Of course.''

Damnation, he thought savagely, recognising what it must be. It's obviously the key to a Chinese safe box. It must be this one. How could I have been so stupid? The box is locked and armed. I never considered the key, or where it was. Yasuko must have sent it to the heir anonymously. A creeping suspicion overcame him. But why didn't she mention it? Certainly there was little time. We met only fleetingly when she gave me the box and implored me to take it to the audience with Sakuma Kiyohide. Even so, could she have forgotten something so important?

"Please, Mister Straker, do me the courtesy of not taking me for a fool in my own house."

"Excellency," Hayden Straker said, meeting the other's eye with difficulty. "The key was missing. I am pleased it has come to you, though by what route it did so I cannot say."

"Why are you doing this? What do you hope to gain from me?"

"I know you will soon rule Yamato unchallenged because your people believe there is a curse on the *menuki*. Even educated people believe the ornament in the hilt of the Sho-gun's sword of office is a test of legitimacy."

"And you?"

"I would prefer your rule on Edo to any pretender's—for my own reasons. My intent in bringing this gift to you will soon be clear enough."

Inside he felt the tension of the moment reach breaking point. Be careful! he thought. This man certainly believes in the Shogun's sword as the symbol of power, but there's more in his mind than that. Look behind his eyes! Look deep, like your father looks deep, right into the soul of a man. Is Sakuma Kiyohide unwilling to test himself against the sword's amyg-dala, like the rest of them? Is his coolness genuine? Or is he really worried? Is he praying to his gods that the new crystal is all I say it is? Or is he trying you? Testing your own belief in its power to disarm the *menuki*?

His eyes give him away! Look at that almost imperceptible tremble in his hand. You must believe, Hayden Straker. Believe in the power of the gift like you've never believed before. Show him you think that crystal's worth half of Known Space.

Sakuma Kiyohide tried to brush the matter off. "The wearing of the sword is no longer important to the Emperor's subjects."

He resisted. "On the contrary. You must have the sword to show them you are great enough to be Shogun, that your name is meant to be added to the history scrolls. No one on Edo, or on all the worlds of Yamato, can understand how the great Sakuma Hidenaga has avoided falling under the power of the *menuki*, despite carrying it with him for years. No one has explained it. Nor can you."

Sakuma Kiyohide's words were razor-edged. "Amerikan, your presumption is dangerous."

"Perhaps so. But it is the hard reality of things that interests me. I am a merchant; what I cannot count I cannot deal in. These specifics are clear enough. And I say that you yourself will not move without knowing precisely how the stars travel in their courses."

"Explain yourself."

He wanted very much to lay it all out before the heir, to tell him, "It's like this, Kiyohide-sama: Either psi-active crystals exist or they do not. If they do, then the sword *menuki* may or may not be one such. So also the item I brought to Osumi may or may not be one such. On the other hand, it may be that the actual power of these crystals is a gigantic fiction, and in that case we are dealing with the morass of human credulity and the desire to believe, and of what constitutes the legitimacy of political power."

He wanted to say that straight, to lay it out like an Amerikan, but he dared not do it. He drew breath, his heart beating like a war drum, and launched into the biggest gamble of his life. "I think you will not move to announce the death of your father, Sakuma Hidenaga, who is most certainly dead and has been these past twenty-four hours—you will not do that until you can be certain Honda Yukio's faction has lost all hope of wresting the shogunate from you." He returned Sakuma Kiyohide's steely gaze steadily. "If only there was a way to squash your father's troublesome grandson, eh, my Lord?"

Not a glimmer of admission crossed Sakuma Kiyohide's immobile face. "And if there was?"

"On behalf of the Amerikan Merchant Traders Corporation, the Controller of the Lease of Osumi, and the President of the United Worlds"—he sat up and took the box in both hands—"I offer this gift to you."

"What for?"

He shrugged very meaningfully.

"We are alone."

"Exclusive trading rights for Straker." He pulled out a sealed sheet of hardcopy. "It's all here."

Sakuma Kiyohide read the conditions and gave the sheet back. He drew himself up, called his retainers and guards and servants back around him. The important among them resumed their places and settled politely to hear Sakuma Kiyohide's words.

"See! The mystery of the key is revealed. The Amerikan trading corporation has a gift for me," he said grandly. "What do you think of that? Should I accept it?"

They looked at the lacquer box, looked at the way it glinted in the gaijin's outstretched hands. Then the chief retainer said "Ah!" and one after another, in a way that laid bare their alliances, they added their own approving noises.

Sakuma Kiyohide hushed them. "And what is the price of this gift?"

"It is freely given, Excellency."

"So." Sakuma Kiyohide took the ion key from around his neck. "This is the key to Yamato." His pun drew no reaction from his retainers. "I have lived long enough," he said with an ironic smile, "to know that nothing is ever freely given to a lord."

He received the box and put the ion key to the lock-plate.

Suddenly Hayden Straker's stomach heaved with a gripping fear. What if this was a setup? What if the Chinese box was like his father's safe aboard the *Chance*—primed to blow on tampering?

Surely the heir's security people would have probed the box properly for explosive mechanisms, he reasoned. Surely the sensor checks they had run on it before Sakuma Kiyohide came within half a *ri* of it would have revealed any danger.

Silently, the ion key operated.

The lid cracked open.

Then Sakuma Kiyohide made a sudden movement and dropped it, his eyes stark with shock. Something long and black fell, then retainers were on their feet, their swords drawn instantly.

By God, what is it? What have I done? he asked himself, his guts turning to water. Sweat began to dew him. For God's sake, what's happened? What's terrified him?

Then the truth crashed in on him as the box was kicked out of Sakuma Kiyohide's vicinity across the tatami. There, weaving menacingly, was the living contents for all to see.

A shocked cry went up. "Hebi! Hebi! Hebi! Get back!"

There was a scramble. Everyone recoiled instantly as the banded krait slithered forward, everyone except Sakuma Kiyohide who was staring, rock-still as if at an assassin.

Sweet Jeezus, how did that happen? he thought frantically, staring at the krait as it came towards him. He knew the bite of the krait was lethal. It was by far the most dangerously

venomous snake known—so venomous that Yamakawa Do-
boku, one of the big terraforming agencies, had proposed
drawing up an unwanted species list and heading it with the
banded krait. Despite that attempt, Earth Central had ruled
that deliberate extinction of a species was a greater evil, since
it crossed the Hamiltonian attractor and therefore warped psi,
distorting unacceptably the lives of people whose rare fate it
would be to die from krait bites.

Momentarily paralysed by childhood terror, he watched as
the krait slid from view. Then one of Sakuma Kiyohide's
generals stroked his sword up, lifting the heir's bolster cush-
ion on its tip. The silk tore and cascaded white feathers and
the snake struck at them, until the second stroke of the sword
cut it neatly in two and its halves twisted in death, leaving
drops of dark blood on the tatami.

Hayden Straker tried to recover himself, but guards rushed
forward and seized him, and despite his protests he was over-
powered and marched struggling from the audience hall.

20

It was the fifth of the month, and her robe was a mass of
violet irises, made to ward off the evil spirits of Shiki who
came to make liars of men.

In the hot darkness the palace drowsed peacefully. No
evening breeze blew in from the east tonight, and the timber
decking surrounding the Tower of Jade was warm. This had

once been a proud place, the private domain of a great lord, high above the sleeping world, amid the shadows of night and the very stars themselves. Tonight they would eat a meal of celebration, and then they would make love, also in celebration. For tonight, the plans of the Amerikan and the faithless wife were in ruin and the victory over them was assured.

Myobu, in her most arousing attire, knelt in the sultry night. She massaged Hideki Shingo's temples and listened as Matsujiro the musician tuned the long-handled *samisen*. It was three-stringed, with a gourdlike body. Behind the windbreak, Matsujiro's attendants would be kneeling beside him with hands folded in their laps, as the cascading music began. Like icy streams at the headwaters of a great river, the notes thrilling and bending, carried high into the air, an ancient composition telling of the days before the universe began when the gods loved one another in cosmic splendor.

With a snap of her fingers Myobu summoned her bodyservant. The windbreak was parted instantly.

"Bring tea." The curl of her lip was commanding.

The servant was young, in his mid-teens, unhappy, scared of her now. He had thought himself better than others, better than her. So he had been brought from Osumi at her special suggestion to learn humility and here he was easy to handle.

She listened to the flat notes of the song for a while, her thoughts coiling and uncoiling, like the lobes of a nexus, like the bodies of serpents. How right I was to side with Isakosan in this dispute, she thought. What a remarkable politician she is! And how clever of her to think of the krait. Shingosama will wake up soon, and then I will find out what happened. That wife of his has played into Isako's hands all along, and now she has ensured her own death, leaving me to control the man who will be the next Prefect of Kyushu Quadrant.

The windbreak parted again, and the young servant put down a tray with tea bowls in black and silver patterns, sparkling like stars, and an elegant pot of jasmine tea.

She watched the young man pour, dismissing him sharply to his station beside the musicians behind the curtain. Then she slid away from Shingo, and offered him a candied cube of melon. Then she began to sing. Her high voice chased the notes of the *samisen* into the air, soaring artfully. She sang to Hideki Shingo a song of the Iris Festival, a song to make him glad, a song to make him pliable. As all men were after food and drink and when feeling the heat of a woman's body.

> *"Oshi takabe*
> *Kamo sae kiiru*
> *Hara no Ike no ya*
> *Tamamo wa*
> *Mane na kiri so ya*
> *Oi mo tsugu ga ni ya*
> *Oi mo tsugu ga ni."*

> *"The mandarin,*
> *The teal,*
> *Even the wild duck*
> *All come to the Pool of Hara.*
> *Do not cut the weed by the roots!*
> *Oh, let it go on growing!*
> *Let it go on growing!"*

She sang, and as she sang she was thinking. Words two thousand years old, and still they have the power to move us. How Shingo-san would scorn them if he realised they were the words of a Kozuke folk song, an invocation against bad psi. But what does it matter where it comes from?—it suits my purpose, the purpose I was trained for.

She massaged the line of his jaw, her long black fingernails crackling over his stubble. The great emerald on her finger glinting poisonously, a secret locket of narcotics, milked from the fangs of highland snakes, dried and crushed to powder with the seeds of the jujube plant. Only the courtesan can truly know the one great truth of the world, which is that while women long for the love of one man, men love to have many women. Who is there better than I to know that? And those who do not perceive that the souls of men and women are truly different cannot understand anything of this existence, so I am wise. How clever of me to have listened to Isako-san. What a marvelous practitioner of politics she is. How she wields her son like a knife.

Myobu pursed her lips, refusing the proffered cube of *midori*. The platinum brooch on her lapel glinted, its weight pulling down the fabric sensually. "No, Lord, I cannot eat. My voice, you see."

"Tonight you shall sing of love," Hideki Shingo said drowsily; his hand began stroking her thigh through the diaphanous material of her robe. His eyes dwelt on the strand of tiny pearls that were stitched into the iris patterns that barely covered her breasts.

"Drink. This is to be your night of pleasure, my Lord. A night when all dreams shall be fulfilled. Now you are to be confirmed Daimyo, anything you desire shall be yours." She poured more tea into a bowl of rare beauty and offered it coyly across the line that connected their eyes. "I live only to serve you."

He took the tea and savored it, enjoying the astringent thrill of its bouquet. "After the victories of today I have now time to appreciate your beauty properly, Myobu-san."

"Thank you, Lord. You do me a great honor, and in return I shall give you pleasure like the geisha of Paradise." Myobu felt suddenly light-headed. The huge paper fretwork lamp that hung overhead cast flickering shadows across the decking in bewildering patterns. All around, the space, surrounded by its rippling multicolored awnings and windbreaks, basked in the light of a thousand stars, and beyond, in the void, the windless sky shimmered. She thought she saw a brief streak of light flare in the darkness—a falling star, a spirit that had become detached from the firmament, one that only she had seen fall—that or, more prosaically, a fragment broken from a lander, reentering. She gathered between her fingertips a morsel of marinaded squid from the tray that was laid out before them, and he opened his mouth.

"The most delicious food is that taken from the hand of a beautiful woman."

"My Lord, it is a poor offering for so great a man as you."

She laid out a delicate repast for him on a jade platter: thin slices of fresh mango and papaya. She took them, hungry herself now, and fed them to him. There were prawns in a salty sauce; cucumber roll; *tai*, or thin slices of red snapper; *akagai*, ark shell; and *awabi*, abalone. There were oiled leaves containing tiny sea slugs, and plum and coconut delicacies, seawater eel and belly of tuna.

And she fed him until he wanted no more, until his eyes wandered in dreamy forgetfulness along the pale path of the sky, absorbing the mystical glow of the galaxy and the light of Edo's wonderful little moons.

"Tell me," she said. "What are you thinking?"

"I am thinking that this is a perfect night."

There were nightingales in the trees, trilling. The Tower of Jade cut a pattern of serrated black out of the Milky Way, across the constellations the Amerikans called Hercules and Eagle.

"Yes. So perfect."

"Now the Amerikan is imprisoned. His amygdala is with Honda Yukio-sama. Tonight his men will break into Sakuma Hidenaga's apartments. They will slay the Shogun, or if he is already dead they will stamp out his memory, and after that, Sakuma Kiyohide will die also."

"And Yasuko-san?" she whispered, hardly wanting to mention her, but desiring to know Shingo's mind.

He gazed straight upwards towards the zenith. "Yasuko-san is a thief and an adulterer. She will return with me to Miyakonojo. Then, when Osumi is ruled by me, she will atone for her crimes as the Imperial law decrees."

"As the law decrees."

Sukeko woke her at a godless hour.

The night seemed almost over. Perhaps dawn was about to break. The little orange moon was sinking into the west like a great bloodied ruby. The flames of the lamps had become so emaciated that they could no longer bear the weight of the night. On the window ledges flowers had withered in their jars. The pollen of the lotuses had been turned to cold paste by the dew.

Sakuma Hidenaga was dead. Hayden Straker was imprisoned by Sakuma Kiyohide. They had been tricked by Isako and Shingo-san. It was very bad, and difficult to see how things could get much worse.

Sukeko shook her again, wordlessly. Since the death of Niso two days ago she had not spoken a single word.

There were footsteps running through the courts and gardens. Shouts and the screams of women. Then arcs. The bright flare of firing casting stark shadows on the ceiling.

She ran to the window.

"No!"

There were mounted soldiers in the square below, their lobster-tail helmets and corded armor reminding her of Haigo Gozaemon. At the ramp a dozen men struggled to manually wind open the doors to the underground bunkers, but horsemen were already spurring towards them. Suddenly a rash of firing began in the outer courtyard; the sounds were magnified inside the echoing halls from which the flashes emanated. Men were running. More were trying to burn the men guarding the gate. Someone fell from the walls, impacting with a sickening thump. Then fire-devils were raining onto the ceremonial gate, flames sticking there and dripping bright fire down the old dry wood.

Sukeko seized her hand, her eyes imploring.

"No! We shall stay here. This is the safest place. They will not harm us here."

Privately, her reason said otherwise. Her greatest fear was being acted out. Shingo-san and his power-thirsty mother had taken the crystal to Honda Yukio, prompting him into a bloody and unnecessary rebellion.

"The fools!" she shouted. "The blind fools!"

Then there was the noise of men on the roof above, the sight of ropes being thrown down from the eaves, and the black-swathed bodies of special troops, fighting men recruited from the famous Kusunoki martial arts school, sliding down the ropes, short, straight swords slung over their muscular backs, steel tiger's claws looped from thumb to little finger of the left hand, their heads bound tightly into strange grilled hoods. Some of them wielded short swords, others flung *shuriken*—razor-sharp throwing stars—silently cutting down the men of the guard.

A rope snaked down just outside the wood-latticed window. The assassin slithered down, agile as a spider. He stopped as he came level with them, the whites of his eyes reddened, his face that of a killer. Sukeko broke away and ran, panic sending her out across the corridor and out to the entranceway. She weaved as she fled. Yasuko tried to follow her, past knots of frightened women and towards the place of escape.

"Sukeko-san! Stop! Come back."

She turned a corner and halted, lost, turning to see which direction Sukeko had gone. There on the raised wooden floor was Uchimaro the steward, his rib cage laid open by a sword slash. Blood lay pooled all around him.

"Sukeko!"

An open door signaled to her. She flung it open to see the girl standing in the threshold, transfixed by fear. No more than twenty yards away, a dozen horsemen were kicking their mounts across the manicured garden outside, swinging swords that were dull with blood. They were chasing the men of the palace guard, men who were being hacked to pieces as they ran screaming for any cover they could find.

She dragged Sukeko back, and slammed the heavy wooden shutters just before the body of a man crashed into it. She heard his terrified screams as he was impaled on a *naginata* lance.

Sukeko, too, was screaming, paralysed by terror. Her strength was great, her limbs stiff as a corpse's. Yasuko pulled her into a dark room where a well head gaped down into the bedrock of the palace, a circular hole full of black echoes, lipped in stone and surrounded by a hundred huge water jars, standing ready to store water for a siege. And there they hid, Yasuko cradling her maid, down on the floor, in the dusty space between the stoneware jars.

"What if they come? What if they find us?"

"No man can lift these jars when they are full of water, Little Squirrel. Look how they have fat bellies and narrow feet. We could crawl into the gaps and hide and no soldier could follow in such a maze."

When the firing stopped and the shouting stopped Sukeko asked her shakily, "Who are those men?"

"Assassins. Supporters of the pretender, men of the clan Honda."

"The great Shogun's grandson?"

"Yes."

"What if he wins, Yasuko-san? What if he kills the Shogun and his true heir, and takes control of the palace? What will happen to us then?"

"Hush, now, Little Squirrel. Try to sleep. I will wake you when the battle is over. When safety has returned. Then we shall go back to the others. Everything is well."

But she knew that everything was not well. That whatever happened now there could be no escape. If that treacherous hyena, Honda Yukio-san, prevails, she thought, we shall remain at Edo—as captives, awaiting death. And equally, if Sakuma Kiyohide-sama has escaped the attempt on his life, then he will cherish no love for those who had made the revolt possible.

I hope you are not dead, Hayden Straker. I hope that with all my heart.

22

The blood had been washed away, the corpses burned, and the fires doused.

Hayden Straker stumbled on the steps; the punishment wheel loading him weighed heavily on his wrists and neck. Last night he had listened to the violence of the coup through the bars of a dark and airless dungeon, trying desperately to fathom which way the fighting was turning. It was the night for which all the forces that would shape the future of Yamato had waited during these last failing years of Sakuma Hidenaga's glorious reign.

He had spent the night in the cell, cursing his luck, damning his stupidity, running through in his mind the possible ways the snake could have got into the box that Yasuko had sworn contained the amygdala.

I pray that she hasn't deserted me, he thought, as he was led solemnly into the shade of the Hall of Audiences. I pray that Sakuma Kiyohide has triumphed, or all hope is gone, we are all dead, and Amerikan interests thrown out of one quarter of human space for at least a generation—maybe forever.

My father was right. Humankind is growing apart. Known Space is a human sphere, mostly civilised after some fashion, but they are inculcated into different ways of thinking. It's not like it was on Old Earth, where as time passed the universe grew smaller. We are no longer integrating, we're differentiating. And only trade can tie us together again. Amerika must not be excluded from Yamato. Nor must the Kan be allowed to take it for their own.

The spacious hall of the Shogun's palace was clean and cool in the morning light, the air perfumed once more as he was propelled through it in shackles, his cap clapped on his head awry. He bore the heavy wheel stoically. Hundreds of armed guards stood motionless in serried ranks along the entire length of the audience room. Everyone was in battle attire. A breeze blew in through open windows, carrying the harsh light of another blistering noonday within. When they reached the Shogun's rostrum, Hayden Straker counted seven noblemen. Two were important enough to warrant their own pages kneeling inconspicuously behind. But it was the eighth man, a bulky man in a brocade robe, who made him exclaim in despair.

"By God! I should have guessed!"

As he approached, Sakuma Kiyohide shifted on his haunches. His calculating eyes watched everything. He was swathed in a gold-threaded *jinbaori* now, a general's jacket for wearing over armor, wide wing shoulders coming up from a corded waist, almost hiding his breastplate.

Then he saw it. It was a sight he knew he would never be able to forget. The hilt of Sakuma Kiyohide's incredibly ornate sword was set with a glowing *menuki*, a glassy object that sparkled with what seemed like the white fire of hell. It was like a diamond, almond-shaped, sparkling against the ray-skin of the handguard. A jewel of power. It made him stop and stand still.

To Sakuma Kiyohide's left on the rostrum, similarly robed and armored, sat his chief retainer and five of his gray-clad generals. All were similarly armed with ornate swords, all wore fearsome masks corded down on their chests. They looked to one another, unsurprised by the Amerikan's astonishment. Then the spell was broken as the Kan general also smiled.

He was wisp-bearded and patrician, he sported three long silver finger cones on each hand, his dress crisp and well cut. He seemed at ease with those at his elbows, in control of the situation.

A secretary/translator introduced him. "Celestial Marshal Chin, of China Products, Secretary of the Assembly of Satsuma and ambassadorial representative of the Dowager Empress of the Central Realm to the Court of His Imperial Highness's Most Exalted Generalissimo."

He put his hands flat above his knees and bowed ironically.

Sakuma Kiyohide's searching gaze broke away from the Kan. He whispered something indistinct to Hayden Straker who deliberately stared past Marshal Chin to where the sentient crystal glittered in the sword hilt. Beyond, a gush of water played from an exquisitely carved dragon fountain; its sound filled his mind with haunting music.

"Well?"

His collar was heavy. The chains clanked as he moved. Insect bites covered the tender parts of his body, itching madly. The filth of the cell stained his sweat-foul clothes. He fought to master himself. The Shogun wants me to bow to Marshal Chin, he thought. Bow to the Kan. I will not do it!

His parched throat was dust-dry from his confinement, and fear tautened his belly, but his voice came strong as he whispered, "This floor sweeper's not fit to sit beside you, Excellency. I refuse to acknowledge him."

Then Sakuma Kiyohide's voice was suddenly raised angrily. "Do as you are told!"

The new Shogun nodded sharply towards the guards who ringed the prisoner. One threw off his cap. Another stepped forward, and he felt a sharp blow crash into the pit of his stomach. He went down on one knee and was held there. A drawn sword was put at his throat, and he began to tremble as a nick at his Adam's apple started to bleed a small red trickle across the upper surface of the wheel.

Fear mingled with guilt in his belly. Terrible regret that he had failed in his mission, failed in his promises, failed as his father's son. His head came up angrily, and his eyes went to the Kan who he knew had him precisely where he wanted him.

"Have you told him the true reason you're here, Marshal?" he asked savagely. "Have you told him about your dealings with Honda Yukio? That together you planned to install him as Shogun? And then to put Shibata Junkei in charge of the Kyushu Quadrant?"

The Marshal thrust out his lips thoughtfully, unruffled by the Amerikan's words and prepared to give him nothing, except perhaps sufficient rope with which to hang himself. "The Shogun doubtless has his own good reasons for tolerating a Chinese embassy," he said toyingly. "For our part, Lord Yu wants merely to see the Kyushu Quadrant ruled by the rightful heir. Only then might we expect to see a proper normalization of trade."

"Kan trade! Kan trade because there'll be no one else here to compete with you. Isn't that right? Get rid of the Amerikans and you'll have got the whole of Yamato under your heel. Have you told the Shogun what Yu Hsien will do with him and his kind when you've succeeded in kicking every last Amerikan back over the Boundary?"

His eyes went to Sakuma Kiyohide's. He was wondering how much the new Shogun knew about Chinese intentions, and the man whom they sought to install at Miyakonojo. Shibata Junkei had lusted for possession of the Kyushu Quadrant since the chaos of the Korean freebooter invasion eight years ago. Though not born a samurai, Shibata had been sold into a Fifth Grade family as a boy. He had married a lesser daughter of Choso Yoshinobu, the then Prefect of Kyushu Quadrant. He had worked himself up the ladder of promotion in Yoshinobu's army. But then the Koreans had come into the system and changed everything. At the battle of Kokubu the plunderers had slain Yoshinobu. As a result the old man's only son, Choso Yoshisaburo, had been forced to contest the succession with his brother-in-law, and first cousin.

Shibata had sided with the Choso and had been rewarded for his support by the daimyoship of Kirishima, but the Koreans had besieged that planet's strongest fortress and taken him alive. They had removed him to their own stronghold on Ulsan, hoping to ransom him. There he had languished in a cell, impotent to prevent his dream from fading.

Yes, he recalled, watching his captor, while Shibata Junkei was locked away on Ulsan, the Kyushu Quadrant passed to Hideki Ryuji on the orders of Sakuma Hidenaga. As Shogun, he asserted his absolute right to choose which of his vassals would rule the Kyushu Quadrant, and Sakuma Hidenaga had no love for the independent-minded Choso clan. *It doesn't surprise me that Hideki Ryuji showed no inclination to ransom him. So he stayed in his freezee for seven years, until someone paid the freebooters what they wanted. Who was it? Who got you out? Who else, but Yu Hsien?*

"How sweet it would have been for you and Honda Yukio-san to plan to sweep Sakuma Kiyohide-sama into oblivion," he said to Marshal Chin. "But your coup failed. You miscalculated. You lost, and now you're trying to repair your position with the new Shogun!"

He faced Sakuma Kiyohide defiantly. "Excellency, I've always maintained that you've every right to rule on Edo. The Kyushu Quadrant is yours, if you have the power to seize it. But by embracing Yu Hsien you'd throw the will of Amerika against you. And that would be very stupid."

Sakuma Kiyohide's eyes half lidded momentarily, then he

answered, "This is my Sector, Amerikan. Not yours. Nor the Kan's. It is the Amerikans who have made a mistake, for they have chosen to make Hideki Ryuji-san their vassal, and to turn him against his rightful lord."

"We have no vassals. And we seek none. Hideki Ryuji-san was the choice of your honorable father. We recognise that the Kyushu Quadrant is just that: a Quadrant of Yamato and not an independent realm. Amerika has no ambitions there. We desire only to survive, and to trade peaceably as we have done since MeTraCor first came to the Osumi Lease more than a decade ago."

He saw Sakuma Kiyohide's languidity leave him. "Hidenaga-sama is dead. Who now shall say Shibata Junkei-san may not rule in the Kyushu Quadrant?"

"I do not say that," he said carefully. "If it is your choice. I only warn that it must never be a Kan choice who rules the Quadrant of Kyushu—Osumi, Satsuma, or any of its provincial worlds."

Suddenly Sakuma Kiyohide sat up, his face thunderous. "My father willed the shogunate to me. Therefore I decide everything. No Kan shall choose! Nor shall any Amerikan!"

Hell of hells, he told himself. One false step and they'll cut out your heart. He hesitated as Sakuma Kiyohide's anger echoed away, but the raw nerve he had exposed astonished him and he knew he must stake his life on it. Clearly, in his most carefully pronounced Japanese, he said, "Sakuma Hidenaga had no right to will the shogunate to anyone. Only the Emperor on Kyoto may—"

Instantly, Sakuma Kiyohide's chief retainer was on his feet. "Hold your mouth, dirty *gaijin*! I say you are an assassin. You tried to murder our Lord. It was you who wanted the despicable Honda clan to rule here. But soon we shall find Honda Yukio, and his head shall be trampled in the dust! That is the reward of usurpers and assassins!"

For Hayden Straker it was like the clearing fogs of early morning seen from a pinnacle above a valley, the lifting of an obscuring cloud. He felt no fear as a great precipice was revealed before him. He felt only sobered as the sweat on his back turned to ice.

He willed himself not to look at Marshal Chin. The Kan's grand strategy had suddenly become terrifyingly clear. Yu Hsien's ambition was not only to seize control of the Kyushu Quadrant, but of all the Shogun's realm. By God! Yu Hsien wants the whole of Yamato. Xanadu domains already stretch clear from the Three Thirty Degree Boundary to something like the Two Eighty-Five Degree beacons. To the west, Xanadu has de facto control far beyond the official beacon of Acrux. Already, the Dowager's functionaries are suggesting how things should be run in the Malay Federation, in Upper and Lower Burma, and in the Khmer-Shan Protectorate. With her nominee in Edo the Dowager would be able to control damned near a quarter of Known Space, and threaten Amerika. If Marshal Chin succeeds in winning the Shogun to him, all Amerikan presence in Yamato must eventually withdraw. The Kan already have the singularity gun. Soon they will have massive access to the Zone. And there'll be nothing we can do to stop them.

He tried to keep his face blank. He realised with relief that the razor-sharp *katana* held against his throat had prevented him from showing any greater fearful reaction.

He looked Sakuma Kiyohide in the eye, the flashing of that astonishing jewel hidden in his blind spot as if under radio black. "Highness, we Amerikans are merchants. We have no interest in your dynastic disputes. We want only to trade peaceably, to pay our due taxes to the legitimate ruler, and in return to enjoy the protection of Yamato law. Remember, it was the Kan who cravenly attacked our Lease on Osumi. They are the aggressors. We asked Hideki Ryuji-sama to help us, not because we had any preference for him, but because he was appointed at the Shogun's order to be Prefect of Kyushu Quadrant—appointed ultimately by the same Imperial authority by which you now sit as master of Edo. To us, the rule of law is paramount. We have done nothing to contradict that.''

"You tried to kill me."

"Excellency, as I have repeated many times from my cell, that was a Kan trick. The box was locked. I did not know what was inside. If I had truly wanted to kill you, would I have chosen to use a snake?''

"The self-consuming serpent is the *mon* of the Sakuma. You knew the significance.''

"You have already said we Amerikans are a direct and practical people. Few of us would have stopped to consider the symbolism of it, much less compromise the chances of a successful outcome by making some kind of ironic joke. That sounds to me like Kan thinking.''

"He's lying to save his own skin!'' Marshal Chin said. "But his absurd lies are transparent. If it was unlikely he sent the snake, how much more unlikely is it that we did so?''

Sakuma Kiyohide considered that, then turned back to his prisoner and asked, "So, you say the Amerikans in the Osumi system recognise my authority?''

"That is beyond dispute. As for myself, I want only to open your eyes to the ambitions of the Kan who surely seek to dominate Yamato, and eject us.''

Sakuma Kiyohide relaxed visibly. "Is that why you came to Edo? To warn me?''

"Yes. And to aid you. And—''

"He's a spy,'' Marshal Chin interrupted scornfully. "He's nothing but an intelligence gatherer sent here to discover the secret of the Nagoya event—and to decide how best to destroy you.''

"I came here to ask a favor of the Shogun."

Sakuma Kiyohide inclined his head questioningly. "What favor?"

"I came here to ask him to send his forces into the Kyushu Quadrant. To oblige the Kan to vacate Osumi. By force. To restore our Lease to us. By force if necessary. As it was before the Xanadu-Amerika war spilled into your systems. By force, Excellency—because that is the only thing that will uncoil this serpent from his stranglehold on your most strategic Quadrant."

Marshal Chin watched the Amerikan with growing insecurity. An hour ago, when Sakuma Kiyohide had ordered him brought before him, he had thought there would be a swift and final end to it. He had accused Hayden Straker of spying, believing he could persuade the Shogun to execute him, but so far he had played his hand with great skill. Also, Sakuma Kiyohide was a notoriously honorable and chivalrous man— for a samurai—and that was dangerous because it made him less pliable. He was the thread from which the entire future hung.

By all the judges of hell, Marshal Chin thought. The Amerikan is too well aware of what we have been doing. Of course. I should have realised earlier that my grip on Sakuma Kiyohide is now at its weakest. Now he is installed on Edo his own ambition is secured. From now on he is less likely to take suggestions from me, and until we can make Honda Yukio Shogun, which we cannot easily do for the moment, we are dependent on Sakuma Kiyohide. This is a most critical time, because once Honda Yukio becomes Shogun, we will have won. It is vital I hold the line now and induce this running dog to dispose of a most troublesome Amerikan.

He thought again about Shibata Junkei. He is already in debt to Honda Yukio for bailing him out of Korean hands. And Honda Yukio only outbid the sum Hideki Ryuji was prepared to pay the Ulsan Koreans to keep Shibata prisoner by borrowing seven aurium tranches from us. If Shibata's sense of honor makes him stick by the original bargain we will have won. I pray the Judges that the alliance does not fall apart.

What did the gods intend by allowing Sakuma Kiyohide to win the contest here? And now this Amerikan government agent is trying to upset everything with his spiteful accusations. Surely they are mere stabs in the darkness. Or does he know how correct he is? How I despise these gross-featured people, and their continued interference in matters that come under the Mandate of Heaven. Of course he's a government man. That must be why he's really here—to prise Sakuma Kiyohide away from us before it's too late.

"You came here to ask for force of arms?" Sakuma Kiyohide asked the prisoner, intrigued by the answer.

"That is so. To restore Osumi, a world that was so treacherously taken by the Kan without any cause, to your own appointee."

Marshal Chin tutted. "Amerikan ships provoked the attack. Amerikan pirates preyed on Kan trade. You had turned Osumi into a veritable pirate base! You had to be chastised vigorously!"

Sakuma Kiyohide raised a hand for silence, and Hayden Straker was invited to continue.

He decided to play his strongest suit. "After crashing in a remote region of the planet, I made Miyakonojo the object of my quest. I promised Hideki Ryuji-sama I would give him an amygdala if he would attempt to relieve Kanoya City. He promised me he would try."

"You went with his army?" Sakuma Kiyohide asked quickly, his eyes sparkling with the reflections of the psi-active crystal at his waist.

"I did. With his son. Aboard his *sora-sensha.*"

"You say you were at the battle where Hideki Shingo-san was wounded? Riding with him in the attack vehicle? Like a warrior? You actually witnessed the destruction of his father's forces?"

"Yes." Straker's head bowed slightly. "I witnessed that. I saw how it was that the Kan won their victory. And I understood the secret of it. They used a singularity gun. A banned weapon! A weapon outlawed under Clause 259 of the Convention of the Central Authority of Old Earth!"

"Look at him!" Marshal Chin said. "He's plainly lying! We have no such weapon. He's just a spy, sent by the Amerikan guerrilla, Colonel Lawton."

"Enough!" Sakuma Kiyohide looked at his captive for a long moment, then he said, "Tell me why I should listen to you now. Tell me why I should prefer the Amerikan view over the Kan view. Tell me why I should not simply execute you as the Celestial Marshal wants."

Ice water trickled down his spine, but he balled his fist and urged Sakuma Kiyohide with all the feeling he could muster. "Because, Excellency, Amerika's war fleet is formidable. Soon, an Amerikan squadron under Admiral Eddison Maskull will appear in Kyushu. I don't know when it will arrive, but it has certainly been called there. And when it does, a powerful army will land. A force that will destroy the Kan. And"— he looked regretfully at Sakuma Kiyohide, inwardly terrified at what he was about to say—"and if you have lent your support to them it will be the worse for you."

Sakuma Kiyohide remained silent. Then he put his hands together, a half smile illuminating his face as Marshal Chin leaned forward and crisply delivered the crushing blow.

"As I have already informed the Shogun, some time ago forty thousand Amerikan troops were landed on Satsuma. Since then, those forty thousand troops have failed to capture eighteen thousand defenders. They have failed to retake

Osumi. They have failed to conquer Satsuma as was their aim. The MeTraCor commander of Amerikan forces on Osumi, Colonel Lawton, has been captured and the only other senior Amerikan officer is dead.''

Hayden Straker felt the blood drain from him, he began to speak, but this time Sakuma Kiyohide motioned him to silence as Marshal Chin went on. ''If you will permit me, Excellency, there is more. Some sixty days ago there was quadrature in the Osumi system. A great psi-storm roared forth from the nexus that the Amerikans designate Teth-Two-Nine. It destroyed the greater part of the Amerikan fleet, including Admiral Maskull's flagship—the *Edward Preble* I believe it was called—as it sought to flee from the system. Since the remains of this squadron have now transited back to the Neutral Zone, it is clear that the salvation which the Kyushu Quadrant Amerikans have looked to their Navy to provide has, for the foreseeable future, evaporated. Their position is now far worse than it was before the great Admiral Maskull arrived. My superior, Celestial Functionary Yu, has ordered more troops to the system of Osumi, to crush the stubborn diehards of Fort Baker with all speed. In view of these facts, let me ask you this question, Mister Straker: Why should the Shogun move himself to aid your—powerful—compatriots now?''

Hayden Straker opened his eyes. What Marshal Chin had said had shut them like blinding light. The news had crushed all his hopes, undermined whatever slim position he had thought was his. How hollow his recent bravado sounded now. He knew the great significance of what Yasuko had told him and he knew also that he must carry it to Fort Baker as quickly as he could.

''I beg leave to go to Osumi,'' he said steadily.

Sakuma Kiyohide inclined his head and looked sidelong at Marshal Chin before answering.

"Strike off the wheel," he said simply.

"But, Excellency—!"

"Marshal Chin, I have made a decision. The embassy of Hideki Ryuji-sama is at an end. Hideki Shingo-san will leave today for Miyakonojo with my blessing: his father will, for the moment, retain the Kyushu Quadrant, but my Court shall deliberate further on the request of the claimant, Shibata Junkei-san."

The Marshal balked at the delay. "You are granting freedom for a man who tried to kill you, Excellency?"

"I find that the matter is not proven. Tomorrow he will have permission to leave Edo. He will carry a card of safe passage, so he may return to Fort Baker as he requests. Perhaps, by that time, your valiant Kan troops might have stormed and taken it. Perhaps another great Amerikan fleet might have arrived to save it. Who but the gods know that? I am therefore placing his life in the hands of those same gods. Permission will be granted tomorrow."

They released him from his chains and he walked from the audience hall unchallenged by the guards. They watched him: Sakuma Kiyohide, all his lords, the retainers of the clan Sakuma, the damnable Kan, and the evil eye of the insane crystal.

He steadied his step as he left, knowing that he must leave the hall with dignity, praying that he still had time to reach the apron to catch Yasuko.

He knew that if she had already lit out he would never see her again. Never, this side of paradise. Do the dead of Yamato sometimes go to our heaven or we to theirs? he wondered absurdly. Do we come back? And will there be a chance to meet in the life that follows? If not, I would rather be reincarnated a dung fly . . .

As he descended the steps, and pulled on his boots, it took

all his composure to suppress the panic inside him. Then he reached the parapet and saw it.

There, moving down the road to the apron, was a procession of tiny figures. They were leaving the citadel and moving towards the gleaming darts of the landers: five, six white craft, and a ceremonial departure. Leaving were two hundred people, bodyguards with swirling Hideki *mon* on their *jin-baori*, and servants in yellow and white robes. At the head, wearing his distinctive crested helmet, strode Hideki Shingo himself, staring unseeingly ahead. Behind, attended by shuffling women who walked alongside, were a half-dozen closed palanquins.

He gasped involuntarily as he looked at the swinging tassels of the suspended box that came second to last in the procession, the opaque paper-white windows of Yasuko's *kago*.

The certainty blew up like storm thunderheads, scattering his hopes and contingencies, all his ifs and buts, like straws in a gale.

Then that was it. That was the truth of it: He had missed her. She had gone, she would be gone forever. Forever.

He burst into a run, alerting the guards at the gate who clashed *naginata* across his path as he tried to pass. His fingers clawed at them, but they held him, and more came from the guardhouse to hold him in their special wrestlers' grip.

The apron was outside the Shogun's citadel. Nobody left without the Shogun's personal authorization. There was no way to get out. No way to get to her. No way to stop her leaving. He shouted out as the horrible thought slitted his guts.

Hideki Shingo craved revenge on his wife. Once out of Edo and into the domain of the Kyushu Quadrant he would have her at his mercy. She had been accused of betraying her

husband. She was going to her destruction. They would offer
her death just as surely as they had executed that poor young
woman who they had watched broken in agony. And there
was nothing he could do.

He broke away, ran back to the wall, gazed helplessly at
the palanquin reaching the first of the landers. He shouted,
and his shout echoed round the canyon walls of the entrance
ramp. Then he saw the side of the palanquin open, and a
delicate figure in an ice-blue kimono turn and touch her fingertips to her lips before the maids walking beside closed her
from view.

23

The deadly barrel of a Molberg Snipe-o-mat jutted out from
behind a rocky outcrop, wavering as it followed its target.
The weapon was aimed at a figure emerging from an un-
marked lander that sat half-hidden in the jungle gully below.
The figure stood still, hands on hips, visor scanning the top
of the gully. It moved like a man, but you never could tell
with the Navy.

The figure wore a plain gray one-piece pilot suit and a big
silvered dragonfly helmet with faceplate down. This was a
good hiding place, Barb Eastman knew, which was why the
lander had dropped his machine in here, and why Eastman
had had to track it so carefully. Stood to reason: eventually
some Kan lander pilot had to get into trouble, and when he

did he would die, and the fifth mission kill could be chalked on the bulkhead.

So far the chop squad had not seen a victim such as this. Eastman's half-dozen volunteers crouched low, watching, their chameleon suits blending with the outcrop. None of them talked now; they had put their slim tobako sticks out, and the waiting had stopped. All eyes were on the leafy gut of the gully. Their own lander had left the Amerikan fort hidden by a new and powerful radio-black generator that Ellis Straker had sold them against MeTraCor credit and Commander Rohan's indebtedness to the trader. But it had been Eastman's own idea to form the guerrilla force and to glide down out of Baker to harry the Kan planetside.

Better than waiting, he thought. Could never stand waiting. Too many secrets bubble out of a man's mind and haunt him . . .

On random days scattered over the past three months, the chop squad had caused the Kan to worry what was wrong with their sensors. They had scored on each mission—nasty accidents started to befall the Kan: two landers destroyed, and another two captured, but this latest patrol had yielded nothing. Until the day before yesterday.

There had been an unusual amount of traffic via Two-Eight. A big ship had transited and made planetfall directly on one of the southern cities, and a day later a smaller vessel had come through, disgorged a lander, then vanished again. It had been nothing the interrogators recognised, so definitely either Yamato or Kan. They had tracked the lander, suspecting a secret mission of diplomacy they might just be able to bust up. But instead of the lander making for Kanoya or Miyakonojo, it had lain hidden in a crack in the southern jungles—as if waiting for some kind of window.

The chirring of insects tore the air softly.

Eastman's hunting Molberg continued to follow the lone

man as he walked round the wing stub and began to tear open
his fly patch. He was now no more than sixty yards away.
The power of the Molberg was sufficient to burn the heart out
of a man at that distance—but its accuracy was questionable
close to the kind of fields that webbed a lander, which was
why he had not yet fired.

C'mon, he thought tensely. Take a leak against that big
old tree right there.

Another ten yards and he could be certain. Already his
finger was tightening on the release.

Just like the first time I killed, he thought. The first time
and the best.

The handling of the attack on Baker had been magnificent.
The Kan had been seen off by a combination of Colonel
Lawton's brilliant tactics and the insane bravery of Eastman
as his squad had flushed the fleeing Kan out of the black, icy
corridors of the fort. He had led the operations of his team in
the deadly closed-down honeycomb of Baker's upper quarters
where at least a third of the men who had cut their way in
had been trapped. His own teams had covered the approaches
just inside the ingress holes, and they had poured arcs and
beams into the tightly packed mass of assault troops struggling
to escape back to the outside.

It was good to send the Kan away hurting, Eastman
thought. The importance of that firefight was immense. The
Kan beat a samurai army, but we kept them out of Baker.
That's something the samurai powers must have noted.

The tall pilot was hung with strange tackle, and he was
dressed kind of odd too, making Eastman ease his finger off
the trigger.

Got to make sure of him, he thought. Better a clean kill
than to wound him and feel we ought to bring him into Baker
where he'll have a chance to recover and cause us trouble.
Rohan in his head-blind way'll swap him for one of our

captured people, and I have the distinct feeling this one's important. He's not wearing Kan gear, but it's not local Yamato gear either. Jeez, look at the mixture of equipment. And what kind of helmet is that? By all that's real, who is he? And why's he lying low here? Almost as if he's waiting for a window to power up to Baker, a window when no Kan ships are close. Maybe we should take him and get all that out of him. But I'd rather put a burn on him. Nothing like uncertainty among the boys when there's tricky business going down.

His forefinger stroked the release again, and he seated the crook of the knuckle against the hot metal while his men watched the pilot, absorbed by his every move.

The lander was plain buff with no markings and a bulging cowl just aft of center. It carried two large panniers and ducts—a regular chemical head. The pilot was standing up to relieve himself. Yes, a male sure enough, but that meant nothing down here. Would a Kan or a samurai be more or less likely to want to use a lander head? What the hell was he? Korean privateer maybe? Ellis Straker says give your average Korean thirty minutes and he'll go somewhere out of sight and before the hour's spent he's scheming with the locals to plot some third party's downfall. Always poking their noses into Yamato unannounced. Always filthying the water for us with the samurai. Interfering sonsabitches is what they are. Born that way. That's why our kicking their hides in the Zone was necessary.

He felt a dark cloud shadow his vision of things: the cloud's name was Admiral Maskull.

Big squatting shame about the attempt on Satsuma. Blew Amerikan standing with the samurai to its roots, and just when we were starting to reestablish contact with Miyako-nojo. Ludicrous fuckup. By all that's real, if the Admiral had only listened to Zev he'd have taken Satsuma inside thirty days! And if he'd listened to Ellis Straker, he'd have got out the system before the Index plunged and not lost the *Edward Preble* to Two-Nine. Our chance to smash them is gone. Theirs is coming next.

I know enough about Sectorpolitik to know that what we do here is going to change history in a big way. Fact is, the campaign has all along been a fight for Amerikan survival in Kyushu Quadrant. Yamato power probably doesn't appear in the equation anymore. That much has now been acknowledged by MeTraCor. But for the long term it's clear to me the future can only be settled by Osumi, and probably by the whole Quadrant being ruled under a joint Amerikan-Yamato, or a Kan-Yamato, alliance. But which is it to be?

We won't be deadlocked here for much longer. Each squadron, Amerikan or Kan, that comes into Yamato will be bigger than the last, sent in an effort to deliver a decisive blow and smash the enemy. So far we've been closely matched, and the prize we're fighting over is too squatting rich for either side to give up the struggle.

The image of Arkali came to him once again as his thoughts leapfrogged forward. But for now it's a purgatory that goes on and on. Unless . . . there's immediate intervention from the Shogun—one way or the other.

He could hear the sound of the man urinating.

So this Kan's waiting for a window, is he? he thought, chewing the skin of his lip. I'll wager Yu Hsien is knotted up in schemes so tight that he's like a python in a longan tree. Short of a miracle Baker will eventually be captured. It makes my blood boil. I can imagine the fence-sitting that's going on on Edo—Sakuma Hidenaga watching to see what happens.

Suddenly there was a chiming console alarm from the portal. A red light began to flash in the darkened interior of the lander. The pilot was caught at the worst possible moment.

He started, tried to do up his patch. He turned and bolted for the portal, ripping out a blaster. Then a big rifle blaster fired, the side arm suddenly jerked out of his hand as an arc snapped down onto his helmet and catapulted him onto the wing. A sudden crisscross of beams targeted the portal and lit up the lander. Then, a split second later, he grounded a fifty kV charge and collapsed.

Slashed foliage rolled down the gully and came to rest. The sound of the ambush echoed into nothingness. Eerily, the insect noises and the alarm had stopped.

"Shit!"

The lone man sat up, scanned the slopes, his heart hammering. He saw his own reflection in the glossy plates of the lander: the chrome dome of his helmet had a carbon-black starburst on one side where the arc had belted him. By the time he got down from the wing, his lander was belching thin blue smoke, bleeding its energy away in death throes as a pool of dark lube dribbled out from it.

Whoever it was hit him had put paid to any escape. He looked up again, nerves shocked to jangles, his mind close to panic. In the half-melted faceplate, the rocks that lipped the gully were glowing in the infrared, the foliage all cool blues and purples, a tumbled maze that deceived the eye. His assailants could be anywhere, in any numbers. To go for the blaster that lay on the wing stub would be to invite instant death. He put his hands up to lift his visor and cup his mouth and shouted into the silence.

"*Anata no o-namae wa?*" What is your honorable name?

An answering shout echoed back. "Stand still!"

The insects began to scream again. He heard footsteps scrambling towards him from behind, and began to turn on a reflex, but the order was shouted again and he obeyed until the feel of a blaster muzzle on his raw neck made him flinch.

Hard hands came round him and pulled off his external gear and his helmet, then he was whirled about to face a rough-faced man in a chameleon suit.

"You!"

Barb Eastman's jaw dropped. "By all that's real! Hayden Straker."

"Barb? Sweet Jeezus, I've never been so relieved to see a human face!" His own was lit by astonished relief. He rubbed at his singed ear.

"What the squat you doing here?"

"Let me ask you the same question! You burned my craft down. Jeezus, you nearly killed me!"

"Mistook you for Kan."

The shock of their meeting wore thin, and he found an unexpected hardness in Eastman's voice. He turned away. "That's fine. Just fine!"

"You weren't looked for here, Straker! The hell you doing, sneaking around in this gully?"

"News for Commander Rohan. How else can I approach Baker except by waiting on a window, then powering up there, hoping to hell they'll believe I'm who I say I am?" His hand hovered over the burn on his cheek, not touching the flesh. "Shit, that stings!"

"That way's a shortcut to getting yourself atomised. We're nervous about anyone slipping into an approach. I mean anyone."

"Is that good enough reason to open fire without a challenge?"

"As good a reason as you'll get from Baker. We're taking no chances these days. Straker, you'd better tell me what your game is."

"I've already told you—what do you mean, game?"

Eastman's manner was unyielding. "You maintain your destination wasn't Kanoya City?"

"Kanoya? Kanoya's still occupied by the Kan, isn't it?"

"Yeah."

"C'mon. What do you take me for?"

"It's been tough for Amerikans on Osumi since you were last around. Heard you been in Miyakonojo. Kissing ass, maybe? Double-dealing, eh? Selling us out, eh? Got any proof you're not a squatting traitor?"

He turned, amazed by Eastman's suspicion. "By Jeez, Barb, what's got into you?" He wiped the sweat from his forehead, then tried to move his jaw sideways. "Are you crazy, or what?"

"I'm as sane as you are. I just want you to know I could drop you. Right now. No one would question it. The reason I don't is mercy. Self-restraint. Control. See?"

"You are crazy."

Eastman shouted after him as he walked away. "Let me tell you something, our chances of making a kill again are totally ruined. Can't properly surprise a Kan machine with a burning lander lying in the jungle like a beacon. Every squatting Kan patrol in the system'll know we're operating planetside now. We hang around much longer we'll be lucky to get back inside Baker alive."

He reacted to the blame in Eastman's manner. "Well, seems to me you shouldn't have burned out my vehicle."

"You're squatting lucky I didn't burn you—friend. I was aiming to."

He faced Eastman and saw the fire burning in the lander reflected in his eyes. "Well, this is a helluva welcome back!"

"If you want a welcome from me, Straker, then you're going to have to wait a long time."

One of the team wearing a headset broke in. "Sir, I've got a vector. We're drawing attention!"

"We ought to get out of here! Now!"

They scrambled then, and some minutes were needed to

reach their own craft. As they blasted skyward under five gee, Hayden Straker considered Eastman's attitude and the newly appeared eagle flash on his collar. It was astonishing and inexplicable. The alteration in his attitude had been total.

He treats me like an enemy, he thought. Where's the black humor I used to find in him? Even in his blackest of black-dog moods he could raise a joke. He was never like this. Look at those dead eyes, and the wolfish way he runs his team. Can it be that a little MeTraCor rank has driven him over the edge?

"So, you're a full Corps lieutenant now?" he asked after the main thrust cut out and he could breathe again.

"As you see."

"Care to tell me about my father, Barb? Did the *Chance* beat the Kan into Two-Nine?"

"Father?" Eastman snorted. "You've got no father."

A fist clenched inside him. "What happened?"

"I don't mean killed. You ought to have more faith in his squatting talent. He not only came down to Kanoya City during the occupation, he got out again too. He's a great man. And a great fighter. Greater than you'll ever realise. But then you think his life's aims and his whole philosophy are a heap of shit. So maybe it's just as well you're shit to him."

Relief flooded him. The samurai were wrong. Beside death, dishonor was nothing. What right did one man have to pronounce judgment on another? Especially a man like Ellis Straker? He was a hard bastard and a bully and a man full of schemes. Like the Adventer prophet said, only throw a rock at a sinner if your own conscience is clean. He said, "My father's disowned me? He announced that?"

"Squatting right he did! He's told everybody. You're dis-graced everywhere as a coward, as a thief, and as a liar. The man who's single-handedly brought ruin over the whole Osumi system. The one who's given everything to the Kan."

He started, his throat suddenly dry. The terror of his father had once seemed a gigantic thing, a threat to his life that filled his vision. But now it had receded and he could view it without emotion. He said, "My father's the thief and the liar. He's an evil charmer. His slanders are skillful and loud, and I know what it is now. It's the psi talent in him that's turning sour. He was a great man once, greater than I ever understood, but his talent caught up with him. It's killing him from the inside."

"You're just a bitter man, Hayden Straker."

"And you're like everyone else! Eye-blinded by him. You never saw the dirty side of Ellis Straker. Don't you know that everyone close to him died? Most of his crews. Two wives. Both of his daughters. Where do you think the miracles come from? He's already used up enough psi for five lives. And that ravening appetite he calls a talent would have had me too, only I wouldn't let it."

"No. You ran. You couldn't go with the flow. You couldn't bring yourself to face destiny like a man."

"I wasn't going with his flow. Because his flow is a whirlpool that would have sucked me down. I did what I had to do. I followed my own psi. I did what was right. And I saw it through. I'll tell him that to his face if ever I get the opportunity."

Eastman grunted. "I'd like to see that very much."

"Where did he go, Barb?"

"I don't know. And I wouldn't discuss it with you even if I did."

He ignored the remark. "Tell me about Arkali? You remember, Jos Hawken's daughter? Do you know if she's safe?"

"She's aboard Baker. And fine. Physically at least."

"Thank psi for that." He rubbed at his forehead. "Yes, thank psi."

Eastman shot him a despising look. "Can't vouch for her state of mind, though. You've messed her up with your running off like you did."

Eastman's mind was in turmoil. "Do I remember Jos Hawken's daughter?" he asks! By all that's real, I think of her every waking hour. Jeezus, Straker, why did you have to show up? Here? Now? Just as we were inching closer together? Just as I was making progress putting my relationship with her back together again? How is it that arc missed burning you down?

Do I remember her?

I've laid siege to her, Hayden Straker! I want her. By all that's real, I'll give her anything she wants, but I'm determined to have her. When she told me she was still going to marry you, I felt it like molten metal burning in me. I asked myself whether I should tell her what I knew about you. I had the chance to show her the real you and to destroy her love for you. But with those weapons in my hands, I still chose not to do anything. I chose to prove I'm a man. A full man. As much a man as anyone. I've got a complete range of attributes and a full spectrum of emotions: I've known excitement and boredom, joy and suffering, pleasure and pain the equal of anyone. I'm as much a man as anyone. And the higher virtues? Courage? I've shown that! Compassion? I've offered that! Hope? I've suffered that! And love? Oh, yes, love! I've suffered that, too.

I talked it over with Bosco. I didn't want to hurt Arkali. Respect her wishes, he said, so I made up my mind to slowly trap her respect, make it so she couldn't do anything but love me. I thought that when she came to accept you were dead, I would be her natural choice. But now you're here, by all that's real, and I'm back in hell again!

As they synched with the orbiter, Eastman seemed to calm down, like a man coming down off a weird high. He told him stiffly the bare essentials of what had happened at Kanoya City, from the *Chance*'s capture, through the occupation, to their own escape to Fort Baker. He did not mention Arkali again, but revealed that Ellis Straker had embarked on a secret voyage, a mission that, if successful, could still save everything.

"Not another psi-twisting ruse with banned technology?" he groaned, thinking that with Sakuma Hidenaga dead and the succession settled on Sakuma Kiyohide there was no need for more complicating factors.

"I don't know what he's doing. Says he's got a rendezvous with Zone pirates. People who owe him some kind of favor."

"Not Kim? Kim Gwon Chung?"

"Don't know."

"Well, was he guarded over it? Or did he shout it around?" Eastman remained unsmiling, his voice flat and terse. "He confided in me. Otherwise he kept it close. I think I only found out about it because he had to give some idea of where he was going to Commander Rohan."

"Why?"

"Because if he hadn't morale aboard Baker might easily have collapsed completely."

"You sure he was secretive about where he was going? Not just trying to excite speculation by appearing to keep it quiet?"

"I told you. He didn't even want to say he was leaving."

"Well, that's a good sign."

They reached Baker as it swung into Osumi's umbra. There was not any intervention by the Kan, but even so Eastman insisted on a careful approach along a fast track that decelerated severely. The less the Kan knew of their comings and goings even under this almost perfect radio black, the better, he said.

Fort Baker had been badly smashed up. The Kan cutter

attacks had made a mess of the orbital fortress, and it was surrounded by a halo of debris that peppered them as they approached. It was incredible to him, looking at the blackened hulk, that anyone was aboard, but Eastman told him that the vital systems of shield, weapons, grav, skin integrity, and life-support were all more or less intact.

The docking was noisy and clanging. The mechanism complained at the modifications they had made to the lander as a half-dozen drones struggled to connect the seals.

Straight out of the umbilicus the first man he met was Bosco Shadbolt. He embraced him and seemed genuinely pleased at his reappearance.

"Waydago, Hayd! This is great! Wait 'til I tell the boys! Half of us thought you had to be dead. Jeez, what happened to your face?"

"Accident I had."

"You should have heard all the rumors that it was you who'd raised the Hideki army that attacked Kanoya. Did you?"

"Something like that."

"Jeezus! Wait 'til Arkali hears that."

They reached the elevator plate. He felt a hollowness in the pit of his stomach. His voice dropped. "Bosco, how's Arkali? I've asked Barb about her, but he won't give me a straight answer."

Shadbolt's eyes seemed to cloud momentarily, but then his smile reappeared. "We've had a hard time up here, but don't worry! She's fine, and she's one person who never doubted you'd come back. You're a lucky man, Hayden Straker."

"That's good." The hollowness grew inside him. "What's eating Eastman? I've never seen a change like that come over anybody. He fires on me without a challenge, or an apology— that's how I got this—then he accuses me of getting in the way of his covert operations. After that he comes tantamount to calling me a spy who's working for the Kan. Is that what warfare does to a man?''

Shadbolt pursed his lips as if picking over a delicate matter. ''I'd say—just the opposite.''

''What do you mean?''

''Not war. Love.''

''Jeezus, if that's love . . . what do you mean?''

Shadbolt's head tilted, and he sucked on his lip. ''Well, see . . . it's kind of personal.''

''You'd better out with it, Bosco. Tell me before we get to the bridge. If you do, I'll tell you something you want to hear.''

Shadbolt chewed his lip. ''I guess I ought to—for your own good. But when you've heard me out you've got to promise me you'll remember that I was only trying to help you. And that I still count myself as Barb Eastman's friend too.''

24

Still stunned by what Shadbolt had said, Hayden Straker met the sentry and told him he had to speak with Commander Rohan immediately. He was admitted to Rohan's private apartments.

Inside, the thermocline was steaming. He gasped as the lock irised and the heat hit him, then he and the sweating sentry exchanged a glance.

"You guarding the Commander, or keeping him from getting out of the steamroom?"

"We had a break-in by Kan units in Upper fourteen through eighteen, sir. We're still not a thousand mils certain that all of them got flushed."

"I'm not sure Rohan would be top target in any case."

"Sure hope you're right, sir."

The warm, humid air oppressed his mind as he waited, and he thought about what he could tell the Commander and how best to put it.

Rohan admitted him and poured two bulbs of Bull's Blood before dismissing his adjutants and sitting down. He was a man with corpse eyes, ten days growth of beard, and a set of narrow teeth that appeared in a strange smile when he was amused or anxious.

Rohan's a one-off, he thought. A psi-avoider. A man unlike anyone else I've ever known. He's certainly been drinking, but it's hard to know what state of mind he's in beyond that.

"So, here's to you, Hayden Straker!"

"To me?"

"Yes, you!"

"Sorry to disappoint you, but I didn't bring any cause to celebrate."

"C'mon! Hard to give credit where it's due. You deserve the full thanks of MeTraCor. Full thanks. Shame we lost Kanoya City. You did what you could."

"In that case, thank you, Commander." He made a vague gesture of acceptance and drank. "Unfortunately, Kanoya City remains lost."

"Them Yambo manners? Been away too long."

"I've been on Edo."

"On Edo? Sheeee . . .''

"That's correct. And I—"

"Must have brought back news. Important news for Me-TraCor?"

He nodded gravely. "It might sour your wine when you hear it."

"Oh, not this wine. Nooo. This is Communion wine. And I'm tasting the Last Rites."

He told Rohan about the death of Sakuma Hidenaga. How Sakuma Kiyohide had taken the lead in the power struggle and had seized the succession at the Shogun's palace. He did not say anything about the persuasive "advice" the Shogun was probably now taking from his very special *menuki*.

"Sakuma Kiyohide has eyes everywhere in Kyushu. Much more so than we realised. There's not a thing happens in the Quadrant that he doesn't get to hear about."

"Mmm," Rohan said, getting up and pacing distractedly. "Should've learned that sixty days ago. Might have goaded Yu Hsien to make his move prematurely. Yeah. As it is— it's bad. Very bad!"

"I regret that circumstances on Edo prevented me from making—"

"No! No criticism. You did good. But that sixty UT . . . would've made a lot of difference."

"What are you going to do?"

Rohan cocked an eyebrow at him. "Get your face fixed. Still hurt?"

He touched the raw skin of his ear and cheek. "It can wait."

"Wait? For what? Our Lieutenant Eastman did it, didn't he?"

"Yes."

"He's a hotshot. Deep-down MeTraCor man. Real tough. Real loyal. Real . . . I apologise for him. Know how he got into MeTraCor? You know what's special about him?"

He saw that Rohan's hand was shaking. "What?"

"He's well connected with the new Administration. I saw his indenture data one time. Principal referee's Kurt Reiner. The Kurt Reiner."

"Head of Halide?" He considered that, and though it was surprising, it was not that remarkable. Derion Reiner had been appointed to the Kanoya City governing board. "So? Plenty of aristo families swing tough positions for their youth. They call it 'a spell of broadening' or 'grand touring,' we both know that."

"Doesn't matter now. None of it matters." Rohan seemed suddenly to remember himself. His tone switched from conspiratorial to official. "By the rules MeTraCor'll reimburse your heirs against injury and death. And the loss of one lander vehicle. Insurance, see? Important paperwork."

"My heirs?"

"Ever hear of the Alamo?"

"It's a famous bar on Liberty, isn't it?"

"Funny man. We're all going to die in the next attack."

"Commander—"

"But don't worry 'bout a thing. I'll get a last message to Seoul. Swear I will. Captain of the *Balkan*'ll do me that favor. Last trade vessel to transit Osumi. Promised me he'd drop by on his return. Hundred eighty-seven days UT. He'll be hitting Two-Eight and lining up on Two-Nine on a burn through. No waiting around. Just a radio burst to *Balkan* is all. By my reckoning she's overdue two days. When you came through, thought you was her. Let me redraft the message with you looking on. I don't want any mistakes."

Rohan sat down at his console, heavily. It was difficult to know if he was feeling total despair or just self-pity, but as he spoke the code preamble at the blank screen his shoulders sagged. He looked up, his fingers holding down the edit bar.

"This is fritzy. Dumb scream for help that can't possibly be answered."

"You really think so?"

"May as well yell it down a megaphone. Seoul can't supply us with reinforcements, and according to Maskull, Liberty's hands are full with Kan threats in the Zone and a big offensive against Taipei. Pusan has even fewer ships than Seoul, and we got no idea if the Kan are sending in another fleet. Nothing Navy's coming here for two hundred days minimum."

"We can still hope."

"Yeah, hope! Even when the stars are going out one at a time. Final snuffing out. One more concerted attack from Yu's ships and we'll blow. Believe it."

As Rohan applied himself to the console Hayden Straker thought over what Shadbolt had said about Arkali and Eastman on the ride up to the bridge:

"We've been fighting for our lives here, but she's had a particularly hard time. Eastman's crazy over her. You'll come to know, sooner or later, so you may as well hear it from me. He's dreamed up this mad idea that their destinies are linked. That they're psi-fated for one another. For a while he talked about her all the time. Now he won't talk about anything at all! He's outside of his right mind with it, but it's more than that. There's something real spooky about him. I don't know what it is, but he makes my skin crawl."

"And she won't see him?"

"She hates the sight of him."

"I see."

Shadbolt had become suddenly intense. "Hayden, you won't like me for saying this but she's almost as mad for you as he is for her. He irritates and repels her so she avoids him, and that deepens his resentment of you. She sees you—not as you are—but as some kind of shining hope. Her future.

A symbol. She wants to cling to you. And he wants to kill you.''

"This is insane."

"That's right. Insane." Shadbolt's face had been full of human concern. He had shaken his head and thrown up his hands. "Unleashed passions are dangerous. Can't say I understand those kinds of emotions all that well. I'm a man of pretty even moods myself. But I've seen the effects, and they're worse than any designer disease. Arkali and Eastman are both in hell with it."

"He sees me as a . . . a rival?"

"For sure. You're plumb in his path, aren't you?"

"Jeezus, if he only knew! Crazy bastard's got it all wrong!"

"Hey, go careful with him. Eastman's already proved he's not afraid to die. I saw him pick a fight with a bunch of mean Navy people, and it damn near froze my blood to see it. I'd say that his experiences since then have done zero to improve his humor."

He had laughed bitterly and told Shadbolt how much crueler the twist of it really was. He had told him about Yasuko and their love and final parting.

Shadbolt had been flabbergasted. "You're as crazy as they are. It's obvious there can't be any future in it. Marry a Yambo? What you going to do? Smuggle her into Amerika? Her husband'll send ninja to cut your pecker off for sure."

"I love her, Bosco."

"Oh, man!"

"I love her."

Shadbolt had shaken his head. Finally he had said, "You realise that if you say that to Arkali you'll waste what little sanity she's got left?"

He had hung his head. "Perhaps I will. But it's the truth."

He looked up and found Rohan expecting an answer.

"I'm sorry, Commander? What did you say?"

"I said your father's been here. Twice." Rohan paused as the information sank in. "He's disinherited you. Know that?"

He was too tired to go through it all again. "Fact is, Commander, I don't give a shit. Not about the credit. Not about the name. Not about him. Or anything."

"Think it's fair to say he bears you some kind of grudge?"

Rohan's understatement amused him, and he laughed. "Yes. I guess that would be fair to say, Commander."

"No laughing matter. Or wouldn't be if the *Chance* ever transited in again. He wants to kill you. But that's kinda academic now."

"I'm ready to face my father man to man. Anytime."

"Braver man than me, feller. Real hard meat, your father. Says you stripped him out. Says you lit out with his property at a delicate time. He ain't about to forgive you."

"Have I completely busted him?"

"Nope. Seems he's fixed his affairs in Seoul. Heavy price, though. He came here twice. Brought us 'quipment and support and news and such. Nobody can judge what's going on inside that head of his, but I tell you this: He's still smoldering. Ruin of Hawken Inc., missing the merger, all that stuff . . . it's put his life's aim out of reach."

"I heard he'd saved his ships by mortgaging himself to a clique of Korean creditspreaders headed by the Ei Cartel."

"Right. Never write off bad debts don't Ei. They kill them."

"Where is he now?"

"Left here couple of days before the *Edward Preble* got mushed."

He nodded, knowing that Rohan meant the Teth-Two-Nine tsunami. More red wine squirted out of the bulb.

"Ellis warned Maskull to get out. Before the Index fell. Said the nexus was turning. Admiral wouldn't listen." Rohan shrugged. "Didn't surprise me when Ellis upped and away. Didn't surprise me when Maskull's astrogators got it all wrong. Turned half a squadron into cranberry juice. Where the *Chance* is now is anyone's guess. Seoul?"

He digested that thoughtfully. Shadbolt had said he had spoken to Eastman about it. It was Eastman's opinion that this time Ellis Straker had not gone back to Seoul at all. According to Barb Eastman, Ellis's departure had been prompted by a piece of intelligence he had bought from one of the Korean pirates with whom he maintained dealings. It was one of Kim Gwon Chung's men. So. Eastman believed Ellis was about to learn something of vast importance. Something so huge it could set everything to rights.

I wonder what that could be, he thought cynically as he drained Rohan's bulb into his own. What can the sonofabitch be up to? And can I trust what Eastman says?

"Read that."

He looked at Rohan's screen and read it over. It failed on style, but set down the situation accurately, and begged Seoul for immediate aid.

"There's not much else to be said, is there?"

"That's my thinking too. Go get the side of your head fixed." Rohan's narrow grin came, and he jerked a thumb towards the senior officer's quarters. "Somebody sleeping downaways. Somebody been asking after you every day for a hundred days UT. Want me to tell her you're here?"

25

The moment she heard the docking mechanism thundering dully through Baker's load structure Arkali's heart began to beat faster, and she knew she was going to be sick. The thought of Barb Eastman being back inside the orbiter sent a pang of dismay through her. For months now she had been avoiding him, feigning illness, dressing exclusively in a baggy one-piece op's suit, locking herself away, thinking of reasons why she could not talk with him, or sit with him in red assembly. The man was an unbalanced imbecile, raving on about destiny and his love—he wouldn't take no for an answer.

She began to cross to the wash. The private quarters that Commander Rohan had provided for her were close by his own. They were clean and spacious and out of bounds to everyone. Since the Navy had lit out, and since the last merchantman to transit had taken away the remaining civilian presence, she was the last woman aboard. She let herself into the wash through the open iris, and gagged over the sluice, bringing up a mouthful of thin vomit.

If it hadn't been for Bosco, she thought, I would've gone spook with Eastman's attentions. Fort Baker's too small a place to be trapped in. It's been like being caged up with a bear. If only Hayden were here to protect me, and love me, and take me away from here. I'll never forgive Ellis Straker for his deceptions. Never!

She hurried back inside her main room and lit a panel. It was a comfortable chamber—if a little small—cool, white walls and holo ceiling, a port, a relaxer, and a midfloor mezzanine where the strap hung.

When there was no alert to jam dense-fleck armor down over the port the view of Osumi could be hypnotic. The corridor outside was hot and humid, and down below was a storage vault in which crazy Rohan had put a collection of salvaged shrubs rooted up from the park he had jettisoned. Some were sizable, all were dying, even though he came here every day to water them, and talk to them. Yellowing banana plants thrust up their huge, mottled fronds against the bars of her mezzanine rail. It smelled like a jungle grave.

She began to throw off the vest she had found for herself, kicked off her shoes, and undid the knee pops on her suit. Today, because of the extra activity planetside, she had walked along the stations of the bridge to watch the macros and scanners, and had stayed for a while to contemplate the patterns of colored light, and imagine Hayden down there, striving to make his way back to her.

Life on Baker was like life on any MeTraCor installation. Life came in three colors: red shift, blue shift, and green shift. It was best to sleep through the hours of green shift. It meant missing dining with the Commander at the end of the period, and it also avoided his guests, who were invariably young men driven to the ends of their tethers. Some MeTra-Cor officers were needing a woman's comfort badly now, and men just couldn't resist making their needs understood.

Rohan had warned her against playing one man's urges off against another. It was clear to him, if not them, that she intended no payoff for anybody. He had warned also that

Eastman's duel down in the ducts had not been prompted entirely by a suspect hand of smart cards, and that to unwittingly incite his moody jealousies further could be dangerous.

She sighed. *Because of him I'm reduced to virtual solitary confinement. I wonder if I'll ever get off this heap of junk? What a terrible thought. To die here. To orbit Osumi, boiling and freezing among the trash for years, until a junker comes along to sweep the lanes clear and render us down into mechanically recovered mush.*

Despite the crisis there was still enough water in the cycle to permit her to wash once a day. It was a relief to peel off her gear and knead the soles of her feet. Doing without servants had been impossible at first. There had been no obedient synth to organise her things, no product of the Halide Corporation's vats to fetch and carry, and no lady's servant to run errands or see to her personal requirements. Damn that Suzi. When Rohan had given her the option to leave, she had upped and gone.

"You just can't get the staff, these days," she said at her reflection in the mirror.

Her hair was tied back. She released it and began to comb it out as she went back to the wash, then she stepped out of her one-piece and pulled her vest over her head. The showerhead was crusted with limescale. A little water dripped onto the molded plex seat. It was in a recess: a semicylindrical door slid shut to contain the usual high-power needles of water. With the faucet put on full only a trickle appeared. She took the sponge and soaked it, then put it to her face. The touch of it was delightful.

Then she dabbed water on her neck and shoulders and chest, and rubbed a smear of liquid soap across her skin, rinsing herself with the sponge. When she had finished, she used towels to dry herself and climbed into the strap webbing.

She would use up a half hour of her precious panel time to write manually in her diary before turning down the grav, then she would sleep.

The knock startled her.

"Who is it?"

"Don't worry, Miz Hawken. It's me, Rohan."

"Commander Rohan? I . . . I'm in my strap."

"Better get out of your strap. Got a surprise for you."

"What kind of surprise?"

She threw a *yukata* around herself and dialed on the ion bolt. The iris opened, she saw, took a step back . . . and felt herself falling.

Hayden Straker had never seen anyone faint from shock before. He caught her as she collapsed. He carried her to the relaxer, and laid her on it while Rohan went to fetch a medikit.

He leaned over her and watched her as she came round. Her eyes opened, cleared, and registered him. Then she put her hand up to touch his injured face: his chin and his unshaven cheeks and his mouth. Her fingertips lingered, and then she burst into tears, and reached up with both her hands to grab his neck and pull herself to him, racked with sobs.

He put his hands on her wrists, tried gently to disengage her, but she would not release him. Her grip was like wire, so he put his arms round her to support her, and she hugged him for a long moment without speaking.

When she did, the words gushed out. "Oh, Hayden! Hayden! Oh, Hayden! Is it really you? I knew you'd come back to me. I knew you would. Oh, Hayden. Tell me it's you. Tell me this is real."

He could not reply to her.

Rohan stepped in with the medikit and saw her clinging to him. He peeled out a sedative and then left tactfully, closing the iris.

She would not release him for many minutes. "Hold me.

Hold me, Hayden,'' she murmured every time he tried to pull away. His cheek was wet; he felt the salt of her tears sting his burn. Her breathing came in gasps.

"Arkali," he said softly. "Arkali, listen to me. We have to talk."

"Oh, yes. We have to. I've got so much to tell you. But we're together now and for always. There's all the time in Creation. I love you, Hayden. Hold me tight. Promise me we'll never be apart again."

"I can't make that promise."

Her eyes questioned him. She was so vulnerable in that moment, her soul so bared and fully open to him that he could not go on. The truth was a dagger to be plunged into her heart. How could he use it?

"Arkali, we . . . we have to talk."

He settled himself beside her, his hands holding hers tightly. The torment of it ate at him. How can I explain that the love she feels for me is not balanced by my own love for her? That fact alone is enough to prevent the full flowering that true love needs. Oh, sweet Jeezus, how can I tell her that Yasuko is the woman I love? Though she's parted from me, and I don't know if I'll ever see her again, my time with her has changed me. I can't marry anyone else now.

He could not bring himself to tell her straightaway, but then he remembered that cowardice could afflict a man in many ways, not just in the heat of battle.

"Arkali, you know I'd do anything to avoid hurting you, but I can't make any promises."

She heard but discarded the tentative regret in his voice. "Hold me, Hayden. Love me, now."

He pulled back. "Please listen to me. I'm relieved to see you, Arkali. And I'm real glad you're well. I hated the thought that you might have come to harm because of me. I never wanted to hurt you."

"Hayden, I'm not hurt. Everything's all right again. We're just as we were before. A ship'll come soon and we'll be married on Seoul, and it'll be just as if this nightmare had never happened."

"No. This isn't a nightmare. This is real. And we're not the same as we were. I've changed. And you too." He released her hands and applied the sedative patch to the back of her hand. "Sleep now. And when you wake, we'll talk about the future."

She stared at the patch. "Sleep? How can I sleep? Don't leave me, Hayden. I need you. You must never leave me ever again."

She pressed herself to him again, hung herself around his neck, and he felt her whole body trembling. She was pale and beautiful, and her red hair cascaded around her face in coppery curls. Her small breasts shaped the thin cotton of her *yukata*. The pupils of her eyes were huge as if drinking in the sight of him thirstily.

Waves of conflicting emotions clashed inside him. Her smell was suddenly cloying. Her hair was in his mouth and eyes. He pulled back. I have to find some way of telling her, he thought desperately. I don't want to hurt her, but I have to tell her. Every minute I allow her to carry on believing in me the wound cuts deeper, and the deception grows dirtier. She has to be told that I can't see her anymore. And she has to be told why.

Her voice was breathy, urgent, and demanding all at once. "I never knew I wanted you so much, Hayden. Stay with me tonight. Ride in my strap. I couldn't bear it if you were to leave me tonight. I won't sleep unless I can feel your arms around me. Love me. Ooh, love me!"

She lay back on the relaxer, her eyes fixed on his, her nostrils flaring astonishingly. The moisture of her lips glistened in the panel light, there was now a red flush in the skin of her face and neck, mottling her chest. She was fighting the drug patch, but it had loosened her in a strange way. She had offered herself in that astonishing invitation. Then she bucked her hips and uncrossed her hands from in front of her, and in the most wanton way discarded the *yukata* across the room.

The agony of his decision was intense. The moment burned A-type hot. His body was screaming at him to do as she wanted, to give her the love she craved in one consummately passionate act of physical lust. And it would have been so easy to do. But he knew also that if he kissed her, or even touched her naked body, the moment would be lost. He knew he must get up and walk out on her, but he could not.

He bent over her and kissed her. Then he threw off her arms and began a halting explanation that he would have given anything not to have had to make.

26

In Rohan's private tropics, the air was close and feverish. The man in the chameleon suit lurked among the corridor shadows, staring at the iris of the room at the back of the Commander's quarters. His enclosed eyes were fixed on the rectangle of translucent light that seemed to pulsate beside the iris, and his ears strained to pick up the muffled, tantalising sounds that came to him. They were impassioned sounds, confessions of regret and remorse uttered in a low voice, then terrible shrieks of denial imploring in a higher pitch.

It had taken that to tear him from his duty. His squad were on watch, at their stations, keeping watch for the imminent Kan attack. An attack that he knew must come soon and destroy them all.

Inside the suit Eastman's whole skin sweated at each indistinct sound. It seemed to him that the deceptive quality of the flexiplex was such that it did not admit words to his ears, as if he could only hear emotions, and the emotions that emanated from the room seared him like Wesson beams.

Under the mask his face was beaded, his neck seal sodden. The stifling heat made him itch from head to toe, but he held his breath and listened motionlessly as the tirade of sobbing screams rose ever more shrill in the room. From his concealed position he could see shadows cast on the ceiling of the darkened corridor, the shades of a struggle projected through the pinhole camera of the ion-locked iris.

"He's raping her," he hissed. "The squatting bastard's taking her against her will!"

His mind went back to the terror that had taken place in the bunkers of Kanoya City. Terrible memories overtook him, and he began to shake with a vengeful wrath that was beyond his power to control.

He tore off his mask and skullcap and vaulted down the shaft to the lower storeroom. MeTraCor regulations, he thought. The lock there would be fail-safe: iris open in an emergency. Like . . . loss of power. Instantly he burned the panel, and the iris sssshushed apart. He burst through into the Commander's private hothouse of rotting memories, his entire being filled suddenly with a maniac's strength. His heartbeats thumped in his head, his arms and legs shivered with rage. He barely realised that he had fired his blaster, and set off a wailing alarm. Wildly his eyes darted about to look for a means to get up to the mezzanine.

But there was no way. Unless he could climb one of the

banana trees high enough to get his hands onto the plex railing.

A piercing scream and the sobbing that followed tortured him. He could hear her words now: "No! No! No! I won't let you. I won't let you!"

He wanted to shout to her, but he wanted to surprise Hayden Straker even more.

Each banana plant had a one-meter plex cube of sodden dirt on its base. A ton of dirt to stabilise him as he climbed. He reached up. His suit slid on the profusion of frond stems that thrust out of the banana trees' primordial forms. The fronds themselves shook fearfully as he leapt in among them. Their fibrous edges ripped at his hands and knees. But it was not so much a tree as a clump of leaves, and unclimbable.

He sprang up from one foot, powerfully, snapping several of the leaves, but even so he found purchase with his hand on the upper deck and hung there, straining to pull himself up.

Then, as he hung, he heard the iris cycle in the room above, and though Arkali's sobbing continued he knew he had done what he must.

"Run, you filthy psi-damned bastard!" he shouted. Then his grip on the plex slipped away, and he was falling ten feet onto his back on the plants below.

He cracked his head, and tore both elbows and a heel, but he was on his feet immediately, swirling round like a ninja, astonished at the three men who surrounded him with spike guns leveled belly high.

He was dazed, shaking his head, but he recovered enough to say, "What are you looking at?"

They stared back at him with wide eyes like he was a crazed tiger, holding their blasters close against their guts as if their lives depended on them. Then an angry Rohan was there, shooting off orders, dressed only in his knee trousers, and with a dozen troopers at his shoulder, one toting a heavy-duty weapon.

Bright panel light flashed on around Eastman among the ruin of banana fronds. Then a figure in a white cotton *yukata* appeared above him on the edge of the mezzanine, a pale oval face, hand to mouth, eyes full of tears, red hair cascading. She saw him and broke into another fit of sobbing, turning away with a noise that made him despair. Then she was gone again.

"Who's that? By Christ, what's going on here? You! Stand still!" Rohan pushed his way forward. "Eastman? What are you doing here?" He picked up a ripped banana leaf and shook it. "Did you do this? Are you drunk or out of your mind?"

At that moment, the warbling alarm ceased abruptly, but only to be replaced by an insistent pulsing sound echoing throughout all of Baker and howling round the talkbacks. It was the event warning signal. Rohan hesitated, then there were voices shouting from the bridge. It was a transit. Mertz energy detected around Teth-Two-Nine. He turned on his heel, turning back to slap the leaf into Eastman's hands and tell him, "I'll deal with you later!"

In his own quarters, Rohan dressed, agitated by the notion the vessel must surely be Kan. Teth-Two-Nine was a couple of light-hours away, and the ship they saw decelerating was already millions of miles closer than the bridge detectors saw it. It appeared to be eating up the distance faster than the speed of light, though its corrected real velocity could not have been much more than 0.5 cee.

If it had come in at half cee, and maintained velocity, he would be seeing it now just after transit, but it would already be halfway to Osumi in actuality. If it had not been shedding kinetic, and not tracking a few degrees ecliptic north, he could have hoped that it was the *Balkan* heading for Two-Eight, but the ship was shedding kinetic at a monstrous rate, and it was heading straight for Osumi. Therefore it could not be the *Balkan*, it could not be friendly, and Armageddon had already begun.

He went to his command seat and was met by Shadbolt whose people were at their instrument stations. He had brought a gaggle of other staffers.

"A ship, Commander. A ship of five thousand tons mass or more. In line and fixing to lock on to Osumi beacon, I think. She's radio quiet."

"Arm and fire the meson device. You know what to do."

Shadbolt looked shocked. "Yes . . . yes, sir."

There was only one meson device aboard. The MeTraCor contingency manuals called it "a weapon of last resort." It was only to be used in a final emergency and required that Baker's argentium power generators be stripped out, and the cones used to arm the bomb. Without power, Baker was dead, and so was everyone aboard. Once the weapon was fired it would be impossible to recall, and, if timed correctly, would almost certainly denature the plex of the incoming ship enough to destroy it as it closed with them.

In the hours that followed, the faces of Shadbolt's technicians were variously full of alarm and anticipation as the station progressively shut down and went on ice. No coded signals were emanating from the enemy ship across the whole electromagnetic spectrum. She was not trying to communicate.

When she started to turn on final, Rohan talked to weapons. "What d'you say? Kan?"

"Has to be, sir."

"What kind?"

"Can't say yet."

"Shit."

He talked to the weapons pylon, where the systems man was waiting, neat in his red jacket and flat-top hairstyle.

"Got the cones in?"

"All but two, Commander," he drawled. "Take out the next one and we lose all ancillary functions. The last one, and there's just enough power on stellar pickup to keep the organix alive and thinking."

"Go ahead."

"Sir. You'd better ask everybody to web in."

An hour later the gravity cut out. There was a general gutsy moan. A tech to Rohan's left threw up over his console, and the vile globules floated out everywhere.

"This is it," the systems man shouted back. "That's a Kan hull all right. No mistaking those engines. She's coming in range and she don't give a damn. Rolling in nice as you please. I can see her burning a hole in my macro right now. All chromed up for a fight by the look of her! She's not scared of us neither. Jeezus, look at that hull go!"

The interrogators filled the talkback and a familiar data tune floated across the bridge.

"Hold it!"

"She can't be Kan!"

Rohan shook his head in disbelief. "Disarm! Loomis, get your fucking hand off of that lever!"

"Thank the living God."

Rohan shouted across the open channel. "Jeezus, we nearly blew your ass to the kingdom come. Who the fuck are you?"

"Probably Navy," systems said.

"Perish the thought." Rohan rubbed his eyes. No MeTra-Cor officer late of the Ohio Marines thought much of the Navy in the best of circumstances. Systems was no different.

Since Admiral Maskull's notable failures he had redoubled his damnations of all things connected with the Admiralty.

The big silver stingray floated in the screens. A product of the Chinese yards on Shang Hai for certain.

"Who is she?"

"Goddamn you, Rohan," a voice growled suddenly on the comms channel. "A man turns up in a brand spanking new ship right off the Admiralty prize lists, and all you want to do is mush him. You'd better get them cones put back where they belong and get that coffee machine of yours powered up again."

27

"An answer to your question, Commander." Ellis Straker slapped a diplomatic satchel down on Rohan's desk. "That's what I've brought you this time. And nothing else. But, as you'll see, it's likely to be enough."

There was a universal gasp.

Twenty men, MeTraCor officials and all of Rohan's remaining officers, stood around him expectantly. Had he brought them weapons? Were the *Chance*'s bays stuffed with provisions? Did he have drones from Seoul to augment their overworked maintenance teams? They had badgered him as he had strode up from the umbilicus, but he had been tight-lipped.

"Yep, none of you have come even close to it yet. And I doubt you will."

"Maskull left us deep in it, Ellis," Lawton said as he sat down.

"A gink in free space, and a blunderer planetside."

"So. You got a new ship?" Rohan said.

"Yep."

"Your accounts on Seoul been set to rights?"

"I expect I'll have the means to settle everything pretty soon."

"They say a wealthy man is a happy man."

"Ain't that a fact, now."

"We thought you'd deserted us, Straker. There was talk of you going to the Thai Quadrant. Of you throwing in with some piratical elements." Rohan turned to Lawton. "Maskull said something about Koreans. Something about a man called Kim."

"They're all called Kim."

"Pirates, Ellis. You know, the parasites that make all trade sicken and die?"

Ellis knew what Rohan meant: the Free Korean "privateers," who now infested a vast tract of the Zone stretching right across the equatorial part of the Sector. In the early days of the Korean revolt they had enlisted the help of *sangokujin*—racial Chinese, but not Xanadu Kan—living on Yamato colony worlds. Some of them were political refugees, some were descended from POWs or escaped criminals, many had fled from the *han* system that had been set up in the Zone, and lived in the various wildernesses of the Sector, or had fled to Free Korea.

Many of these men had long since fallen out with the Koreans as they had once fallen out with their nominal samurai governors. For years a notable few had made a living from preying on Zone traffic. Ellis Straker's dealings with them went back a long time, to the days of his first ventures in the Zone. He had had to point out to Kim Gwon Chung the tremendous benefits that might be made to flow from mutual respect—and also the unutterable price that would have to be paid should bad relations develop.

Under difficult circumstances the negotiations had proceeded well. The terms had been good. Kim's ships hunted like wolves, falling on whoever they could. They had heaped up a considerable treasure on their uncharted bases, weird, inhospitable places like fortresses built inside asteroids or attached to the lesser moons of giant worlds residing in uninhabited systems. It was said that their spy network reported two hundred thousand cubic parsecs of the Zone, from the Serpent's Head down to the Region of Microscopium. In return for protection for his ships, his cargoes, and the lives of his men, Ellis would do them favors.

Ellis doffed tobako ash as he recalled the deal he had solemnly sworn with Kim Gwon Chung years ago. He had been uncommonly luckless with a ship and allowed himself to be put at Kim's mercy.

A spy in the very midst of the MeTraCor camp is what I offered. Yep, it was when he was about to torture my balls off for having got caught.

"Now, Kim, you can't spend a man's balls," I told him. "They're no damn use to anybody but me." And I could see his eyes cloud over then and there. It disappointed him some not to have his fun, but I rightly judged him to be a man of business.

"See, Kim," I said, "your big problem is that all ships look alike to your sensors. You can't say what you've got 'til you're up close and it's too late. You might have got a juicy freighter, or a well-armed Minuteman, or even a Navy frigate holoed-up to deceive you. Now, this is what I propose . . ."

An accomplice to the biggest pirate in Known Space, I was called to my face by that bitch, Aziza Pope, when she found out. But not publicly—no, she wasn't ever that straight, nor so brave.

Ah, well, I don't deny it. I was aider and abettor. But it was a good working arrangement, simple and with nobody worth a slottee the loser. I'd feed info to Kim's contacts: the schedule times of MeTraCor freighters, lading data, cargo manifests, whatever I'd decide on. Once his jacknasties knew which ships were MeTraCor corvets—which were the real wasps with stingers in their asses, and not just shit-flies holoed-up to look like it—well then he'd know what to avoid. He was better guided, getting rid of the likes of Kan interlopers, and ships belonging to Yamato, and some of my lesser competition. Ah, that's how I grew so big so quick. I had an acquisitive heart in those days, psi save me. Yep, days when I wasn't as mellow as I am now. I always knew what I wanted.

He raised his eyebrows innocently. "Pirates, you say?"

Lawton grunted. "It's common knowledge you've had dealings with them, Straker."

"I like you as a man, Lawton. So I'll let that slander pass. You may not have been here long enough to know that some inquiries it just ain't quite prudent to make of me."

Rohan examined the beam-scorched diplomatic satchel balefully. Stitched into the flexiplex in big serif letters was the legend:

F.M.S. BALKAN
BAR HARBOR, LIB.

"I hoped she might've made Seoul. Or been delayed in Pusan. So, she's been taken?"

"No. She was smashed up by a nexus. Vav-Three-Oh, in

the Palawan side-chain.'' Ellis's stogie burned bright red at the tip as he sucked on the other end. "You might like to see the hardcopy she was carrying."

"Hardcopy? You mean diplomatic correspondence?"

"I don't mean a beefie wrapper."

"They're always sealed, Ellis."

"So?"

"By law, and by MeTraCor rules, only an accredited dipl—"

"MeTraCor rules? C'mon, Commander. Besides, I already opened it."

"You did what?"

"I opened it and read it. What you expect me to do? Pay big credit sight unseen? That's off the record."

"So you admit you did meet with pirates," Lawton jumped in. "And traded with them for this? We got your ass in a slingshot now, Bubb!"

"Keep your damned hair on, Colonel. Last government we had, Kim was our ally. He hasn't changed."

There was general muttering. Rohan's eyes were alight. The *Balkan* had been cruising from Liberty. The MeTraCor ship was long months overdue, but had she survived she would have been the only ship to deliver word from Amerika since Maskull's arrival.

"You know it's a capital offense to tamper with diplomatic material."

Ellis shrugged. "Aw, I'd deny it."

"You know they could probe you over this."

"They'd have to catch me first. Like my new ship? Think I'll call her the 'Up Yours.' "

It was probably obvious to Lawton and Rohan he had traded her hull-for-hull with Kim's people, probably against the Federal Mail Ship *Balkan*.

"Lepers don't ever change their sores, do they?" Lawton

said disgustedly. "Straker, your attitude's a disgrace. And your methods stink."

Ellis was stung by that. "Colonel, like it or not, I just saved all your lives. You could try showing a little gratitude."

"Gratitude? You sonofabitch, you're doing it out of self-interest."

"C'mon. Quit horse-assing. Why don't you open the damned thing."

Silence fell.

"How did you come by it?" Lawton demanded. "Diplomatic bags don't just float out of nexi."

"I told you before not to make inquiries into my affairs."

The silence deepened. Lawton sat back, a significant look on his face. "Let's suppose you did obtain it from pirates."

"You can suppose what you like. I'm a man who listens far and wide. I just came by an interesting piece of debris, and thought it might be worth buying—on behalf of MeTra-Cor, that is, you understand?"

Ah, what a cost, he thought. A big favor repaid by Kim: his life back free when it was mine to give having saved it up against the future. The honor of thieves, of a Korean, and an honorable man as he is, and where would we be without honor? But it's a fact I could've let him die, in summary execution on the Pennsylvania in 'forty-six, if I'd wanted. What use is a dead man? That's what I asked myself as I blundered up the Navy's best-laid ambush since the invasion. A vigorous man in business he is for sure, old Kim, and self-effacing when it comes to setting a value on his own neck. So it was a big debt canceled plus a quarter tranche of aurium, a full fortieth part my life's hoard, all for that little bag. But Kim knew what was in it, all right. The price I paid him was nothing compared to its value.

"Whaddaya mean 'on behalf MeTraCor'?" Rohan was

warily suspicious. He reached out towards the satchel but Ellis's hand banged down over it.

"Ah, no!"

"How much?"

"For a peep in this here bag?" He sucked in his breath.

"What's in there, Straker?"

"That's for me to know, and you to find out."

"How much, Straker."

"Ten tranches, and that's a bargain."

"Ten tranches?" Lawton exploded. "You've got real nerve to try selling us Federal property! For God's sake, Straker! Ten tranches is a monstrous figure!"

Ellis grinned. "How do you know that when you don't know what you're buying?"

Rohan sighed. "Is it worth the credit?" he asked flatly, ignoring Lawton's protests.

"I guarantee you this: The hardcopy in here will save Baker. And more."

"Save the fort?" Rohan digested that, sucking on his lips. He walked up and down, turning suddenly. "Really? You're certain? How?"

"I said, it'll save Fort Baker. And more."

"What more?" Lawton asked.

"It'll get you back Kanoya City too."

"That's impossible!"

"No, sir!"

Lawton's jowls quivered. "When Maskull brought thirty vessels here, including thirteen assault ships? With twelve companies of a thousand regulars each? Eight thousand marines? Goddammit, Straker, if those men couldn't do it, how can a miserable letter?"

"Ah, you pack of ingrates," he said, turning to Rohan, his voice larded with pathos an inch thick. "Here I am a

simple trader who lost all his capital because of other folks'
conniving. MeTraCor took away my due payment, leaving
me twenty tranches adrift on the deal. How can you blame
me for trying to pull myself halfways back? And think who
it was brought you supplies in your darkest hour of need. If
it hadn't been for me why—''

''Okeh, Straker—''

''—if it hadn't been for me, you'd all have starved, or
asphyxiated, or been killed dead by the Kan who—''

''Straker—''

''—who are despicable murderers as is well known, yet
when ol' Ellis Straker jumps into the system with more gifts
than you could've thought possible at such a time, what
reception does he get but quibbles and mis'ble—''

''Ellis!''

Ellis stopped, then his voice changed abruptly. ''What?''

Rohan composed himself. ''You know, Ellis, there's an
awful strong Kan force planetside? See, tonight we were
expecting their terms of surrender. Unconditional. You're
aware of Yu Hsien's stated intention? He wants Baker busted
down.''

''None of that surprises me, though it's all irrelevant to
us.''

Rohan's fists clenched. ''Ellis, there's going to be fighting.
I'll not sanction any exodus. Or the stripping of any of our
superheavy assets. I'd be obliged if you'd agree to take Miz
Hawken away.''

''I didn't come here to play rescue. Nor to strip your
goddamned argentium. Nor to nanny Arkali Hawken.''

''Then what?''

''Like I said. To bring you this.'' He slapped the diplomatic
bag again. ''But the cost of it is just ten tranches.''

''One tranche. Payable on condition the hardcopy has the
effect you say!''

"If you can't trust my word. Seven. And I guarantee that bag'll frustrate the Kan's ambitions to take Baker."

"Three. And we'll have a pledge to that effect."

"Five. And you'll authorise payment on a MeTraCor bill expeditiously redeemable in Seoul."

"Yeah, yeah."

"Done at five, then?"

"Done."

Ellis nodded with satisfaction. "Then it's yours as soon as the MeTraCor code's locked in my datachord."

The contract was drawn and coded and geno-printed and the transmission made to the ship. Lawton watched with increasing anger. Then he picked up his cap.

"I won't stay and watch any more of this bullshit."

"Don't you want to know what's in the li'l bag, Colonel?" Ellis asked.

"No, sir! I do not!"

Ellis's eyes followed him. As Lawton reached the iris, the segments pulled back automatically. The Major narrowly missed bumping into someone who had just arrived to see what was going on.

Suddenly Ellis's jaw dropped. The stogie almost fell off his lip, but he recovered. Heads turned. All eyes went to the door to see what Ellis Straker was staring at. Those who knew what had passed between father and son gasped.

"Hello, Dad."

Ellis's jocularity evaporated instantly. The self-satisfied humor of the last few minutes had frozen solid in the silence.

"So it's you, is it?"

"As you see."

"And did you bring back the property you stole?"

"I stole nothing."

"My jacket? And my best side arms? And a ship's lander? And a little something else?"

"I don't owe any debt to you."

"Ah, don't you? And what about Dannyl Quinn? Have you lost him too?"

"Quinn's dead."

"Yep, like you should be." He spat and turned back to Rohan. "Open the bag, Commander."

The seal broke, and the flap cracked back stiffly. Rohan drew out the packet. Government papers marked with the golden eagle of Aquila. Hardcopy vellums folded like legal instruments, waxy and indelible with optically readable authentication tabs. No doubt about these.

Rohan opened the documents and read, and as he read, his face changed. He looked up at two dozen expectant faces.

"It's incredible," he said shakily. "The communication confirms that the Kan war is over. Let me quote: '. . . in wake of the decision to once more deploy the singularity gun on Amerikan Navy warships, the Celestial Court has agreed to cease hostilities. All conflicts between contestants are to cease forthwith in whatever system, and further, the Secretary of State of the Federal government has negotiated a peace treaty with the Imperium on Muscovi' "—his eyes widened—" 'in which the return to Xanadu of her system of Ulan Bator in the Autonomous Mongolian Quadrant is ordered, and so in consequence is the restitution of Kanoya City to the Amerikan Merchant Traders Corporation.' "

A cheer went up. Great jubilation overwhelmed everyone on the bridge.

"Yu Hsien's been sold out!" someone shouted.

"And by his own government!"

"The Dowager's sued for peace. She knows she can't do anything against a Sector that possesses the singularity gun and is prepared to use it."

"The war's over!"

"Get on the comms desk and raise them! Let the Kan know hostilities are at an end!"

Rohan led them off to comms, the notification grasped in his hand. Soon only two were left, father facing son across an empty command chamber.

"Father, I—"

"Don't call me that, by psi!"

Hayden Straker hung his head, trying to master the intense feelings inside him. He faced his father, man to man.

"Sweet Jeezus, give me an opportunity to be myself. That's all I want. All I've ever wanted from you. We should be thanking psi that the war's over. Loosen your pride just this once. Can't you allow yourself to make peace with me now?"

Ellis was contained but fearsomely volcanic. "So. You think this can be the end of it?" he asked softly. "That you can worm your way back now? That it'll be business as usual, just like it was before, when I'm still fifteen tranches adrift?"

He shook his head. All the little things that nauseated him about his father flooded back, washing away the image he had built up in his mind, the version of an Ellis Straker he wanted to know. That version was the one he was sure lay somewhere inside his father, but it was never allowed to emerge.

"I don't want to hear about your business. I just want to be able to call you father again. I want your respect, don't you see that? And I want you to want mine."

"Respect?" Ellis said. "The only reason I've not kicked you all over this floor is that you somehow got that crystal to Edo. But you'll get no praise for that. You botched it and botched it again. Your interference ruined all my stratagems, and you never went about it once in the way it ought to be done. And if it's respect you want from me—then you'll have to do better'n that!''

"I did what I set out to do. Maybe not the way you would have done, but I'm not you. I'm me. And proud to say it."

Ellis shook his head. "It's a good job your mother never lived to see how you turned out. You're bad psi, boy. A drain, not a source. You always have been. One day you'll be the death of me too."

His own anger blazed up, just as it had under the dome of the *Chance*, but an eon had passed and he was a different man from the one who had stood there on that awesome bridge. He was able to douse his rage and face his father's magnificence coolly.

"Okeh, tell me what more you want from me."

They faced each other, and then Ellis spoke, in a strangely muted voice, all chewed up with recriminations. "By psi, Hayden, you talk of respect. What respect have you ever had for me? You were never a good son. You'd never listen to me. I tried to tell you about fighting the Kan. How it was in my young days. About the war and all, but you never once wanted to hear me out. You weren't interested! You threw it all back in my face, the vastest moments of my life, all my philosophies, shrugged away by my own no-good know-nothing son as worthless. Every time you did it, it cut me up good. And when I tried to give you the means to make your living in the chains you told me it was pissy poetry and the mansions of Liberty that you wanted. If it weren't a slight on your mother's memory I'd say that such a damned ingrate could never have been my son!"

"That's too bad! The fact is, I am your son. Like it or not. And nothing you can say will ever undo that."

Ellis broke off his stare, chewed mightily on his tobako stub. "You asked me what I wanted from you?"

"Yes. I did."

"Only this: I want to feel good psi when I look at you. I want you to return what you stole and cheated from me. Only then will you be my son again, and that day you'll prove to me your worth as a man."

He watched his father stand up. Watched him walk from the room. Saw the way he doffed ash inconsiderately as he passed out of sight without looking back. Hayden Straker punched the table hard enough to make his knuckle bleed, hard enough to release the rage he had saved up.

The hard trader, he thought, full of rage. The tough, unforgiving man of commerce! Where's his heart? I'll have to cut him again to find it. By the Adventer God, I will!

The fire stung his eyes. Inside he was taut as harp wire. He collapsed down into the Commander's big seat and held his head, his thoughts a furious jumble. All I've ever done is a great mistake to him. He wants me as his pawn, a lapdog heir to train up in his mind tricks. But I'll never be that. Since I last saw him I've labored day and night to accomplish what I promised. I did it all and more. When he learns I've rejected Arkali there'll be fury. Now the war's over, the union of Hawken and Straker is more necessary than ever. How will he take that? What could he have meant? Restore what? What did I steal? How did I cheat him? What does he want, by psi? He won't be satisfied until I bring him the Shogun's crystal itself!

"The hell with him," he said, and meant it.

Outside, Ellis turned a corner in the gangway and ran flat into Barb Eastman. A blaster was in his hand; his anger was boundless.

"Where is he? I swear I'll kill him!"

"Hey! Don't you know the war's finished?"

"It's not any Kan I mean, but your squatting son!"

Ellis seized Eastman's wrist without any loss of civility and broke it back in the Chinese style until Eastman shouted.

"Well, let the Wesson drop, man. What are you, a fool who'd prefer a broken elbow to a little polite conversation?"

Eastman gasped, but the blaster fell. He cradled his arm.

"I'll teach you how you do that, if you like." His voice was unruffled, slightly humorous, but he had hold of Eastman's lapel just in case. "Ah, don't scowl at me. You're ugly enough in the face as it is. Now what's the panic?"

"He's dishonored her!"

"Who?"

"Miz Hawken—"

"Ah, little Arkali. Yep, and you have a thing about her still, don't you?" Eastman's jaw clenched but Ellis shook him. "Don't you?"

"Yes."

"Well and good. Because Hayden doesn't want her anymore, and that's fresh from Rohan. From what he told me your path's likely as clear as it'll ever be."

Eastman stared back, astounded. "You think that—"

"Well? Do you want her or don't you? It's all a case of valuation, lad. What's credit except a notion of worth in the mind of some organix, a bunch of ohs and ones that we all agree means power, eh?" He pulled Eastman up, put an arm around his shoulders, and began to walk him away from the bridge. "What say we have a drink, you and me, to wet the Peace?"

They went out through the umbilicus, Eastman uncertain, but unable to decide what else to do, and all the while as Ellis led him away, the staffers were jigging about like madmen, shouting and whooping.

Soon they reached the tube that stretched out to the lander.

In the dormant vehicle there was a bottle of the best Zwiss fivestar and Ellis told a patient *gishi* to unpop it.

"I been saving this, in case I ever set eyes on you again. Did I ever tell you a tale I heard about the mighty Kan tyrant who had a weakling for a son?"

"I don't recollect that."

"Then listen, and maybe learn." Ellis looked up at the blinking indicator lights and paused long enough to hitch his jacket and lodge his backside on the arm of the pilot's seat. Then he began in a faraway voice.

"There's this father, see, a tyrant of some damned Xanadu Quadrant, in a system that lives by trade, like we do. And he sends his heir, the Prince, across the chains to make his fortune against the smack of events and the enemies of his Sector and all. But the boy only jumps into the next system, and he sends in secret to his mother who always doted on him. Then, see, he tells her his plight, and he asks her for aurium to fill up his holds, and she obliges him in that, and so he lights out back.

"What happens then is, after a space he comes and lands on the main apron, and he applies to see his father who as a Xanadu tyrant needed that kind of formality."

Eastman smiled.

"Well, the tyrant has this great pit filled with reengineered saurians, ichthyosaurs, and plesiosaurs and the like, and he receives his son on the lip of it. And the Prince brings by the aurium and he says: 'There y'go, Father, look at the fortune what I got through trading, just like you asked me.' And the tyrant takes a looksee at an ingot of it, and looks at his son, then he throws it in the pit. And the Prince just stares at it and says: 'Why did you do that?' And the father calls him a damned liar and sends him off to trade again."

He handed Eastman the fivestar. Eastman quaffed and wiped his mouth. "I don't see—"

"Let me finish. So. This time the Prince goes out and starts to trade. He makes his way along the chains. He overcomes local rulers and psi and all the deceits of men's devising, and he wins his own profit, by sweat and ingenuity. And when he comes back safe to his homeworld he comes up to his father who's back down beside the pit. And again the Prince shows an ingot to his father. And again the father throws it in down by the saurians. Ah! But this time, the Prince vaults over the side of the pit and grabs the ingot from out of the snapping jaws, and he brings it out. And this time the father lays his hands on the son's shoulders and tells him he's proud of him."

Ellis paused and saw Eastman nod his head, then he went on. "That's my favorite parable. One I told my son when he was young, though I guess he's forgotten that. You see the meaning, don't you, Barb?"

"Yes. I've always thought it's not what a man is, but what a man does that's important."

"That right? I'd put it different: It's not what a man has, it's the way he gets it that makes him."

He handed the blaster back to Eastman. "Mind how you go. And take no heed of anyone who says I want Hayden Straker dead. Y'hear me?"

As Eastman sullenly took the Wesson back, Ellis swigged at the fivestar again, then handed it back to a *gishi*. That's a pissy shallow reading of my parable, he thought. And I supposed young Eastman knew a thing or two about Yamato and the ways of fate. Hayden's changed. My lad's returned from his first journey. He's learned to recognise destiny, but he's yet to go on his second where he'll discover how to mold it to his will. That's the work of a man of forty or more, but who says it can't be done by him? After all, he is my son.

"So the war's over, is it?" Eastman said desolately, turning in the mouth of the umbilicus. "That was it. And I'd counted on ten years."

"Take that long to get all your rage out?"

Eastman grunted. "I guess it's my destiny to be a squatting credit op after all, because that's what MeTraCor'll put me back to now."

The word jolted Ellis. It was as if Eastman had heard his thoughts.

"Courage!" he told him. "You don't think Celestial Functionary Yu's going to give up the war just because the Dowager's ordered it, do you? You don't suppose Kanoya City'll be handed back by the Kan just like that?"

Eastman's face lit as he heard Ellis's fingers snap. "But the treaty's signed and sealed. MeTraCor and China Products, both our government and theirs, all have agreed. How can Yu Hsien go ahead with his megalomaniac plans now?"

Ellis laughed shortly. "Think about it. Think about it hard in coming time. Yep, and keep your powder dry."